AT THE SIGHT OF BLOOD

I saw it first, a blue slipper on its side on the floor with a foot in it, extending beyond the edge of a couch. I moved automatically but stopped short. Let the cop do his own discovering. He did; he saw it too and went; and when he had passed the end of the couch he stopped shorter than I had, growled, "God-almighty," and stood looking down. Then I moved, and so did Vance. When Vance saw it, all of it, he went stiff, gawking, then he made a sort of choking noise, and then he crumpled. It wasn't a faint; his knees just quit on him and he went down, and no wonder. Even live blood on a live face makes an impression, and when the face is dead and the blood has dried all over one side and the ear, plenty of it, you do need knees.

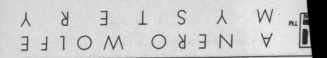

BANTAM BOOKS

NEW YORK • TORONTO • LONDON • SYDNEY • AUCKLAND

A NERO WOLFE THREESOME

TRIO FOR BLUNT INSTRUMENTS

BY REX STOUT

OPM   19   18

Contents

Kill Now—Pay Later

1

That Monday morning Pete didn't give me his usual polite grin, contrasting the white gleam of his teeth with the maple-syrup shade of the skin of his square leathery face. He did give me his usual greeting, "Hi-ho, Mr. Goodwin," but with no grin in his voice either, and he ignored the established fact that I expected to take his cap and jacket and put them on the rack. By the time I turned from shutting the door he had dropped his jacket on the hall bench and was picking up his box, which he had put on the floor to free his hands for the jacket.

"You're an hour early," I said. "They going barefoot?"

"Naw, they're busy," he said, and headed down the hall to the office. I followed, snubbed; after all, we had been friends for more than three years.

Pete came three days a week—Monday, Wednesday, and Friday—around noon, after he had finished his rounds in an office building on Eighth Avenue. Wolfe always gave him a dollar, since it was a five-minute walk for him to the old brownstone on West 35th Street, and I only gave him a quarter, but he gave my shoes as good a shine as he did Wolfe's. None better. I never pretended to keep busy while he was working on Wolfe because I liked to listen. It was instructive. Wolfe's line was that a man who had been born in Greece, even though he had left at the age of six, should be familiar with the ancient glories of his native land, and he had been hammering away at Pete for forty months. That morning, as Wolfe swiveled his oversized chair, in which he was seated behind his desk, and Pete knelt and got his box in place, and I crossed to my desk, Wolfe demanded, "Who was Eratosthenes and who accused him of murder in a great and famous speech in four-oh-three B.C.?"

Pete, poising his brush, shook his head.

"Who?" Wolfe demanded.

"Maybe Pericles."

"Nonsense. Pericles had been dead twenty-six years. Confound it, I read parts of that speech to you last year. His name begins with L."

"Lycurgus."

"No! The Athenian Lycurgus hadn't been born!"

Pete looked up. "Today you must excuse me." He tapped his head with the edge of the brush. "Empty today. Why I came early, something happened. I go in a man's room, Mr. Ashby, a good customer, two bits every day. Room empty, nobody there. Window wide open, cold wind coming in. Tenth floor. I go and look out window, big crowd down below and cops. I go out to hall and take elevator down, I push through crowd, and there is my good customer, Mr. Ashby, there on the sidewalk, all smashed up terrible. I push back out of crowd, I look up, I see heads sticking out of windows, I think it's no good going up to customers now, they will be looking out of windows, so I come here, that's why I come early, so today you must excuse me, Mr. Wolfe." He lowered his head and started the brush going.

Wolfe grunted. "I advise you to return to that building without delay. Does anyone know you were in his room?"

"Sure. Miss Cox."

"She saw you enter?"

"Sure."

"How long were you in his room?"

"Maybe one minute."

"Did Miss Cox see you leave?"

"No, I go out another door to the hall."

"Did you push him out the window?"

Pete stopped brushing to raise his head. "Now, Mr. Wolfe. In God's name."

"I advise you to return. If a crowd had already gathered when you looked out the window, and if Miss

Cox can fix the exact time you entered the room, you are probably not vulnerable, but you may be in a pickle. You should not have left the premises. The police will soon be looking for you. Go back at once. Mr. Goodwin's shoes can wait till Wednesday—or come this afternoon."

Pete put the brush down and got out the polish. "Cops," he said. "They're all right, I like cops. But if I tell a cop I saw someone—" He started dabbing polish on. "No," he said. "No, sir."

Wolfe grunted. "So you saw someone."

"I didn't say I saw someone, I only said what if I told a cop I did? Did they have cops in Athens in four-oh-three B.C.?" He dabbed polish.

That took the conversation back to the ancient glories of Greece, but I didn't listen. While Pete finished with Wolfe and then shined me, ignoring Wolfe's advice, I practiced on him. The idea that a detective should stick strictly to facts is the bunk. One good opinion can sometimes get you further than a hundred assorted facts. So I practiced on Pete Vassos for that ten minutes. Had he killed a man half an hour ago? If the facts, now being gathered by cops, made it possible but left it open, how would I vote? I ended by not voting because I would have had to know about motive. For money, no, Pete wouldn't. For vengeance, that would depend on what for. For fear, sure, if the fear was hot enough. So I couldn't vote.

An hour later, when I walked crosstown on an errand to the bank, I stopped at the corner at Eighth Avenue for a look. The smashed-up Mr. Ashby had been removed, but the sidewalk in front of the building was roped off to keep the crowd of volunteer criminologists from interfering with the research of a couple of homicide scientists, and three cops were dealing with the traffic. Looking up, I saw a few heads sticking out of windows, but none on the tenth floor, which was third from the top.

The afternoon *Gazette* is delivered a little after five o'clock at the old brownstone on West 35th Street which is owned and lived in and worked in—when he works—by Nero Wolfe, and when we have no important operation going it's a dead hour in the office. Wolfe is up in the plant rooms on the roof with Theodore for his four-to-six afternoon session with the orchids, Fritz is in the kitchen getting something ready for the oven or the pot, and I am killing time. So when the *Gazette* came that day it was welcomed, and I learned all it knew about the death of Mr. Dennis Ashby. He had hit the sidewalk at 10:35 A.M. and had died on arrival. No one had been found who had seen him come out of the window of his office on the tenth floor, but it was assumed that that was where he had come from, since the receptionist, Miss Frances Cox, had spoken with him on the phone at 10:28, and no other nearby window had been open.

If the police had decided whether to call it accident or suicide or murder they weren't saying. If anyone had been with Ashby in the room when he left by the window, he wasn't bragging about it. No one had gone to the room after 10:35, when Ashby had hit the sidewalk, for some fifteen minutes, when a bootblack named Peter Vassos had entered, expecting to give Ashby a shine. A few minutes later, when a cop who had got Ashby's name from papers in his pocket had arrived on the tenth floor, Vassos had departed. Found subsequently at his home on Graham Street on the Lower East Side, Manhattan, he had been taken to the district attorney's office for questioning.

Dennis Ashby, thirty-nine, married, no children, had been vice-president of Mercer's Bobbins, Inc., in charge of sales and promotion. According to his business associates and his widow, he had been in good health and his affairs had been in order, and he had had no reason to kill himself. The widow, Joan, was grief-stricken and wouldn't see reporters. Ashby had been below average in stature, 5 feet 7, 140 pounds. That bit, saved for the last, was a typical *Gazette* touch, suggesting that it would be no great feat to shove a man that size through a window, so it had probably been murder, and buy the *Gazette* tomorrow to find out.

At six o'clock the sound came from the hall of the elevator groaning its way down and jolting to a stop.

and Wolfe entered. I waited until he had crossed to his desk and got his seventh of a ton lowered into the oversized chair to say, "They've got Pete down at the DA's office. Apparently he didn't go back to the building at all, and they—"

The doorbell rang. I got up and stepped to the hall, switched on the stoop light, saw a familiar brawny figure through the one-way glass, and turned. "Cramer."

"What does he want?" Wolfe growled. That meant let him in. When Inspector Cramer of Homicide South is not to be admitted, with or without reason, Wolfe merely snaps, "No!" When he is to be admitted but is first to be riled, again with or without reason, Wolfe says, "I'm busy." As for Cramer, he has moods too. When I open the door he may cross the sill and march down the hall without a grunt of greeting, or he may hello me man to man. Twice he has even called me Archie, but that was a slip of the tongue. That day he let me take his hat and coat, and when I got to the office he was in the red leather chair near the end of Wolfe's desk, but not settled back. That chair has a deep seat, and Cramer likes to plant his feet flat on the floor. I have never seen him cross his legs. He told Wolfe this wouldn't take long, he just wanted a little information to fill in, and Wolfe grunted.

"About that man that came this morning to shine your shoes," Cramer said. "Peter Vassos. What time did he get here?"

Wolfe shook his head. "You should know better, Mr. Cramer. You do know better. I answer questions only when you have established their relevance to your duty and to my obligation, and then at my discretion."

"Yeah." Cramer squeezed his lips together and counted three. "Yeah. Never make it simple, no matter how simple it is, that's you. I'm investigating what may have been a murder, and Peter Vassos may have done it. If he did, he came straight to you afterwards. I know, he's been coming more than three years, three times a week, to shine your shoes, but today he came early. I want to know what he said. I don't have to remind you that you're a licensed private detective, you're not a lawyer, and communications to you are not privileged. What time did Vassos come this morning and what did he say?"

Wolfe's brows were up. "Not established. 'May have' isn't enough. A man can get through a window un-aided."

"This one didn't. Close to certain. There was a thing on his desk, a big hunk of polished petrified wood, and it had been wiped. A thing like that on a man's desk would have somebody's prints or at least smudges, and it didn't. It had been wiped. And at the back of his head, at the base of his skull, something smooth and round had hit him hard. Nothing he hit when he landed could have done that, and nothing on the way down. This hasn't been released yet, but it will be in the morning."

Wolfe made a face. "Then your second 'may have.' Supposing that someone hit him with that thing and then pushed him out the window, it couldn't have been Mr. Vassos, by his account. A woman, a Miss Cox, saw him enter Mr. Ashby's room; and within seconds after entering, finding no one there, he looked out the window and saw a crowd gathered below. If Miss Cox can set the time within—"

"She can. She does. But Vassos might have been in there before that. He could have entered by the other door, direct from the outer hall. That door was kept locked, but he could have knocked and Ashby let him in. He hit Ashby with that thing, killed him or stunned him, dragged or carried him to the window and pushed him out, left by that door, went down the hall and entered the anteroom and spoke to Miss Cox, went to Mercer's room and gave him a shine, went to Busch's room and gave him a shine, went to Ashby's room by the inner hall, speaking to Miss Cox again, looked out of the window or didn't, left by the door to the outer hall he had used before, took the elevator down and left the building, decided he had better come and see you, and came. What did he say?"

Wolfe took a deep breath. "Very well. I won't pretend that I'm not concerned. Aside from the many pleasant conversations I have had with Mr. Vassos, he is an excellent bootblack and he never fails to come. He would be hard to replace. Therefore I'll indulge you, Archie. Report to Mr. Cramer in full. Verbatim."

I did so. That was easy, compared to some of the lengthy and complicated dialogues I have had to report to Wolfe over the years. I got my notebook and pen and shorthanded it down as I recited it, so there would be no discrepancy if he wanted it typed and signed later. Since I was looking at the notebook I couldn't see Cramer's face, but of course his sharp gray eyes were fastened on me, trying to spot a sign of a skip or stumble. When I came to the end, Pete's departure, and tossed the notebook on my desk, he looked at Wolfe.

"You advised him to go back there at once?"

"Yes, Mr. Goodwin's memory is incomparable."

"I know it is. He's good at forgetting too. Vassos didn't go back. He went home and we found him there. His account of his conversation with you agrees with Goodwin's, only he left something out or Goodwin put something in. Vassos says nothing about telling you he saw someone."

"He didn't. You heard it. It was an if—what if he told a cop he saw someone."

"Yeah. Like for instance, if he told a cop he saw someone going into Ashby's room by the hall door, would that be a good idea, or not? Like that?"

"Pfui. You're welcome to your conjectures, but don't expect me to rate them. I'm concerned; I have said so; it would be a serious inconvenience to lose Mr. Vassos. If he killed that man a jury would wonder why. So would I."

"We're not ready for a jury," Cramer stood up. "But we've got a pretty good guess at why. Granting that Goodwin has reported everything Vassos said today, which I don't, what about other days? What has Vassos ever said about Ashby?"

"Nothing."

"He has never mentioned his name?"

"No, Archie?"

"Right," I said, "Not before today."

"What has he ever said about his daughter?"

"Nothing," Wolfe said.

"Correction," I said. "What Pete talked about wasn't up to him. Mr. Wolfe kept him on the ancient glories of Greece. But one day more than two years ago, in June nineteen fifty-eight, when Mr. Wolfe was upstairs in bed with the flu, Pete told me his daughter had just graduated from high school and showed me a picture of her. Pete and I would know each other a lot better if it wasn't for ancient Greece."

"And he has never mentioned his daughter since?"

"No, how could he?"

"Nuts. Greece." Cramer looked at Wolfe. "You know what I think? I think this. If you know Vassos killed Ashby, and you know why, on account of his daughter, and you can help nail him for it, you won't. If you can help him wriggle out of it, you will." He tapped Wolfe's desk with a finger. "Just because, by God, you can count on him to come and shine your shoes, and you like to spout to him about people nobody ever heard of. That's you." His eyes darted to me. "And you." He turned and tramped out.

2

It was exactly twenty-eight hours later, Tuesday evening at half past ten, that I went to answer the doorbell and saw, through the one-way glass of the front door, a scared but determined little face bounded at the sides by the turned-up collar of a brown wool coat and on top by a fuzzy brown thing that flopped to the right. When I opened the door she told me with a single rush of breath, "You're Archie Goodwin I'm Elma Vassos."

It had been a normal nothing-stirring day, three meals, Wolfe reading a book and dictating letters in between his morning and afternoon turns in the plant rooms, Fritz housekeeping and cooking, me choring. It was still in the air whether I would have to find another bootblack. According to the papers the police had tagged Ashby's death as murder, but no one had been charged. Around one o'clock Sergeant Purley Stebbins had phoned to ask if we knew where Peter Vassos was, and when I said no and started to ask a question he hung up on me. A little after four Lon Cohen of the *Gazette* had phoned to offer a grand for a thousand-word piece on Peter Vassos, a dollar a word, and another grand if I would tell him where Vassos was. I declined with thanks and made a counter offer, my autograph in his album if he would tell me who at Homicide or the DA's bureau had given him the steer that we knew Vassos. When I told him I had no idea where Vassos was he pronounced a word you are not supposed to use on the telephone.

I usually stick to the rule that no one is to be ushered to the office when Wolfe is there without asking him, but I ignore it now and then in an emergency. That time the emergency was a face. I had been in the kitchen chinning with Fritz. Wolfe was buried in a book, we had no case and no client, and to him no woman is ever welcome in that house. Ten to one he would have refused to see her. But I had seen her scared little face and he hadn't, and anyway he hadn't done a lick of work for more than two weeks, and it would be up to me, not him, to find another bootblack if it came to that. So I invited her in, took her coat and put it on a hanger, escorted her to the office, and said, "Miss Elma Vassos, Peter's daughter." Wolfe closed his book on a finger and glared at me. She put a hand on the back of the red leather chair to steady herself. It looked as if she might crack, and I took her arm and eased her into the chair. Wolfe transferred the glare to her, and there was her face. It was a little face, but not too little, and the point was that you didn't see any of the details, eyes or mouth or nose, just the face. I have supplied descriptions of many faces professionally, but with her I wouldn't know where to begin. I asked her if she wanted a drink, water or something stronger, and she said no.

She looked at Wolfe and said, "You're Nero Wolfe. Do you know my father is dead?" She needed more breath.

Wolfe shook his head. His lips parted and closed again. He turned to me. "Confound it, get something! Brandy. Whisky."

"I couldn't swallow it," she said. "You didn't know?"

"No." He was gruff. "When? How? Can you talk?"

"I guess so." She wasn't any too sure. "I have to. Some boys found him at the bottom of a cliff. I went and looked at him—not there, at the morgue." She set her teeth on her lip, hard, but it didn't change the face. She made the teeth let go. "They think he killed himself, he jumped off, but he didn't, I know he didn't."

Wolfe pushed his chair back. "I offer my profound sympathy, Miss Vassos." Even gruffer. He arose. "I'll leave you with Mr. Goodwin. You will give him the details." He moved, the book in his hand.

That was him. He thought she was going to flop, and a woman off the rail is not only unwelcome, she is not to be borne. Not by him. But she caught his sleeve and stopped him. "You," she said. "I must tell you. To my father you are a great man, the greatest man in the world. I must tell you."

"She'll do," I said. "She'll make it."

—here are few men who would not like to be told they are the greatest in the world, and Wolfe isn't one of them. He stared down at her for five seconds, returned to his chair, sat, inserted the marker in the book and put it down, scowled at her, and demanded, "When did you eat?"

"I haven't—I can't swallow."

"Pfui. When did you eat?"

"A little this morning. My father hadn't come home and I didn't know . . ."

He swiveled to push a button, leaned back, closed his eyes, and opened them when he heard a step at the door. "Tea with honey, Fritz. Toast, pot cheese, and Bar-le-Duc. For Miss Vassos."

Fritz went.

"I really can't," she said.

"You will if you want me to listen. Where is the cliff?"

It took her a second to go back. "It's in the country somewhere. I guess they told me, but I don't—"

"When was he found?"

"Sometime this afternoon, late this afternoon."

"You saw him at the morgue. Where, in the country?"

"No, they brought him; it's not far from here. When I had—when I could—I came here from there."

"Who was with you?"

"Two men, detectives. They told me their names, but I don't remember."

"I mean *with* you. Brother, sister, mother?"

"I have no brother or sister. My mother died ten years ago."

"When did you last see your father alive?"

"Yesterday. When I got home from work he wasn't there, and it was nearly six o'clock when he came, and he said he had been at the district attorney's office for three hours, they had been asking him questions about Mr. Ashby. You know about Mr. Ashby, he said he told you about him when he came here. Of course I already knew about him because I work there. I *did* work there."

"Where?"

"At the office. That company, Mercer's Bobbins."

"Indeed. In what capacity?"

"I'm a stenographer. Not anybody's secretary, just a stenographer. Mostly typing and sometimes letters for Mr. Busch. My father got me the job through Mr. Mercer."

"How long ago?"

"Two years ago. After I graduated from high school."

"Then you knew Mr. Ashby."

"Yes, I knew him a little, yes."

"About last evening. Your father came home around six, then?"

"I had dinner nearly ready, and we talked, and we ate, and then we talked some more. He said there was something he hadn't told the police and he hadn't told you, and he was going to go and tell you in the morning and ask you what he ought to do. He said you were such a great man that people paid you fifty thousand dollars just to tell them what to do, and he thought you would tell him for nothing, so it would be foolish not to go and ask you. He wouldn't tell me what it was. Then a friend of mine came—I was going to a movie with her—and we went. When I got home father wasn't there and there was a note on the table. It said he was going out and might be late. One of the detectives tried to take the note but I wouldn't let him. I have it here in my bag if you want to see it."

Wolfe shook his head. "Not necessary. Had your father mentioned before you left that he intended to go out?"

"No. And he always did. We always told each other ahead of time what we were going to do."

"Had he given you no hint— Very well, Fritz."

Fritz crossed to the red leather chair, put the tray on the little table that is always there for people to write checks on, and proffered her a napkin. She didn't lift a hand to take it. Wolfe spoke.

"I'll listen to more, Miss Vassos, only after you eat." He picked up his book, opened to his page, and swiveled to put his back to her. She took the napkin. Fritz went. I could have turned to my desk and pretended to do something, but I would have been reflected to her in the big mirror on the wall back of my desk, which gives me a view of the door to the hall, and she would have been reflected to me, so I got up and went to the kitchen. Fritz was at the side table putting the cover on the toaster. As I got the milk from the refrigerator I told him, "She's the daughter of Pete Vassos. I'll have to scare up a bootblack. He's dead."

"Him?" Fritz turned. *"Dieu m'en garde."* He shook his head. "Too young. Then she is not a client?"

"Not one to send a bill to." I poured milk. "Anyhow, as you know, he wouldn't take a paying client if one came up the stoop on his knees. It's December, and his tax bracket is near the top. If she wants him to help and he won't, I'll take a leave of absence and handle it myself. You saw her face."

He snorted. "She should be warned. About you."

"Sure. I'll do that first."

I don't gulp milk. When the glass was half empty I tiptoed out to the office door. Wolfe's back was still turned and Elma was putting jam on a piece of toast. I finished the milk, taking my time, and took the glass to the kitchen, and when I returned Wolfe had about-faced and put the book down and she was saying something. I entered and crossed to my desk.

". . . and he had never done that before," she was telling Wolfe. "I thought he might have gone back to the district attorney's office, so I phoned there, but he hadn't. I phoned two of his friends but they hadn't seen him. I went to work as usual, he goes to that building every morning, and I told Mr. Busch and he tried to find out if he was in the building, but no one had seen him. Then a detective came and asked me a lot of questions, and later, after lunch, another one came and took me to the district attorney's office, and I—"

"Miss Vassos." Wolfe was curt. "If you please. You have eaten, though not much, and your faculties are apparently in order. You said you must tell me, and I would not be uncivil to your father's daughter, but these details are not essential. Give me brief answers to some questions. You said that they think your father killed himself, he jumped off. Who are 'they'?"

"The police. The detectives."

"How do you know they do?"

"The way they talked. What they said. What they asked me. They think he killed Mr. Ashby and he knew they were finding out about it, so he killed himself."

"Do they think they know why he killed Mr. Ashby?"

"Yes. Because he had found out that Mr. Ashby had seduced me."

I lifted a brow. You couldn't be much briefer than that. There wasn't the slightest sign on her face that she had said anything remarkable. Nor was there any sign on Wolfe's face that he had heard anything remarkable. He asked, "How do you know that?"

"What they said this afternoon at the district attorney's office. They used that word, 'seduced.' "

"Did you know that your father had found out that Mr. Ashby had seduced you?"

"Of course not, because he hadn't. My father

wouldn't have believed that even if Mr. Ashby had told him, or even if I had gone crazy and told him, because he would have known it wasn't so. My father knew me."

Wolfe was frowning. "You mean he thought he knew you?"

"He did know me. He didn't know I couldn't be seduced—I suppose any girl *could* be seduced if her head gets turned enough—but he knew if I was I would tell him. And he knew if I ever was seduced it wouldn't be Mr. Ashby or anyone like him. My father knew me."

"Let's make it clear. Are you saying that Mr. Ashby had not seduced you?"

"Yes. Of course."

"Had he tried to?"

She hesitated. "No." She considered. "He took me to dinner and a show three times. The last time was nearly a year ago. He asked me several times since, but I didn't go because I had found out what he was like and I didn't like him."

Wolfe's frown had gone. "Then why do the police think he had seduced you?"

"I don't know, but someone must have told them. Someone must have told them lies about Mr. Ashby and me, from what they said."

"Who? Did they name anyone?"

"No."

"Do you know who? Or can you guess?"

"No."

Wolfe's eyes came to me. "Archie?"

That was to be expected. It was merely routine. He pretends to presume that he knows nothing, and I know everything, about women, and he was asking me to tell him whether Elma Vassos had or had not been seduced by Dennis Ashby, yes or no. What the hell, I wasn't under oath, and I did have an opinion. "They don't go by dreams," I said. "She's probably right, someone has fed them a line. Say thirty to one."

"You believe her."

"Believe? Make it twenty to one."

She turned her head, slowly, to look straight at me.

to Wolfe.

"Thank you, Mr. Goodwin," she said and turned back to Wolfe.

His eyes narrowed at her. "Well. Assuming you have been candid, what then? You said you must tell me, and I have listened. Your father is dead. I esteemed him, and I would spare no pains to resurrect him if that were possible. But what can you expect me to tender beyond my sympathy, which you have?"

"Why . . ." She was surprised. "I thought—isn't it obvious, what they're going to do? I mean that they're not going to do anything? If they think my father killed Mr. Ashby on account of me and then killed himself, what can they do? That will end it, it's already ended for them. So I'll have to do something, and I don't know what, so I had to come to you because my father said—" She stopped and covered her mouth with her spread fingers. It was the first quick, strong movement she had made. "Oh!" she said through the fingers. Her hand dropped. "Of course. You must forgive me." She opened her bag, a big brown leather one, stuck her hand in, and took something out. "I should have done this before. My father never spent any of the money you paid him. This is it, all dollar bills, the bills you gave him. He said he would do something special with it some day, but he never said what. But he said—" She stopped. She clamped her teeth on her lip.

"Don't do that," Wolfe snapped.

She nodded. "I know, I won't. I haven't counted it, but it must be nearly five hundred dollars; you paid him three times a week for over three years." She got up and put it on Wolfe's desk and returned to the chair. "Of course it's nothing to you, it's nothing like fifty thousand, so I'm really asking for charity, but it's for my father, not for me, and after all it will mean that you got your shoes shined for nothing for more than three years."

Wolfe looked at me. I had let her in, I admit that, but from his look you might have thought I had killed Ashby and Pete and had seduced her into the bargain. I cocked my head at him. He looked at her. "Miss

Vassos. You are asking me to establish your father's
innocence and your chastity. Is that it?"

"My chastity doesn't matter. I mean that's not it."

"But your father's innocence is."

"Yes. Yes!"

Wolfe wiggled a finger at the stack of dollar bills,
held by rubber bands. "Your money. Take it. It is, as
you say, nothing for a job like this, and if I am quixotic
enough to undertake it I don't want a tip. I make no
commitment. If I said yes or no now it would be no;
it's midnight, bedtime, and I'm tired. I'll tell you in the
morning. You will sleep here. There's a spare bedroom,
adequate and comfortable." He pushed his chair back
and rose.

"But I don't want . . . I have no things . . ."

"You have your skin." He frowned down at her.
"Suppose this. Suppose the assumptions of the police
are correct: that Mr. Ashby had in fact seduced you,
that your father learned about it and killed him, and
that, fearing exposure, he then killed himself; and suppose that under that burden of knowledge you go home
to face the night alone. What would you do?"

"But it's not true! He didn't!"

"I told you to suppose. Suppose it were true. What
would you do?"

"Why . . . I would kill myself. Of course."

Wolfe nodded. "I assume you would. And if you
die tonight or tomorrow in circumstances which make
it plausible that you committed suicide, others, including the police, will make that assumption. The murderer knows that, and since his attempt to have Ashby's death taken for suicide might have succeeded, and
his attempt to have your father's death taken for suicide apparently *has* succeeded, he will probably try
again. If he knows you he knows that you are not
without spirit, as you have shown by coming here, and
you will be a mortal threat to him as long as you live.
You will sleep here. I shall not be available before
eleven in the morning, but Mr. Goodwin will, and you
will tell him everything you know that may be useful.
If I decide to help you, as a service to your father,

I'll need all the information I can get. Don't try withholding anything from Mr. Goodwin; his understanding of attractive young women is extremely acute. Good
night." He turned to me. "You'll see that the South
Room is in order. Good night." He went.

As the sound came of the elevator door closing the
client told me, "Take the money, Mr. Goodwin. I don't
want—" She started to shake, her head dropped, and
her hands came up to cover her face. It was a good
thing she had fought it off until the great man had left.

3

At a quarter to eleven Wednesday morning I was
at my desk, typing. When I had knocked on the door
of the South Room, which is on the third floor, directly
above Wolfe's room, at seven forty-five, Elma had been
up and dressed. She said she had slept pretty well, but
she didn't look it. I eat breakfast in the kitchen, but
Fritz wouldn't want her to, so he served us in the dining room, and she did all all right—all her orange juice,
two griddle cakes, two slices of bacon, two shirred eggs
with chives, and two cups of coffee. Then to the office,
and for nearly an hour, from eight-forty to nine-thirty,
I had asked questions and she had answered them.
Since she had started to work for Mercer's Bobbins,
Inc., two years back, their office space had doubled
and their office staff had tripled. That is, their sales
and executive office in the Eighth Avenue building;
she didn't know what the increase had been in the factory in New Jersey, but it had been big. It was understood by everybody that the increase had been due to
the ability and effort of one man, Dennis Ashby, who
had been put in charge of sales and promotion three
years ago. He had boosted more than bobbins; the firm
now made more than twenty items used in the gar-
ment industry.

Of the dozen members of the staff she named and
described, here are some samples:

JOHN MERCER, president. There had been an office

party, with cake and punch, on his sixty-first birthday in September. He had inherited the business from his father; it was generally understood that he owned most of the stock of the corporation. He spent most of his time at the factory and was at the New York office only two days a week. The firm had been about to go under when he had made Ashby vice-president and put him in charge of sales and promotion. He called the employees by their first names and they all liked him. They called him, not to his face, the Big M. He had children and grandchildren, Elma didn't know how many. None of them was active in the business.

ANDREW BUSCH, secretary of the corporation and office manager, was in his early thirties, not married. Up to a year ago he had been merely the head bookkeeper, and when the office manager had died of old age Mercer had promoted him. He had a room of his own, but three or four times a day he would appear in the rumpus and make the rounds of the desks. (The rumpus was the big room where twenty-eight girls did the work. One of them had called it the rumpus room and it had been shortened to rumpus.) He had instructed the stenographers that when Ashby sent for one of them she was to stop at his room and tell him where she was going, so they called him, not to his face, Paladin.

PHILIP HORAN, salesman, in his middle thirties, married, two or three children. I include him because a) he was seldom at the office before four in the afternoon but had been seen there Monday morning by one of the girls, b) he had expected to get the job Mercer had given Ashby and was known to be sore about it, and c) he had asked one of the girls, an old-timer who had been with the firm as long as he had, to find out what had happened and was happening between Ashby and Elma Vassos, and had kept after her about it.

FRANCES COX, receptionist, Elma said she was thirty, so she was probably twenty-seven or twenty-eight. I do know a few things about women. I include her because if she had seen Pete entering Ashby's room she might have seen someone else on the move, and that might be useful.

DENNIS ASHBY, dead. He had told Elma a year back that he was thirty-eight. Had started with Mercer's Bobbins long ago, Elma didn't know how long, as a stock clerk. Small and not handsome. When I asked Elma to name the animal he was most like, she said a monkey. He had spent about half of his time out of the office, out promoting. He had had no secretary; when he had wanted a stenographer he had called one in from the rumpus, and he had handled his appointments himself, with the assistance of Frances Cox, the receptionist. He had kept a battery of flies in his own room. The girls had called him the Menace, naturally, with his name Dennis, but also because they meant it. Elma had no knowledge of any seduction he had actually achieved, but there had been much talk.

JOAN ASHBY, the widow. I include her because the widow of a murdered man must always be included. She had once worked at Mercer's Bobbins, but had quit when she married Ashby, before Elma had got her job there. Elma had never seen her and knew next to nothing about her. Ashby had told Elma across a restaurant table that his marriage had been a mistake and he was trying to get his wife to agree to a divorce.

ELMA VASSOS. One point: when I asked her why she had gone to dinners and shows with a married man she said, 'I told my father he had asked me, and he told me to go. He said every girl is so curious about married men she wants to be with one somewhere, and she does, and I might as well go ahead and have it over with. Of course, my father knew me.'

As for Monday morning, Elma had been in Busch's room from nine-forty to ten-fifteen, taking dictation from him, and then in the rumpus with the crew. About half past eleven John Mercer had entered with a man, a stranger, and called them together, and the man had asked if any of them had been in Ashby's room that morning, or had seen anyone entering or leaving it, and had got a unanimous no; and then Mercer had told them what had happened.

Even with my extremely acute understanding of attractive young women, I didn't suspect that she was holding out on me, except maybe on one detail, near the end, when I asked who she thought had lied to the cops about her and Ashby. She wouldn't name anyone even as a wild guess. I told her that was ridiculous, that any man or woman alive, knowing that someone or ones of a group had smeared him, would darned well have a notion who it was, but nothing doing. If any of them had it in for her she didn't know it, except Ashby, and he was dead.

At a quarter of eleven I was at my desk typing that part, nearly finished, when the house phone buzzed and I turned and got it. Wolfe rarely interrupts himself in the plant rooms to buzz me. Since he eats breakfast in his room and goes straight up to the roof, I hadn't seen him, so I said good morning.

"Good morning. What are you doing?"

"Typing my conference with Miss Vassos. The substance. Not verbatim. About done."

"Well?"

"Nothing startling. Some facts that might help. As for believing her, it's now fifty to one."

He grunted. "Or better. What could conceivably have led her to come to me with her story if it weren't true? Confound it. Where is she?"

"In her room. Of course she isn't going to work."

"Has she eaten? A guest, welcome or not, must not starve."

"She won't. She ate. She phoned the DA's office to ask when she can have the body. She'll do."

"The account in the *Times* supports her conclusion that the police assume that her father killed Ashby and committed suicide—not, of course, explicitly. You have read it?"

"Yes. So has she."

"But the *Times* may be wrong, and certainly she may be. It's possible that Mr. Cramer is finessing, and if so we can leave it to him. You'll have to find out. Conclusively."

"Lon Cohen may know."

"That won't do. You'll have to see Mr. Cramer. Now."

"If he's finessing he won't show *me* his hand."

"Certainly not. It will take dexterity. Your intelligence, guided by experience."

"Yeah. That's me. I'll go as soon as I finish typing this—five minutes. You'll find it in your drawer." I hung up, beating him to it.

It took only three minutes, I put the original in his desk drawer and the carbon in mine, went to the kitchen to tell Fritz I was leaving, got my coat from the hall rack, and departed. It's a good distance for a leg-stretcher from the old brownstone to Homicide South, but my brain likes to take it easy while I'm walking and I had to consult it about approaches, so I went to Ninth Avenue and flagged a taxi.

The dick at the desk, who was not my favorite city employee, said Cramer was busy but Lieutenant Rowcliff might spare me a minute, and I said no thank you and sat down to wait. It was close to noon when I was escorted down the hall to Cramer's room and found him standing at the end of his desk. As I entered he rasped, "So your client bought a one-way ticket. Want to see him?"

It seldom pays to prepare an approach. It depends on the approachee. The frame of mind he was in, it was hopeless to try smoothing him, so I switched. "Nuts," I said offensively. "If you mean Vassos, he wasn't a client, he was just a bootblack. You owe Mr. Wolfe something and he wants it. Elma Vassos, the daughter, slept in his house last night."

"The hell she did. In your room?"

"No, I snore. She came and fed him a line that her life was in danger. Whoever killed Ashby and her father, she didn't know who, was going to kill her. Then the morning paper has it different. Not spelled out, but it's there, that Vassos killed Ashby and when you started breathing down his neck he found a cliff and jumped off. So you knew about it when you came to see Mr. Wolfe Monday, you knew then about Ashby and Elma Vassos. Why didn't you say so? If you had, when she came last night she wouldn't have got in. So you owe him something. When he turns her out he wants to make a little speech to her, and he wants to know who gave you the dope on her and Ashby. Off the record, and you won't be quoted."

He threw his head back and laughed. Not an all-out laugh, just a ha-ha. He stretched an arm to touch my chest with a forefinger. "Slept in his house, huh? Wonderful! I'd like to hear his speech, what will he call her? Not trollop or floozy, he'll have some fancy word for it. And he has the nerve—on out, Goodwin."

"He wants to know—"

"Nuts. Beat it."

"But dammit—"

"Out."

I went; and since there was now nothing to work the brain on, I walked back to 35th Street. Wolfe was at his desk with the book he was on, *The Rise and Fall of the Third Reich*, by Shirer. A tray on his desk held beer bottle and a glass, and beside it was the report I had typed of my talk with Elma. I went to my desk and sat, and waited until he finished a paragraph and looked up.

"You will," I said "We'll have to bounce her, I would prefer to marry her and reform her, but Cramer would take my license away. Do you want it in full?"

He said yes, and I gave it to him. At the end I said, "As you see, it didn't take any dexterity. The first thing he said, 'So your client bought a one-way ticket,' was enough. He is not finessing. You can't blame him for laughing, since he honestly believes that you have a floozy for a house guest. As for his refusing to name—"

"Shut up."

I leaned back and crossed my legs. He glowered at me for five seconds, then closed his eyes. In a moment he opened them. "It's hopeless," he said through his teeth.

"Yes, sir," I agreed, "I suppose I could disguise myself as a bootblack and take Pete's box and try to—"

"Shut up! I mean it's intolerable. Mr. Cramer cannot be permitted to flout . . ." He put the book down without marking his place, which he never did. "There's no way out, I could have shined my shoes myself. I considered this possibility after reading your report, and here it is. Get Mr. Parker."

I didn't have to look at the book for the number of
Nathaniel Parker, the lawyer. I turned to the phone
and dialed it, and got him, and Wolfe lifted his re-
ceiver.

"Good morning, sir. Afternoon. I need you. I am
going to advise a young woman who has consulted
me to bring actions against a corporation and five or six
individuals, asking for damages, say a million dollars
from each of them, on account of defamatory statements they have made. Slander, not libel, since as far
as I know the statements have been made orally and
not published. She is here in my house. Can you come
to my office? . . . No, after lunch will do. Three
o'clock? . . . Very well, I'll expect you."

He hung up and turned to me. "We'll have to keep
her. You will go with her to her home to get whatever
she needs—not now, later. Mr. Cramer expects me to
turn her out, does he? Pfui. She would be dead within
twenty-four hours, and that would clean the slate for
him. Tell Fritz to take her lunch to her room. I will
not be rude to a guest at my table, and the effort to control myself would spoil the meal."

4.

I asked Parker once how many law books he had
in his office, and he said about seven hundred. I asked
how many there were in print in the English language,
and he said probably around ten thousand. So I suppose you can't expect to give a lawyer an order for a
lawsuit the way you give a tailor an order for a suit
of clothes. But they sure do make a job of it. Parker
came on the dot at three, and they barely got it settled
in time for Wolfe to keep his afternoon date with the
orchids. At three minutes to four Wolfe got to his feet
and said, "Then tomorrow as early as may be. You'll
proceed as soon as Archie phones you that he has explained the matter to Miss Vassos."

Parker shook his head. "The way you operate. You
actually haven't mentioned it to her?"

"No. It would have been pointless to mention it un-til I learned if it was feasible."

Wolfe went to the hall to take the elevator to the roof. Parker went along, and I went to hold his coat and let him out. Then I mounted two flights to the South Room and knocked on the door, heard a faint "Come in," and did so. Elma was sitting on the edge of the bed running her fingers through her hair. "I guess I fell asleep," she said. "What time is it?"

I would have been willing to help her with the hair. Any man would; it was nice hair. "Four o'clock," I said. "Fritz says you ate only two of his Creole fritters. You don't care for shrimps?"

"I'm sorry. He doesn't like me, and I don't blame him, I'm a nuisance." She sighed, deep.

"That's not it. He suspects any woman who enters the house of wanting to take it over." I pulled a chair around and sat. "There have been developments. I went to see a cop, an inspector named Cramer, and you're right. They think your father killed Ashby and then himself. You are now Mr. Wolfe's client. That stack of bills in the safe is still your property, but I have taken a dollar from it as a retainer. Do you ap-prove?"

"Of course—but take all of it. I know it's noth-ing . . ."

"Skip it. That's no inducement for him. And don't thank him. He would rather miss a meal than have anyone think he's a softy, that he would wiggle a finger to help anyone. Don't even hint at it. The idea is that Cramer has flouted him, his word, and therefore he will make a monkey of Cramer, and I admit that that may be the main point. So he has to prove that your father didn't kill Ashby, and the only way he can do that is to find out who did. The question is how. He would have to send me to that building to go over the set-up and see people, and to invite some of them to come to his office, since he never leaves the house on business, but he can't expect the impossible even of me. They would toss me out, and they wouldn't come. So he must—"

"Some of the girls might come. And Mr. Busch might."

"Not enough. We need the ones who wouldn't. So he must drop a bomb. You are going to sue six people for damages, a million dollars each. Slander. He was going to have you sue the corporation too, but the lawyer vetoed it. The lawyer is preparing the papers and will go ahead as soon as you phone him to. His name is Nathaniel Parker and he's good. It isn't expected that any of the cases will ever get to a court or that you will collect anything, that's not the idea. The idea is that the fur will begin to fly. Do you want to consult anybody before you tell Parker to go ahead? Do you know a lawyer?"

"No." Her fingers were clasped tight. "Of course I'll do anything Mr. Wolfe says. Who are the six people?"

"One, John Mercer. Two, Andrew Busch. Three, Philip Horan. Four, Frances Cox. Five, Mrs. Ashby. Six, Inspector Cramer. Anything Cramer says in his official capacity is privileged, but there's a point of law. He may have said something to a reporter, and he told me you're a floozy, or implied it. At least it will be a threat to get him on the witness stand under oath and ask him who told him what about you and Ashby, and just having him summoned will be a pleasure for Mr. Wolfe and you might as well humor him. You're not listening."

"Yes, I am. I don't think I — Can't you leave Mr. Busch out?"

"Why should we?"

"Because I don't think he said anything like that about me. I'm sure he wouldn't."

"Neither did some of the others, probably. It's even conceivable that none of those five did. This is only to get in there, to get at them."

She nodded. "I know," I understand that, but I wouldn't want Mr. Busch to think that I think he might slander me. If what you want—it Mr. Wolfe wants to talk to him, I'm pretty sure he would come if I asked him."

I eyed her. "There seems to be an angle you didn't

mention this morning. When you told me about Busch you didn't say he would come if you whistled."

"I'm not saying it now!" She was indignant. "All I'm saying, he's a nice man, and he's decent, and he wouldn't do that!"

"Have you seen much of him out of the office?"

"No. After Mr. Ashby, I decided I wouldn't make any dates with any man in the office, married or not."

"Okay, we'll exclude Busch, with the understanding that you'll produce him if and when we need him," I got up. "We'll go down to the office and phone Parker, and then we'll go and get whatever you want for an indefinite stay. It may be two days and it may be two months. When Mr. Wolfe—"

"Stay here two months? I can't!"

"You can and will if necessary. If you got killed it would be next to impossible for Mr. Wolfe to get back at Cramer, and that would sour him for good and he would be unbearable. If you want to do things to your face and hair, not that I see anything wrong with them, I'll be down in the office." I went.

Waiting to call Parker until she came down, since he would want to hear his client's voice as evidence that she existed, I had a notion to buzz the plant rooms and ask Wolfe if he wanted to see Andrew Busch at six o'clock, but since he would probably have insisted on Busch getting a summons along with the others I decided against it. I'm a softy. Elma came down much sooner than most girls would have after a nap, and I dialed and got Parker, told him it was all set but that Busch was to be crossed off, and put Elma on. He asked her if he was to proceed on her behalf as he had been instructed by Wolfe, and she said yes, and that was it. I told her I had another call to make, dialed the number of the *Gazette*, got Lon Cohen, and asked him if his offer of a grand for a piece on Pete Vassos was still open. He said he'd have to see the piece first.

"We haven't got time to write it," I said. "We're busy. But if you want something for nothing, Miss Elma Vassos, his daughter, has engaged the services of Nero Wolfe, the famous private detective, and is staying at his house, and is not accessible. On his advice, she has engaged Nathaniel Parker, the famous counselor, to bring an action against five people: John Mercer, Philip Horan, Frances Cox, Mrs. Dennis Ashby, and Inspector Cramer of the NYPD. She is asking for a million dollars for damages for slander from each of them. They will be served tomorrow, probably in time for your first edition. I'm giving you this, exclusive, on instructions from Mr. Wolfe. Parker has been told that you'll probably be phoning him for confirmation, and you'll get it. Yours truly. See you in court."

"Wait a minute, hold it! You can't just—"

"Sorry, I'm busy. No use calling back because I won't be here. Print now, pay later."

I hung up and went to the kitchen to tell Fritz we were leaving, and by the time I got to the hall rack Elma had her hat and coat on. Since her place was downtown we went to Eighth Avenue for a taxi. She was all right at walking. Walking with a girl, you can tell pretty well if you'd want to dance with her. Not if she keeps step, she may not have the legs for that, but if she naturally stays with you without doing a barnacle.

Another mark for her, she didn't apologize for the neighborhood she lived in as the cab turned into Graham Street and stopped in front of Number 314. At that, it wasn't as bad in the December dark as it would have been in daylight; no street is. Dirt doesn't look so dirty. But I must say the vestibule she led me into would have appreciated some attention, and when she used her key and we entered, the inside was no better. She said, "Up three flights," and went to the stairs, and I followed. I admit I thought she was overdoing it a little. She might at least have said something like, "When I got a job I thought we ought to move, but my father didn't want to," just casually. Not a word.

On the third landing she started down the hall toward the rear, stopped after a couple of steps, and said, "Why, the light's on!"

I was at her elbow. I whispered, "Which door?" She pointed to the right, to where a strip of light showed through the crack at the bottom of a door. I whispered, "Is there a bell?" and she whispered back, "It isn't working." I went to the door and knocked on it, and after a short wait it opened, and facing me was a man about my height with a broad flat face and a lot of tousled brown hair.

"Good evening," I said.

"Where's Miss Vassos?" he said. "Are you a police— Oh! Thank God!"

Elma was there. "But you—how did you—this is Mr. Busch, Mr. Goodwin."

"I seem to be . . ." he let it hang, apparently undecided how he seemed to be. He looked at me and back at her.

"I'll trade you even," I said. "I'll tell you why I'm here if you'll tell me why you're here. I came to carry a bag of clothes and accessories for Miss Vassos. She is staying at Nero Wolfe's house on Thirty-fifth Street. My name is Archie Goodwin and I work for him. Your turn."

"Nero Wolfe the detective?"

"Right."

He went to her. "You're staying at his house?"—

"Yes."

"You were there last night and today?"

"Yes."

"I wish you had let me know. I came here from the office. I just got here. I was here last night. I got the janitor to let me in; he's worried too. I was afraid you might—I'm glad to see—I thought perhaps . . ."

"I guess I should have phoned," she said.

"Yes, I wish you had; then at least I would have known. . . ."

He didn't sound much like Paladin. Or even an office manager. "If you don't mind," I said, "Miss Vassos would like to come in and pack a bag. She has hired Nero Wolfe to find out who killed Dennis Ashby, and she'll stay at his house until he does. Of course, since you think her father killed Ashby, I don't suppose—"

"I don't think her father killed Ashby."

"No? Then why did you tell the police that he had found out that Ashby had seduced her?"

He hauled off and swung at me. He meant well, but was so slow that I could have landed a poke while he was still on his backswing. Elma was quicker, jumping between us. He was going through with it anyhow, looping around her, and he would finally have reached the target if I had moved my head eight inches to the left and waited till he got there, but instead I caught his wrist and jerked it down and gave it a twist. That twist hurts, but he didn't squeak. Elma, between us, turned to face me, protesting, "I told you he wouldn't!"

"I didn't," he said.

"Do you know who did?"

"No."

"Okay, you can come along for a talk with Nero Wolfe. You can carry her bag. If there are two, we'll each take one. Go ahead, Miss Vassos, I won't let him hurt me. If he gets me down I'll yell."

She slipped in past him. Busch looked at his wrist and felt at it, and I told him it might swell a little. He turned and went inside, and I followed. It was a medium-sized room, very neat, good enough chairs and nice plain rugs, a TV set in a corner, magazines on a table, shelves with books. A framed picture on top of the book shelves looked familiar and I crossed over, and darned if it wasn't Wolfe on the cover of *Tick* magazine. That had been more than a year ago. I allowed myself a healthy grin as I thought of how Sergeant Stebbins, or anyone else from Homicide, had felt when he came to have a look at the home of a murderer and found a picture of Nero Wolfe in a place of honor. I would have liked to take it and show it to Wolfe. I had heard him quote what someone said, that no man is a hero to his valet, but apparently he could be to his bootblack.

When Elma came out of an inner room with a suitcase and a small bag, Busch, who had put his overcoat on, went to relieve her of the load. I looked at my watch: five fifty-five. Wolfe would be down from the plant rooms by the time we got there.

"I'll take one," I offered. "Better give the wrist a rest."

"The wrist's all right," he said, trying not to set his jaw.

A hero.

5

There can be such a thing as too damn much self-control. I should have resigned that day, for the forty-third time, when Wolfe glared at me and said, "I won't see him." It was inexcusable, being childish in front of a client. Leaving Busch in the front room, I had gone with Elma to the office, explained why I had told Parker to leave Busch out, reported the episode at Graham Street, said that I had checked with the janitor on the way out and he had admitted that he had let Busch into the Vassos apartment, and asked if he wanted Elma present while he talked with Busch; and he said, "I won't see him." Top that. He knew he was going to have to see a bunch of them and he was paying a lawyer to pull a stunt that would make them come, but that would be tomorrow and this was today and he was reading a book, and I hadn't phoned to warn him. I should have walked out on him, but there was Elma, so I merely said, "He can have my room and I'll sleep here on the couch."

His eyes narrowed at me. He knew I meant it and that I wouldn't back down, and that it was his fault for starting it in front of a witness. If I had just sat and met his gaze it would have had to end either by his firing me or my quitting, so I arose, said I would take Miss Vassos' luggage up to her room, shook my head no at her on my way to the hall, picked up the bag and suitcase, mounted the two flights, put them in the South Room, returned to the landing, and stood and listened.

That simplified it for him. With me there it would have been impossible; with me gone, all he had to do was to get her to say that it might help if he talked to

Busch. Which he did. I could hear the voices, though not the words, for three minutes; then nothing; and then voices again, including Busch's. I descended. Of course I kept my eyes straight ahead as I entered and crossed to my desk, detouring around Busch, who was in one of the yellow chairs that had been drawn up to face Wolfe's desk. Wolfe was talking.

". . . and I intend to do so. I'm not obliged to account for the springs of my interest. Call it pique, Mr. Vassos kept my shoes presentable and never failed me; it won't be easy to replace him; and whoever deprived me of his services will be made to regret it. Let's consider you, since you're here. Discovered by Mr. Goodwin and Miss Vassos in her apartment, you affected concern for her welfare. Real concern, or assumed?"

Busch was sitting straight and stiff, his palms on his knees. "I don't have to account to you either," he declared, louder than necessary. "How do I know what you're going to do?"

"You don't. But you will. I won't debate it. Go. You'll be back."

I gritted my teeth. He was taking the trick after all. He was putting him out, with a dodge that tied my tongue. If there had been a cliff handy I would have pushed him off. But it didn't work. Busch looked at Elma, who was in the red leather chair. That turned his head so I couldn't see his face, but there must have been a question on it, for she answered it.

"He's going to do what he says, Mr. Busch. He's going to make a monkey of an inspector named Cramer. If he wants you to tell him anything—and if you want to—"

"I want—Will you marry me?"

Her eyes widened. "What?"

"Will you marry me?"

She stared, speechless.

"Effective, Mr. Busch," Wolfe growled. His dodge wasn't going to work. "For establishing briefly and cogently that your concern is real, admirable. Then you don't believe that Miss Vassos was seduced by Mr. Ashby?"

"No, I know she wasn't."

"You told Mr. Goodwin that you don't know who told the police that she had been."

"I don't."

"But you knew that someone had."

"I didn't exactly know. I knew that the police thought that, or suspected it, from questions they asked me."

"Was that why you were so concerned for Miss Vassos' welfare that you went to her home last night and persuaded the janitor to let you in and repeated the performance today?"

"It was partly that, but I would have done that anyway. Yesterday she was worried about her father because he hadn't come home, and I tried to find out if he was in the building. Then last night the news came that he was dead, his body had been found. I phoned her home and there was no answer, and I went there, and there was no word from her today, and the police didn't know where she was, so I went again. I know what you're getting at, you want to know if I was there waiting for her because I was worried about her or because I wanted to kill her. Because someone must want to kill her, someone must have lied about her to her father and then lied to the police."

Wolfe nodded. "You're assuming that her father believed the lie and killed Ashby and then killed himself."

"No, I'm not. I only know he might have. I haven't seen her, I haven't had a chance to talk with her. I could talk with her about this all right. From the way I'm talking to you, you probably think I'm a pretty good talker, that I don't have any trouble speaking my piece, but I've been wanting for more than a year to tell her how I feel, that I know how wonderful she is, that there's no girl on earth like her, that I have never—"

"Yes. You established that point by asking her to marry you. She has probably grasped it. As you will no doubt hear from her when you get a chance, she is certain that her father would not have believed such a lie about her, so he did not kill her, so he did not kill himself. Therefore I need to know as much as possible about people's movements at the critical times. According to the medical examiner as reported in the paper, Peter Vassos landed at the bottom of that cliff and died between ten o'clock and midnight Monday evening. Since Miss Vassos certainly won't marry you if you killed her father, let's eliminate you. Where were you those two hours?"

"I was at home. I went to bed about eleven o'clock."

"You live alone?"

"Yes."

"Good. You have no alibi. A man with an alibi is suspect *ipso facto*. Now for Mr. Ashby. Where were you at ten thirty-five Monday morning?"

"In my room. My office."

"Alone?"

"Yes. I've gone over this with the police. Miss Vassos had been there taking letters, but she left about a quarter past ten. Pete came about a quarter to eleven and gave me a shine. In between those two times I was alone."

"You didn't leave your room?"

"No."

"Was the door open and did you see anyone pass?"

"The door was open, but my room is at the end of the hall. I never see anyone pass."

"Then you can't help much. But you do corroborate Mr. Vassos' account of his movements. If he came to your room at ten forty-five, shined your shoes, and went straight to Mr. Ashby's room, he entered it about ten fifty-two. He arrived here at three minutes past eleven. Do you know where he had been just before coming to you?"

"Yes, he had been in Mr. Mercer's room, giving him a shine."

"And before that?"

"I don't know. That's what the police wanted to know. They think he had already been in Ashby's room, that he went in by the other door and killed him."

"Did they tell you that?"

"No, but it was obvious from their questions—about him and about that other door."

"Does your room also have a door into the outer hall?"

"No. Ashby's is the only one."

Wolfe turned his head to look up at the wall clock. Half an hour till dinnertime. He looked at Busch. "Now, sir. As I told you at the beginning, I have concluded that Mr. Vassos did not kill Mr. Ashby, and I intend to find out who did and expose him. On this perhaps you *can* help. Who is safe or satisfied or solvent because Ashby is dead? *Cui bono?*"

"I don't get— Oh." Busch nodded. "Of course. That's Latin. The police asked me too, but not like that. I told them I didn't know, and I don't. I saw very little of Ashby personally, I mean outside of business. I knew his wife when she worked there, her name was Snyder then, Joan Snyder, but I've only seen her a couple of times since she married Ashby two years ago. The way you put it, safe or satisfied or solvent because he's dead—I don't know."

"What about people in the office?"

"Nobody liked him. I didn't. I don't think even Mr. Mercer did. We all knew he had saved the business, he was responsible for its success, but we didn't like him. I had complaints from the girls about him. They didn't like to go to his room. A few months ago one girl quit on account of him. When I took it up with Mr. Mercer he said Ashby had the defects of his qualities, that when he wanted something he never hesitated to go after it, and that was why the corporation's income was ten times what it had been four years ago. But when I say nobody liked him maybe I ought to say except one." His eyes went to Elma and back to Wolfe.

"Miss Vassos?"

"Good Lord, no." He was shocked. "Because I looked at her? I just happened— I just wanted to. Miss Cox, Frances Cox, the receptionist. Ashby wouldn't have a secretary, and Miss Cox did the things for him that a secretary does, appointments and so on, except stenography. Maybe she liked him; I suppose she must have. There was a lot of office gossip about them, but you can't go by office gossip. If an office manager took all the gossip seriously he'd go crazy. Only one day last spring Ashby's wife—I told you she was Joan Snyder when she worked there—she came and asked me to fire her."

"To fire Miss Cox?"

"Yes. She said she was a bad influence on her husband. I had to laugh, I couldn't help it—a bad influence on Dennis Ashby. I told her I couldn't fire her, and I couldn't. Ashby had had her salary raised twice without consulting me."

Wolfe grunted. "Another name Miss Vassos has mentioned. Philip Horan. Since he's a salesman, I presume he worked under Ashby?"

"Yes."

"He had expected to get the promotion that Ashby had got?"

"Yes."

"And he resented it?"

"Yes."

"Then Ashby's death is no bereavement for him?"

"No."

"You are suddenly laconic. Have I touched a nerve?"

"Well . . . I thought Phil Horan deserved to get that job, and I still think so."

"And he'll get it now?"

"I suppose he will."

"I won't ask if he might have killed Ashby to get it; you're partial and would of course say no." Wolfe looked up at the clock. "Have you ever sat at table with Miss Vassos, had a meal with her?"

"I don't see what bearing that has on—"

"None, but it's a civil question. Have you?"

"No. I asked her twice, but she declined."

"Then it was foolhardy to ask her to marry you. You can't know what a woman is like until you see her at her food. I invite you to dine with us. There will be chicken sorrel soup with egg yolks and sherry, and roast quail with a sauce of white wine, veal stock, and white grapes. You will not be robbing us; there is enough."

I didn't catch his response because I was commenting to myself. The rule no business at meals was strictly enforced, but I would have to work right through the soup and quail on to the cheese and coffee, as an expert, taking Busch in. When he left I would be asked if his concern for Miss Vassos was real or phony, yes or no. If I couldn't say, some good grub would have been wasted.

It was wasted.

6

The fur started to fly, the first flurry, a little after two Thursday afternoon, when Parker phoned while we were eating lunch—Elma with us—to say that he had just had a talk with an attorney representing John Mercer, Philip Horan, and Frances Cox. He had called before noon to say that all five of them had been served. He had told the attorney that his client, Elma Vassos, had retained him and told him to bring the actions after she had been advised to do so by Nero Wolfe, who was investigating the situation for her; that he was satisfied that his client had a valid complaint but he wouldn't discuss it with the opposing counselor until the investigation had progressed further; that after careful consideration he felt that it would probably be impossible to arrive at a settlement without a court trial; and that he would of course report the conversation to his client, who was staying at Nero Wolfe's house. I returned to the dining room and relayed it to Wolfe, who would not interrupt a meal to speak on the phone, and he muttered, "Satisfactory."

The next flurry came two hours later, from the widow. Wolfe had gone up to the plant rooms, and Elma had gone with him to look at the orchids. Not that he had thawed any; he had got the notion that she was working on me and the less we were alone together the better. The phone rang and I answered it. "Nero Wolfe's office, Archie Goodwin speaking."

"I want to talk to Elma Vassos." A woman's voice, peevish.

"Your name, please?"

"Oh, indeed. Is she there?"

"Not in the room, but I can get her. If you don't mind giving me your name?"

"I don't mind a bit. Joan Ashby. Don't bother to get her; you'll do, if you're Archie Goodwin. I've just been talking to that lawyer, Parker, and he told me she's at Nero Wolfe's house. I told him if she wants to sue me for a million dollars she can go right ahead, and I thought I might as well tell her too. He said he would prefer to speak with my attorney, and I said that would be fine if I had one. What would I pay an attorney with? Tell Elma Vassos if she gets some of those millions from those others I would deeply appreciate it if she would pay some of my husband's debts, and then maybe I could eat. I'd like to see her at that, I'd like to see the one that got him killed."

"Why don't you, Mrs. Ashby? Come, by all means. It's not far, if you're at home. The address is—"

"I know the address, but I'm not coming. When I went out this morning, from the bunch of reporters and photographers on the sidewalk waiting for me you might think I was Liz Taylor. I'd like to see her, but not enough to face that gang again. Just tell her all she gets out of me wouldn't buy her a subway token. If she wants—"

"She'd like to see you too."

"I'll bet she would."

"She really would. She said so last night. Why don't I take her there? We can be there in twenty minutes. You've lost a husband, and she has lost a father. It would do you both good."

"Sure. We can swap tears. Come ahead, but bring your own hankies. I use paper towels."

She hung up. I buzzed the plant rooms on the house phone, got Wolfe, and reported. He growled, "She's probably lying about the debts, and bluffing. I'll send

Miss Vassos down at once. Don't bring that wretch back with you."

"But you wanted to see all of them."

"Not that one. Not unless it becomes imperative. Pfui. You will judge. Your intelligence guided by experience."

When Elma came—down the stairs, not in the elevator—I was waiting for her in the hall with my coat on. When I told her it might be a little hard to take, judging from Mrs. Ashby on the phone, she said she could stand it if I could, and when, after we got a taxi on Ninth Avenue and were crawling crosstown, I gave her the conversation verbatim, she said, "She sounds awful, but if he left a lot of debts— Of course that doesn't matter, since we don't expect to get anything . . ."

The number on East 37th Street, which had been in the papers, was between Park and Lexington. If there were any journalists on post they weren't visible, but daylight was gone, nearly five o'clock. Pushing the button marked Ashby in the vestibule, getting a voice asking who is it, and telling the grill our names, I pushed the door when the click came, and we entered. It was a small lobby, aluminum-trim modern, and the elevator was a do-it-yourself. I pushed the "3" button, we were lifted and emerged on the third floor, and there was the widow, leaning against the jamb of an open door.

"Double wake," she said. "I just thought that up." She focused on us as we approached. "I thought up another one too. My husband liked what the ads said, go now, pay later. Eat now, pay later. I thought up kill now, pay later. I like it. I hope you like it." She didn't move.

It had been fairly obvious on the phone that she was tight, and she must have had another go. Under control and in order, she could have been a fine specimen, with big dark eyes and a wide warm mouth, but not at the moment. Elma had started to offer a hand but changed her mind. I said distinctly, "Mrs. Ashby, Miss Vassos. I'm Archie Goodwin. May we come in?"

"You're a surprise," she told Elma. "You're so little. Not teeny, but little. He liked big girls, like me, only he made exsheptions. You've got a nerve, suing me for a

million dollars. I ought to be suing you for what he
spent on you. Did he give you a gold flower with a pearl
in the middle? You haven't got it on. There was one in
a Jensen box when I went there that morning, the day
he got killed. Kill now, pay later. I like it. I hope you
like it." She fluttered a hand. "Thank you for coming,
thank you very much. I just wanted to look at you. My
God, you're little."

I was smiling at her, a broad, friendly smile. "About
that gold flower with a pearl in the middle, Mrs. Ashby.
That you saw on his desk Monday morning. You didn't
expect Miss Vassos to be wearing that, did you?"

"Certainly not. They've got that one, the police. I
told them I saw it there and they said they had it." Her
eyes went back to Elma, with an effort. "Of course
you've got one. They all got one. Eighty bucks at Jensen's, sometimes more."

Elma parted her lips to say something, but I got in
ahead. "I suppose your husband was in his room when
you were there Monday morning, Mrs. Ashby? What
time was it?"

"It was ten o'clock." She grinned at me. "You're a
detective." She pointed a wobbly finger at me. "Answer
yesh or no."

"Yes, but I'm not a cop."

"I know, I know. Nero Wolfe. Look here, if I'm high
I know it. I know what I said and what I signed. I went
there that morning at ten o'clock, and I knocked on
the door, and he opened it, and I went in, and he gave
me forty dollars, and I came out, and I went and
bought a pair of shoes with the forty dollars because the
accounts at the stores had been stopped." She straightened up, swaying a little, reached and caught the edge
of the door, backed up, and swung the door shut with a
loud slam.

I could have stuck a foot in to stop it, but didn't
bother. The shape she was in, it would have taken more
than intelligence guided by experience to sort her out,
and I already had a better fact than I had expected to
get, that she had been in Ashby's room Monday morning and the cops knew it. Of course they had checked
it, and if the clerk who sold her the shoes had confirmed

her timetable she was out. Maybe. I followed Elma to the elevator.

In the taxi Elma said nothing until it stopped at Fifth Avenue for a red light, then turned her head to me and blurted, "It's so ugly!"

I nodded. "Yeah. I told you she'd be hard to take, but I had to have a look at her. That kill now, pay later, that's okay, but the trouble is who does the paying?"

"Did she kill him?"

"Pass. She says he left her nothing but debts."

"It's so ugly. I don't want to sue her. Couldn't we stop it, I mean for her?"

I patted her shoulder. "Quit fussing. The damage has been done, and whoever gets it now has got it coming. You came and asked Mr. Wolfe for something and you're going to get it, so relax. You have just convinced me, absolutely, that you never went very far with Ashby. Knowing you were going to meet Mrs. Ashby, you put your lipstick on crooked. Not that I had any real doubt, but that settles it."

She opened her bag and got out her mirror.

Paying the hackie at the curb in front of the old brownstone, mounting the stoop with Elma, and using my key, I was surprised to find that the chain bolt was on, since it was only five-thirty and Wolfe would still be up in the plant rooms. I was starting my finger to the button when the door opened and Fritz was there; he must have been in the hall on the lookout. He had his finger to his lips, so I kept my voice low to ask as we entered, "Company?"

He took Elma's coat and put it on a hanger as I attended to mine, then turned. "Three of them, two men and a woman, in the office. Mr. Mercer, Mr. Horan, and Miss Cox. The door is closed. I don't like this, Archie, I never do, you know that, having to watch people—"

"Sure. But if they brought a bomb it won't go off till they leave." I didn't bother about my voice since the office was soundproofed, including the door. "When did they come?"

"Just ten minutes ago. Mr. Wolfe said to tell them to come back in an hour, but they insisted, and he said to put them in the office and stay in the hall. I told him I was making *glace de viande,* but he said one of them is a murderer. I want to do my share, you know that, Archie, but I can't make good *glace de viande* if I have to be watching murderers."

"Certainly not. But he could be wrong. It's possible that Miss Vassos and I have just been interviewing the murderer, who is plastered." I turned to Elma. "This could be even uglier, so why don't you go up to your room? If you're needed later we'll let you know."

"Thank you, Mr. Goodwin," she said and headed for the stairs. Fritz made for the kitchen, and I followed. He went to the big table, which was loaded with the makings of meat glaze, and, after getting the milk from the refrigerator and pouring a glass, I went to the small table against the wall, where the house phone was, and buzzed the plant rooms.

"Yes?"

"Me. Miss Vassos has gone to her room and I'm in the kitchen. Report on Mrs. Ashby." I gave it to him. "So it's just as well I wasn't supposed to bring her; I would have had to carry her up the stoop. Notice that I didn't pry it out of her that she was there Monday morning, she tossed it in. Verdict reserved. Any instructions about the company in the office?"

"No."

"Do you want me up there?"

"No. I've been interrupted enough." He hung up.

The genius. If he had a program beyond a fishing party, which I doubted, I could guess my part as we went along. I finished the milk, taking my time, and went to the alcove in the hall and slid the panel, uncovering the hole. On the alcove side the hole is an open rectangle; on the office side it is hidden by a picture of a waterfall which you can see through from the alcove.

John Mercer, president of Mercer's Bobbins, Inc., was leaning back in the red leather chair, patting the chair arms with his palms. His white hair was thin but still there, and he looked more like a retired admiral than a bobbin merchant. Fritz had put yellow chairs in front of Wolfe's desk for the other two. They were talking in the low voices people use in a doctor's waiting room, something about a phone call that had or hadn't come from some customer. Philip Horan was broad-shouldered and long-armed, with a long bony face and quick-moving brown eyes. Frances Cox was a big girl, a real armful, but her poundage was well distributed. Nothing about her smooth smart face suggested that she had been through three tough days, though she must have been. I stayed at the hole, sizing them up, until the sound came of the elevator, then rounded the corner to the office door, opened it, and stayed there as Wolfe entered. He crossed to his desk, stood, and sent his eyes around. He fixed them on Mercer and spoke.

"You are John Mercer?"

"I am." It came out hoarse, and Mercer cleared his throat. "Miss Frances Cox. Mr. Philip Horan. We want—"

Wolfe cut him off. "If you please." I had gone to my desk, and he sent me a glance. "Mr. Goodwin." He stayed on his feet. "I question the propriety of this, Mr. Mercer. Miss Vassos has brought an action at law against you three, and communication should be between her counselor and yours. I'm a detective, not a lawyer."

Mercer had straightened up. "Your attorney told mine that you had told Miss Vassos to bring the action."

"I did."

"And that she's here in your house."

"She is. But you're not going to see her."

"Isn't that a little high-handed?"

"No. It's merely circumspect. She has resorted to the law to right a wrong; let the lawyers do the talking."

"But her lawyer won't talk! He says he won't discuss it until you have gone further with the investigation!"

Wolfe's shoulders went up an eighth of an inch and down. "Very well. Then what are you doing here? Did your attorney tell you to come?"

"No. We're here to tell you there's nothing to investigate. Have you seen the afternoon paper? The *Gazette?*"

"No."

"It's on the front page. Inside are pictures of us and Inspector Cramer, and you. That kind of sensational publicity is terrible for a respectable business firm, and it's outrageous. All we've done, we've answered the questions the police asked us, investigating a murder, and we had to. What is there for you to investigate?"

"A murder. Two murders. In order to establish the ground for Miss Vassos' action for slander I need to learn who killed Mr. Ashby and Mr. Vassos. It seems discreet and proper for Miss Vassos' attorney to decline to discuss it with your attorney until I have done so."

"But that's ridiculous! Who killed Ashby and Vassos? *You* learn that? The police already have! My attorney thinks it's just a blackmailing trick, and I think he's right!"

Wolfe shook his head. "He's wrong; attorneys often are. He doesn't know what I know, that the police have *not* identified the murderer. The point is this: whoever killed those men is almost certainly responsible for the defamation of Miss Vassos' character, and I'm going to expose him. The actions brought by her are merely a step in the process, and manifestly a potent one, for here you are, you and Miss Cox and Mr. Horan, and it is highly likely that one of you is the culprit."

Mercer gawked at him. "One of *us?*"

"Yes, sir. That's my working hypothesis, based on a supportable conclusion. You may reject it with disdain and go, or you may stay and discuss it, as you please."

"You don't mean it. You *can't* mean it!"

"I can and do. That's what I'm going to investigate. The only way to stop me would be to satisfy me that I'm mistaken."

"Of course you're mistaken!"

"Satisfy me."

Mercer looked at Philip Horan and Frances Cox. They looked back and at each other. Miss Cox said, loud, "It *is* blackmail." Horan said, "We should have brought the lawyer." Miss Cox said, "He wouldn't come." Mercer looked at Wolfe and said, "How do you expect us to satisfy you?"

Wolfe nodded. "That's the question." He sat, brought the chair forward, and swiveled. "Conceivably you can, and speedily; there's only one way to find out. Mr. Horan. Did Mr. Vassos ever shine your shoes?"

The doorbell rang. I got up and detoured around the yellow chairs to the hall, and switched on the stoop light. There facing me, his blunt nose almost touching the glass, was Inspector Cramer. From the expression on his big round red face, he hadn't come to bring the million dollars.

7

It was sometimes necessary, when we had company, to use an alias when announcing a caller who might or might not be welcome, and any name with two Ds in it meant Cramer. I stepped into the office and said, "Mr. Judd."

"Ah?" Wolfe cocked his head at me. "Indeed." His brows went up. He turned to the company. "It's a question. Mr. Cramer of the police is at the door. Shall we have him join us? What do you think?"

They just looked. Not a word.

"I think not," Wolfe said, "unless you want him." He pushed his chair back and rose. "You will excuse me." He headed for the door. I stepped aside to let him by and followed him to the front. He slipped the bolt in, opened the door the two inches the chain would allow, and spoke through the crack. "I'm busy, Mr. Cramer, and I don't know when I'll be free. Miss Frances Cox, Mr. John Mercer, and Mr. Philip Horan are with me. I came to tell you instead of sending Mr. Goodwin because it seemed—"

"Open the door!"

"No. I wouldn't object to your presence while I talk with these people, but you would—"

"I want to see Elma Vassos. Open the door."

"That's it." Wolfe turned his head, and so did I, at a noise from behind. Philip Horan's head was sticking out at the office door. Wolfe turned back to the crack. "That's the point. Miss Vassos will not see you. As I have said before, a citizen's rights vis-à-vis an officer of the law are anomalous and nonsensical. I can refuse to let you into my house, but once I admit you I am helpless. You can roam about at will. You can speak to anyone you choose. I dare not touch you. If I order you to leave you can ignore me. If I call in a policeman to expel an intruder I am laughed at. So I don't admit you—unless you have a warrant!"

"You know damn well I haven't. Elma Vassos has filed a complaint against me at your instigation, and I'm going to discuss it with her."

"Discuss it with her attorney."

"Bah, Nat Parker. You call the tune and he plays it. Are you going to open this door?"

"No."

"By God, I *will* get a warrant."

"On what ground? I advise you to watch the wording. You can't claim the right to enter my house in search of evidence. Evidence of what? You can't charge an attempt to obstruct justice; if you say I'm hindering an official investigation, I ask what investigation? Not of the death of Dennis Ashby; from the published accounts and from what you said to Mr. Goodwin yesterday morning, I understand that that is closed. As for a warrant to search my house for Miss Vassos, that's absurd. In your official capacity you can assert no right to see her or touch her. She has violated no law by bringing a civil action against you, I advise——"

"She's a material witness."

"Indeed. In what matter? The People of the State of New York versus Peter Vassos for the murder of Dennis Ashby? Pfui. Peter Vassos is dead. Or have you abandoned that theory? Do you now think that the one who killed Ashby is still alive? If so, who are the suspects and how can Miss Vassos be a material witness against one or more of them? No, Mr. Cramer; it's no good, I'm busy; the cold air rushes through this crack; I'm shutting the door."

"Wait a minute. You know damn well she can't get me for damages."

"Perhaps not. But there's a good chance she can get you put under oath and asked who told you that she had improper relations with Dennis Ashby. Mr. Goodwin asked you that yesterday and you were amused. Offensively. Will you tell me now, not for quotation?"

"No. You know I won't. Are you saying that she didn't? That Vassos didn't kill Ashby?"

"Certainly. That's why I got those people here. That's what I'm going to discuss with them. The actions brought—"

"Damn it, Wolfe, open the door!"

"I'm shutting it. If you change your mind about answering my question, you know my phone number."

Cramer has his points. Knowing that it would be silly to try to stop the door with his foot, since Wolfe and I together weigh 450 pounds, he didn't. Knowing that if he stood there and shook his fist and made faces we would see him through the one-way glass, he didn't. He turned and went. Wolfe and I about-faced. Horan was no longer peeking; he had stepped into the hall and was standing there. As we approached he turned and moved inside, and as we entered the office he was speaking.

"It was Inspector Cramer. Wolfe shut the door on him. He's gone."

Frances Cox said, loud, "You don't shut the door on a police inspector."

"Wolfe does. He did." Horan was back in his chair. Wolfe and I went to ours. Wolfe focused on Horan.

"To resume. Did Peter Vassos ever shine your shoes?"

Horan's quick-moving eyes darted to Mercer, but the president was frowning at a corner of Wolfe's desk and didn't meet them. They went back to Wolfe. "No, he didn't. I suppose what you're getting at is did I tell Vassos about Ashby and his daughter? I didn't. I have never seen Vassos. I understand he always came around ten-thirty, and I am never there at that time. I'm out calling on customers. I was there Monday morning and was with Ashby a few minutes, but I left before ten o'clock."

Wolfe grunted. "Your observed presence there Monday morning is immaterial. Anyone could have got into Ashby's room unobserved by the door from the hall, including you. I'm not after—"

"Then why pick on us, if *anyone* could have got in?"

"I have two reasons: a weaker one, the attack on Miss Vassos' character, and a stronger one, which I reserve. I'm not after who told Vassos about Ashby and his daughter; I don't think anybody did; I'm after who told the police. Did you?"

"I answered their questions. I had to."

"You know better than that if you're not a nincompoop. You did not have to. Telling them even about yourself and your movements was at your discretion; certainly you were under no compulsion to jabber about others. Did you?"

"I don't jabber. What I told the police is on record. Ask them."

"I have. You just heard me ask Mr. Cramer. You have more than once asked a female employee of your firm to find out about the relations between Mr. Ashby and Miss Vassos. What did she tell you?"

"Ask her."

"I'm asking you."

"Ask her."

"I hope I won't have to." Wolfe's eyes went right. "Miss Cox. What terms were you on with Mr. Vassos?"

"I wasn't on any terms with him." Her head was up and her chin was pushing. It was a nice chin when she left it to itself. "He was the bootblack."

"He was also the father of one of your fellow employees. Of course you knew that."

"Certainly."

"Did you like him? Did he like you?"

"I never asked him. I didn't like him or dislike him. He was the bootblack, that's all."

"Affable exchanges even with a bootblack are not unheard of. Did you speak much with him?"

"No. Hardly any."

"Describe the customary routine. He would appear in the anteroom where you were stationed, and then?"

"He would ask me if it was all right to go in. He always went to Mr. Mercer's room first. If someone was in with Mr. Mercer, it depended on who it was. Sometimes he wouldn't want to be disturbed, and Pete would go to Mr. Busch first. Mr. Busch's room is across the hall from Mr. Mercer's."

"Are the two doors directly opposite?"

"No, Mr. Mercer's door comes first on the left. Mr. Busch's door is nearly at the end of hall on the right."

"After he had finished with Mr. Mercer and Mr. Busch, Mr. Vassos would go to Mr. Ashby?"

"Yes, but that that took him past the reception room and he would ask me on his way. If Mr. Ashby had an important customer with him he wouldn't want Pete butting in."

"Are there any others in that office whom Mr. Vassos served?"

"No."

"Never?"

"No."

"Was the routine followed on Monday morning?"

"Yes, as far as I know. When Pete came there was no one in with Mr. Mercer and he went on in. Then later he came and put his head around the corner and I nodded, and he went on to Mr. Ashby's room."

"How much later?"

"I never timed it. About fifteen minutes."

"Did you see him enter at Mr. Ashby's door?"

"No, it's down the other hall. Anyway, I couldn't see him enter any of the doors because my desk is in a corner of the reception room."

"What time was it when he put his head around the corner and you nodded him on to Mr. Ashby's room?"

"It was ten minutes to eleven, or maybe eight or nine minutes. The police wanted to know exactly, but that's as close as I could come."

"How close could you come to the truth about Mr. Ashby and Miss Vassos?"

It took her off balance, but only for two seconds, and she kept her eyes at him. She raised her voice a little. "You think that's clever, don't you?"

"No, I'm not clever, Miss Cox, I'm either more or less than clever. What did you tell the police about Mr. Ashby and Miss Vassos?"

"I say what Mr. Horan said. Ask them."

"What did you tell them about Mr. Ashby and your-self? Did you tell them that you and he were intimate? Did you tell them that Mrs. Ashby once asked an offi-cer of the corporation to discharge you because you were a bad influence on her husband?"

She was smiling, a corner of her mouth turned up. "That sounds like Andy Busch," she said. "You don't care who you listen to, do you, Mr. Wolfe? Maybe you're less than clever."

"But I'm persistent, madam. The police let up on you because they thought their problem was solved; I don't, and I won't. I shall harass you, if necessary, be-yond the limit of endurance. You can make it easier for both of us by telling me now of your personal relations with Mr. Ashby. Will you?"

"There's nothing to tell."

"There will be." Wolfe left her. He swiveled to face John Mercer in the red leather chair. "Now, sir, I ap-plaud your forbearance. You must have been tempted a dozen times to interrupt and you didn't. Commend-able. As I told you, the only way to stop me would be to satisfy me that I'm mistaken, and Mr. Horan and Miss Cox have made no progress. I invite you to try. Instead of firing questions at you—you know what they would be—I'll listen. Go ahead."

When Mercer had finished his study of the corner of Wolfe's desk he had turned his attention not to Wolfe, but to his salesman and receptionist. He had kept his eyes at Horan while Wolfe was questioning him, and then at Miss Cox, and, since I had him full-face past the profiles of the other two, I didn't have to be more than clever to tell that his immediate worry wasn't how to satisfy Wolfe but how to satisfy himself. And from his eyes when he moved them to Wolfe, he still wasn't sure. He spoke.

"I want to state that I shouldn't have said that my attorney thinks this is a blackmailing trick and I agree with him. I want to retract that. I admit it's possible that Miss Vassos has persuaded you—that you believe she has been slandered and you're acting in good faith."

Wolfe said, "Umm."

Mercer screwed his lips. He still wasn't sure. He unscrewed them. "Of course," he said, "if it's just a trick, nothing will satisfy you. But if it isn't, then the truth ought to. I'm going to disregard my attorney's advice and tell you exactly what happened. It seems to me—"

Two voices interrupted him. Horan said, "No!" emphatically, and Miss Cox said, "Don't, Mr. Mercer!"

He ignored them. "It seems to me that's the best thing to do to stop this—this publicity. I told the police about Miss Vassos'—uh—her association with Mr. Ashby, and Mr. Horan and Miss Cox corroborated it. All three of us told them. It wasn't slander. You may be right that we weren't legally *compelled* to tell them, but they were investigating a murder, and we regarded it as our duty to answer their questions. According to my attorney, if you go on with it and the case gets to court, it will be dismissed."

Wolfe's palms were flat on his desk. "Let's make it explicit. You told the police that Miss Vassos had been seduced by Mr. Ashby?"

"Yes."

"How did you know that? I assume that you hadn't actually witnessed the performance."

"Spontaneously? Voluntarily?"

"No, I asked him. There had been complaints about his conduct with some of the employees, and I had been told specifically about Miss Vassos."

"Told by whom?"

"Mr. Horan and Miss Cox."

"Who had told them?"

"Ashby himself had told Miss Cox. Horan wouldn't say where he had got his information."

"And you went to Ashby and he admitted it?"

"Yes."

"When?"

"Last week. Wednesday. A week ago yesterday."

Wolfe closed his eyes and took it in air, through his nose, all the way down, and let it out through his mouth. He had got more than he had bargained for. No wonder the cops and the DA had bought it. He took it on another load of air, held it a second, let it go, and opened his eyes. "Do you confirm that, Miss Cox? That Ashby himself told you he had seduced Miss Vassos?"

"Yes."

"Who told you, Mr. Horan?"

Horan shook his head. "Nothing doing. I didn't tell the police and I won't tell you. I'm not going to drag anyone else into this mess."

"Then you didn't regard it as your duty to answer all their questions."

"No."

Wolfe looked at Mercer. "I must consult with Miss Vassos and her attorney. I shall advise her either to withdraw her action, or to pursue it and also to prefer a criminal charge against you three, conspiracy to defame her character—whatever the legal phrase may be. At the moment I don't know which I shall advise." He pushed back his chair and arose. "You will be informed, probably by her attorney through yours. Meanwhile—"

"But I've told you the truth!"

"I don't deny the possibility. Meanwhile, I am not clear about the plan of your premises, and I need to be. I want Mr. Goodwin to inspect them. I wish to discuss the situation with him first, and it is near the dinner hour. He'll go after dinner, say at nine o'clock. I presume the door will be locked, so you will please arrange for someone to be there to let him in."

"Why? What good will that do? You said yourself that anyone could have got into Ashby's room by the other door."

"It's necessary if I am to be satisfied. I need to understand clearly all the observable movements of people—particularly of Mr. Vassos. Say nine o'clock?"

Mercer didn't like it, but he wouldn't have liked anything short of an assurance that the heat was off or soon would be. The others didn't like it either, so they had to lump it. It was agreed that one of them would meet me in the lobby of the Eighth Avenue building at nine o'clock. They left together, Miss Cox with her chin up, Mercer with his down, and Horan with his long bony face even longer. When I returned to the office after letting them out, Wolfe was still standing, scowling at the red leather chair as if Mercer were still in it.

I said emphatically, "Nuts. Mercer and Miss Cox are both quoting a dead man, and Horan's quoting anonymous. They're all double-breasted liars. I now call her Elma. If she passes Busch up I'll probably put in a bid myself after I find out if she can dance."

Wolfe grunted. "Innocence has no contract with bliss. Confound it, of course she's innocent, that's the devil of it. If she had misbehaved as charged, and as a result her father had killed that man and then himself, she wouldn't have dared to come to me unless she's a lunatic. There is always that possibility. Is she deranged?"

"No. She's a fine sweet pure fairly bright girl with a special face and good legs."

"Where is she?"

"In her room."

"I'm not in a mood to sit at table with her. Tell Fritz to take up a tray."

"I'll take it up myself, and one for me. She'll want to know how you made out with them. After all, we've got her dollar."

8

Every trade has its tricks. If he's any good a detective gets habits as he goes along that become automatic, one of them being to keep his eyes peeled. As I turned the corner of Eighth Avenue at 8:56 that Thursday evening I wasn't conscious of the fact that I was casing the neighborhood; as I say, it gets automatic; but when my eye told me that there was something familiar about a woman standing at the curb across the avenue I took notice and looked. Right; it was Frances Cox in her gray wool coat and gray fur stole, and she had seen me. As I stopped in front of the building I was bound for she beckoned, and I crossed over to her. As I got there she spoke.

"There's a light in Ashby's room."

I rubbernecked and saw the two lit windows on the tenth floor. "The cleaners," I said.

"No. They start at the top and they're through on that floor by seven-thirty."

"Inspector Cramer. He's short a clue. Have you got a key?"

"Of course. I came to let you in. Mr. Mercer and Mr. Horan are busy."

"With the lawyer?"

"Ask them."

"The trouble with you is you blab. Okay, let's go up and help Cramer."

We crossed the avenue and entered. It was an old building and the lobby looked it, and so did the night man sprawled in a chair, yawning. He gave Miss Cox a nod as we entered the elevator, and on the way up she asked the operator if he had taken anyone to the tenth floor and he said no. When we got out she pointed to a door across the hall to the left and said, "That's Ashby's room."

There were two doors in range across the hall, the one she had pointed to, six paces to the left, and one six paces to the right with the number 1018 and below it MERCER'S ROBBINS, INC., and below that ENTRANCE. I asked if that was the reception room, and she said yes.

"This takes generalship," I said. "If we both go through the reception room and around, he hears us and ducks out this way. This door can be opened from the inside?"

"Yes."

"Then I'll stick here. Maybe you'd better get the elevator man to go in and around with you. He might get tough."

"I can take care of myself. But I'm not taking orders from you."

"Okay, I'll get the elevator man."

"No." Her chin was stiff again—too bad, for it was a nice chin. She moved. As she headed for the door to the right I told her back, not loud, "Don't try to stalk him. Let your heels tap."

As I went to the door on the left and put my back to the wall, near its edge that would open, I was regretting that I had disregarded one of my personal rules, made some years back when I had spent a month in a hospital, that I would never go on an errand connected with a murder case without having a gun along. When you're just standing and listening, your mind skips around. For instance, what if Ashby had been in with a narcotics ring, and he kept bobbins full of heroin in the files in his room, and one or more of his colleagues had come Monday and bumped him, and they had come back to look for bobbins, and they now emerged with hardware? Or, for instance, what if a competitor, knowing that Ashby was responsible for Mercer's Bobbins taking over his customers, had got desperate and decided to put an end—

The door opened, and the opener, not seeing me, was coming out backward, pulling the door shut, easy, easy. I put my hand in the small of his back and pushed him back in, not too easy, and followed him. He stumbled but managed to recover without going down. Frances Cox's voice came. "Oh, it's you!"

I spoke. "This is getting monotonous, Mr. Busch. A door opens, and there you are. Are you surprising me, or am I surprising you?"

"You dirty double-crosser," Andrew Busch said. "I can't handle you, I know that, I found that out. I wish to God I could, and Nero Wolfe too. You lousy rat." He started for the door, not the one to the outer hall, the one where Miss Cox was standing.

"Wrong number," I said. "I didn't know who I was shoving. We don't owe you anything; we're working for Elma Vassos." He had turned and I had approached.

"As for my being with Miss Cox, I wanted to have a look around and someone had to let me in. That's why I'm here. As I asked you once before, why are you here?"

"Go to hell, I think you're a damn liar and a rat."

"You're wrong, but I can't right you now. Of course you were looking for something, and if you found it I want to know what it is. I'm going over you. As you say, you can't handle me, but that's no disgrace. I'm bigger and stronger, and you're an office manager and I'm a pro. Stand still, please." I moved behind him.

I frisked him. Since he hadn't been expecting visitors it wasn't necessary to have him take off his shoes, but I made sure that he had no paper or other object on him that he might have found in that room. He didn't. Miss Cox had moved away from the door and stood and watched, saying nothing. Busch stood stiff, stiff as stone. When I stepped back and said, "Okay, I guess you hadn't found it," he walked to the door, the inner one, and on out, without a word.

I looked around. Everything seemed to be in order; not even a drawer or a file was standing open. It was an ordinary executive office, nothing special, except that most of one wall was lined with filing cabinets. There was no hunk of polished petrified wood on the desk; it was probably still at the police laboratory. I went to the door Busch had left by, crossed the sill, turned right, stepped nine paces to a door on the right, turned through it, and was in the reception room. Miss Cox was at my heels. Facing me was the door to the outer hall with MERCER'S BOBBINS, INC. on it. To the right of it were chairs. The wall on the left was lined with shelves displaying Mercer's Bobbins products. Near the corner at the right were a desk and a switchboard. On the chair nearest the door was Andrew Busch, sitting straight and stiff, his palms on his knees.

"I'm an officer of this corporation," he said. "I belong here. You don't."

I couldn't dispute that, so I ignored it and turned to Miss Cox. "That's your desk?"

"Yes."

"Where are Mercer's and Busch's rooms?"

She showed me, and I went for a look. It was like this: When you entered the reception room from the outer hall the desk and switchboard were near the far left corner, and at the far right corner was the door into the inner hall. Passing through that door, if you turned left you went down a short stretch of hall with only one door in it, Ashby's, on the left; if you went straight ahead you were in a longer hall with a window at the end, and you came to Mercer's door first, on the left, and then Busch's door farther on, on the right. So, as Miss Cox had said, she could see none of the doors from her desk. Another habit a detective forms is looking in drawers and cupboards and closets, on the principle that you sometimes find things you're not even looking for, and I would have pottered around a little in Mercer's and Busch's rooms, and Ashby's too, if Miss Cox hadn't been tagging along. I made a rough plan of the layout on a sheet of paper she furnished on request, folded it and put it in my pocket, and went to the chair where I had put my hat and coat.

"Just a minute," Andrew Busch said. He stood up. "Now *I'm going to search you.*"

"I'll be damned. You are?"

"I am. If you're taking something I want to know what it is."

"Good for you." I dropped my coat on the chair. "I'll make a deal. Tell me what you were after in Ashby's room and I'll let you finger me if you don't tickle."

"I don't know. I was going through his files. I thought I might find something that would give me an idea who killed him. I'm for Elma Vassos, and I think you're lying when you say you are. You came here with *her.*" He aimed a finger at Frances Cox. "She's a liar too. She lied to the police."

"Can you prove it?"

"No. But I know her."

"Watch it. She'll sue you for slander. Did you find anything helpful in Ashby's files?"

"No."

"Since you're an officer of the corporation, why did you scoot to the hall when you heard footsteps?"

"Because I thought it was her. I was coming back in this way and see what she was up to."

"Okay. You're wrong about Nero Wolfe and me, but time will tell. Frisking me will be easier with my hands up." I put them up. "If you tickle, the deal's off."

He wasn't as clumsy as you would expect, and he didn't miss a pocket. He even flipped through my notebook. With some practice he would have made a good dipper. When he was through he said all right and returned to his chair and I put on my coat and went to the door; and there was Miss Cox with her coat and stole on. Evidently she was seeing me out of the building. Not a word had passed between her and Busch since she had said, "Oh, it's you," and no more than necessary between her and me. I opened the door and followed her through, and at the elevator she pressed the button, touched my sleeve with fingertips, and said, "I'm thirsty," in a voice I hadn't thought she had in her. It was unquestionably a come-on.

"Have a heart," I said. "First Busch is suddenly a bulldog, and now you're suddenly a siren. I'm being crowded."

"Not you." The same voice. "I'm no siren. It's just that I've realized what you're like—or what you may be like. I'm curious, and when a girl's curious . . . I only said I'm thirsty. Aren't you?"

I put a fingertip under her nice chin, tilted her head back, and took in her eyes. "Panting," I said, and the elevator came.

An hour and ten minutes later, at a corner table at Charley's Grill, I decided I had wasted seven dollars of Wolfe's money, including tip. Her take-off had been fine, but she hadn't maintained altitude. After only a couple of sips of the first drink she had said, "What was that about asking Andy Busch once before why he was here? Where? I didn't know you had met." I don't mind being foxed by an expert, it's how you learn; but that was an insult. I hung on, quenching her thirst with Wolfe's money and no expense account for a client's bill, as long as there was a chance of getting something useful out of her, and then put her in a taxi and gave my lungs a dose of fresh cold December air by walking home. It was eleven-thirty as I mounted the seven steps of the stoop; Wolfe would probably be in bed.

He wasn't. There were voices in the office as I put my coat and hat on the rack—voices I recognized, and the click of my typewriter. I proceeded down the hall and entered. Wolfe was at his desk. Elma was at my desk, typing. Saul Panzer was in the red leather chair, and Fred Durkin was in one of the yellow ones. I stood. No one had a glance for me. Wolfe was speaking.

". . . but the sooner the better, naturally. It must be conclusive enough for me, and through me for the police, but not necessarily for a judge and jury. You will phone every hour or so whether or not you have got anything; one of you may need the other. Archie will be out much of the day; he will be with Miss Vassos arranging for the burial of her father and attending to it; but the usual restrictions regarding nine to eleven in the morning and four to six in the afternoon will not apply. Call as soon as you have something to report. I want to settle this matter as soon as possible. Whatever you must disburse can't be helped, but it will be my money; it will not be billed to anyone. Have that in mind, Archie. Give them each five hundred dollars."

As I went and opened the safe and pulled out the cash reserve drawer I was remarking to myself that that sounded more lavish than it actually was, since it would be deductible as business expense. Even if they shelled it all out the net loss would be less than two Cs of the grand. Of course there would also be their pay— ten dollars an hour for Saul Panzer, the best free-lance operative this side of outer space, and seven-fifty an hour for Fred Durkin, who wasn't in Saul's class but was way above average.

By the time I had it counted, in used fives, tens, and twenties, Saul and Fred were on their feet, ready to go, the briefing apparently finished. As I handed them the lettuce I told Wolfe I had a sketch of the Mercer's Bobbins office if that would help them, and he said it wouldn't. I said it might be useful for them to know that I had found Andrew Busch in Ashby's room, hoping, according to him, to find something that would give him an idea about who killed Ashby, and Wolfe said it wasn't. Evidently I had nothing to contribute except my services as an escort for Saul and Fred to the door, opening it, and closing it after them, which I supplied, with appropriate exchanges between old friends and colleagues. When I returned to the office, Wolfe was out of his chair but Elma was still at the typewriter. I handed him the sketch, and he looked it over.

He handed it back. "Satisfactory. Who let you in?"

"Miss Cox. Shall I report, or have you gone on ahead with Saul and Fred?"

"Report."

I did so, and he listened, but when I had finished he merely nodded. No questions. He told me Miss Vassos was typing the substance of a conversation she had had with him, said good night, and went out to his elevator. Elma turned to say she was nearly through and did I want to read it, and I took it and sat in the red leather chair. It was four pages, double-spaced, not margined my way, but nice and clean, no erasing or exing out, and it was all about her father—or rather, what her father had told her at various times about his customers at Mercer's Bobbins, and one who hadn't been a customer, Frances Cox. Apparently he had told her a lot, part fact and part opinion.

DENNIS ASHBY. Pete hadn't thought much of him except as a steady source of a dollar and a quarter a week. When Elma had told him that Ashby was responsible for pulling the firm out of the hole it had been in, Pete had said maybe he had been lucky. I have already reported his reaction when Elma told him that Ashby had asked her to dinner and a show, and now add that he said that if she got into trouble with such a man as Ashby she was no daughter of his anyway.

JOHN MERCER. Not as steady a customer as Ashby, since he spent part of his days at the factory in Jersey, but Pete was all for him. A gentleman and a real American. However, Elma said, her father had been very grateful to Mercer because he had given her a good job just because Pete asked him to.

ANDREW BUSCH. Pete's verdict on Busch had varied from week to week. Before Elma had started to work there he had—But what's the use? This was what Elma saw fit to report of what her father had said about a man who had asked her to marry him just yesterday. That affects a girl's attitude. What she had put in was probably straight enough, but what had she left out?

PHILIP HORAN. Nothing. Elma corroborated Horan. Pete had never shined Horan's shoes and had probably never seen him.

FRANCES COX. I got the feeling that Elma had toned it down some, but even so it was positively thumbs down. The general impression was that Miss Cox was a highnose and a female baboon. Evidently she had never turned siren on him.

"I don't see what good this is," Elma said as we collated the original and carbons. "He asked me a thousand questions about what my father said about them."

"Search me," I told her. "I just work here. If it comes to me in a dream, I'll tell you in the morning."

6

At the moment, half past three Friday afternoon, that Saul Panzer was finding what Pete Vassos had scrawled on a rock with his finger dipped in his blood, I was at the curb in front of a church on Cedar Street, Greek Orthodox, getting into a rented limousine with Elma Vassos and three friends of hers. The hearse, with the coffin in it, was just ahead, and we were going to follow it to a cemetery somewhere on the edge of Brooklyn. I had offered to drive us in the sedan, which was Wolfe's in name but mine in practice, but no, it had to be a black limousine. I had asked Elma if she wanted the stack of dollar bills from the safe, but she said she would pay for her father's funeral with her own money, so apparently she had some put away.

I wouldn't have been jolly even if it had been a wedding instead of a funeral, with Saul and Fred somewhere doing something, I had no idea where or what, and me spending the day convoying, on her personal errands, a girl on whom I had no designs, private or professional. The idea, according to Wolfe when I had gone up to his room at eight-thirty A.M. for instructions, was that it would be risky to let her go anywhere unattended. If I would prefer, I could get an operative to escort her and I could stay in the office to stand by. He knew damn well what I would prefer, to join Saul and Fred, and I knew damn well, he wouldn't be blowing $17.50 an hour plus expenses if he hadn't had a healthy notion that he was going to get something for it. But we had had that argument time and again, and there would have been no point in repeating it, especially when he was at breakfast.

So I spent the day bodyguarding, and it didn't help much that the body I was guarding was 110 pounds of attractive female with a sad little face. I have nothing against sympathy when my mind is free, but it wasn't. It was with Saul and Fred, and that was very frustrating because I didn't know where they were. No doubt Elma's friends got the impression that I was a fish.

When we finally got back to Manhattan and the friends had been dropped off at their addresses, and the rented limousine stopped in front of the old brownstone, it was after six o'clock. Elma paid the driver. Mounting the stoop with her and finding that the door wasn't bolted, I knew that at least nothing had blown up, but, stepping inside, I saw that someone had blown in. There on the hall rack were objects that I recognized: a brown wool cap, a gray hat, a blue hat, and three coats. As I took Elma's coat I told her, "Go up and lie down. There's company in the office, Inspector Cramer, Saul Panzer, and Fred Durkin."

"But what—why are they . . ."

"The Lord only knows, or maybe Mr. Wolfe does. You're all in. If you want—"

Her look stopped me. She was facing the door. I turned. There on the stoop was John Mercer, with a finger on the bell button, with Frances Cox and Philip Horan behind him. I told Elma to beat it and waited until she had turned up the stairs to open the door. So Wolfe thought he had it. I wondered, as I let them in and took their things and sent them to the office. More than once I had seen him risk it when all he had hold of was the tip of the tail, even with a big fee at stake, and with no intake but a dollar bill already spent and then some—he could be trying it with no hold at all. He knew I was home, since Saul had appeared at the office door when the bell had rung and had seen me admitting the guests, and I had a notion to go to the kitchen and sit down with a glass of milk. If I joined the party I would be merely a spectator, and it might be a bum show. But while I was considering it another guest appeared on the stoop, Andrew Busch. I had the door open before he pressed the button. Since I had crossed him off and I thought Wolfe had too, his coming meant there would be a real showdown, all or nothing, so I took him to the office and followed him in. And found that it was the full cast: Joan Ashby was on the couch at the left of my desk, with a mink coat, presumably not paid for, draped on her shoulders. Cramer was in the red leather chair. Saul and Fred were over by the big globe. Mercer, Horan, and Miss Cox were on yellow chairs in a row facing Wolfe's desk, and there was a vacant one waiting for Busch. As I circled around the chairs Wolfe told Busch he was late, and Busch said something, and, as I sat, Cramer said he wanted Elma Vassos there.

Wolfe shook his head. "You are here by sufferance, Mr. Cramer, and you will either listen or leave, as agreed. As I told you on the phone, you can't expect to interfere in your official capacity, since you have closed your investigation of the only death by violence in your jurisdiction that these people are connected with. Or you *had* closed it. You agreed to listen or leave. Do you want to leave?"

"Go ahead," Cramer growled, "But Elma Vassos ought to be here."

"She's at hand if needed," Wolfe's eyes left him. "Mr. Mercer, I told you on the phone that if you would bring Miss Cox and Mr. Horan I thought we could come to an understanding about the actions Miss Vassos has brought. It seemed desirable for Mrs. Ashby and Mr. Busch to be present, and I asked them to come. I'm on better ground than I was yesterday. Then I only knew that Mr. Vassos had not killed Dennis Ashby; now I know who did. I'll tell you briefly—"

Cramer cut in. "*Now* I'm here officially! Now you're saying you can name a murderer! How did you know Vassos hadn't killed Ashby?"

Wolfe glared at him. "I have your word. Listen or leave."

"I'll listen to your answer to my question!"

"I was about to give it," Wolfe turned to the others. "I was saying, I'll tell you briefly how I knew that.

Miss Vassos came to me Tuesday evening to engage my services. She said that someone had lied to the police about her; that the police were persuaded that she had been seduced by Ashby and her father had found out about it and had killed Ashby and then himself; that none of that was true; that her father had told her I was the greatest man in the world; that she wanted to hire me to discover and establish the truth; and in payment she would give me all the dollar bills, some five hundred, I had paid-her father for shining my shoes over a period of more than three years."

He turned a palm up. "Very well. If she had in fact misbehaved, and if her misbehavior had been responsible for her father's committing murder and suicide, what on earth could possibly have impelled her to come to me—the greatest man in the world to her father, and therefore a man not to be hoodwinked—and offer me what was for her a substantial sum to learn the truth and expose it? It was inconceivable. So I believed her."

He turned his hand back over. "But I won't pretend that I was moved to act by the dollar bills, by the pathos of Miss Vassos' predicament, or by a passion for truth and justice. I was moved by pique. Monday afternoon, the day before Miss Vassos came, Mr. Cramer had told me that I was capable of shielding a murderer in order to avoid the inconvenience of finding another bootblack; and the next day, Wednesday, he told Mr. Goodwin that I had been beguiled by a harlot and ejected him from his office. That's why—"

"I didn't eject him!"

Wolfe ignored it. "That's why Mr. Cramer is here. I could have asked the district attorney to send someone, but I preferred to have Mr. Cramer present."

"I'm here and I'm listening," Cramer rasped.

Wolfe turned to him. "Yes, sir. I'll pass over the actions at law I advised Miss Vassos to bring; that was merely a ruse to make contact. I needed to see these people. I already had a strong hint about the murderer. So had you."

"If you mean a hint about somebody besides Vassos, you're wrong. I hadn't."

"You had. I gave it to you, half of it, or Mr. Good-win did, when he reported verbatim my conversation with Mr. Vassos Monday morning. He said he saw someone. He said that he had only said what if he told a cop he saw someone, but it was obvious that he actually *had* seen someone. Also he told his daughter that evening that there was something he hadn't told either me or the police, and he was going to come and tell me in the morning and ask me what he ought to do; and he wouldn't tell his daughter what it was. Surely that's a strong hint."

"Hint of what?"

"Then he knew, or thought he knew, who had killed Ashby. Where and when he had seen someone can only be conjectured, but it is highly probable that he had seen someone leaving Ashby's room. Not entering; you know the times involved as well as I do, or bet-ter; he must have seen him leaving, at a moment which made it likely that he had been in that room when Ashby left it by the window. And it was someone whom he did not want to expose, for whom he had affection or regard, or who had put him under obligation. There I have the advantage of you, Mr. Vassos and I had formed the habit, while he was shining my shoes, of discussing the history of ancient Greece and the men who made it, and I knew the bent of his mind. He was tolerant of violence and even ferocity, and the qualities he most strongly contemned were ingratitude and disloyalty. That was, of course, not decisive, but it helped."

Wolfe wiggled a finger. "So. The person, call him X, whom Mr. Vassos had seen in compromising circum-stances and who was probably the murderer, was one who had earned his affection, his high regard, his grat-itude, or his loyalty." He left Cramer and surveyed the others. "Was it one of you? That was the point of my questions yesterday afternoon when you were here, and of a discussion I had with Miss Vassos last evening. It isn't necessary to elaborate; as you know, only one of you qualifies. You, Mr. Mercer. You fit admirably; Mr. Vassos owed you gratitude for giving his daughter a job. By which door were you leaving Ashby's room when he saw you, the one to the outer hall or the other?"

"Neither one," Wolfe had telegraphed the punch, and Mercer had got set. "You're not intimating that I killed Dennis Ashby. Are you?"

"I am indeed." Wolfe turned to Cramer. "The question of which door isn't vital, but the inner one is more likely. You are of course familiar with the arrangement. If Mr. Mercer left by the door to the outer hall after killing Ashby, he would have had to get back in through the reception room and would have been seen by Miss Cox and anyone else who happened to be there. The other way, there was a good chance of being seen by no one, and he was seen only by Mr. Vassos, who had just entered the reception room and been nodded in by Miss Cox."

"You say," Cramer growled. "So far, damn little. I'm still listening."

Wolfe nodded. "I thought it proper to explain what directed my attention to Mr. Mercer. After my talk last evening with Miss Vassos I called in Saul Panzer and Fred Durkin. You know them. Mr. Goodwin wouldn't be available today. There was a possibility that Mr. Mercer was not the only likely candidate, that there was someone in another office in that building who qualified—whom Mr. Vassos would have been reluctant to expose and who might have had a motive for killing Ashby. Mr. Durkin's job—"

"Did Mercer have a motive?"

"I'll come to that. Confound it, don't interrupt Mr. Durkin's job was to explore that possibility, and he has spent the day at it. No negative can be established beyond question, but he found no one who met the specifications; and he got some suggestive information. On the sixth floor of that building is a firm which is the chief competitor of Mercer's Bobbins, and its president told Mr. Durkin that Ashby's death was a blow to him because he had been discussing with him the possibility of Ashby's coming to his firm and they had been approaching agreement on terms. It could be that that man had been so harassed by a competitor that he had killed him, but he fails the other test. He had never had his shoes shined by Mr. Vassos. Only two people in that office had, and only occasionally, and neither of them had put him under any obligation of affection or gratitude or loyalty."

Wolfe took a breath. His eyes stayed at Cramer. "Before calling on Mr. Panzer, I'll dispose of Miss Vassos. Your information about her came from three sources, and probably you would have tested them further if her father had not died as he did outside your jurisdiction, but even so you are open to a charge of nonfeasance. Miss Cox and Mr. Mercer gave Ashby as their source, and he was dead. Were they lying? Mercer's reason for lying is of course manifest, since he had himself killed both Ashby and Mr. Vassos. As for Miss Cox, Ashby may have boasted to her of a feather he had not in fact gathered, or she may be a born liar, or she— Pfui. She's a woman. Pry it out of her when you have nothing better to do. As for—"

"I still believe it," Frances Cox said, loud. Her chin was thrust forward.

Wolfe didn't give her a glance. "As for Mr. Horan, you know, of course, that he coveted Ashby's job. He has refused to name the source of his information. He may have been lying, or he may have himself been misled. That's immaterial now; I'll move to what is material, Saul!"

Saul Panzer got up, went to Mercer's chair, and stood behind it, facing Cramer. There was nothing about him to catch the eye; he looked just ordinary, but people who had dealt with him knew better, and Cramer was one of them.

"My job," he said, "was to check on John Mercer for Monday evening, Mr. Wolfe's theory was that he knew Vassos had seen him leaving Ashby's room that morning, and that evening he phoned him and arranged to meet him. They met, and Mercer had a car, and he drove across the river to Jersey and to a place he knew about. He slugged Vassos with something, stunned him, or killed him, and pushed him over the edge of the cliff. That was the theory, and—"

"To hell with the theory," Cramer snapped. "What did you get?"

"I was lucky. I couldn't start at Mercer's end, for instance at the garage where he kept his car, because I had no in. So I went to Graham Street to try to find someone who had seen Vassos leaving the house that evening. You know how that is, Inspector, you can spend a week at it and come out empty, but I was lucky. Within an hour I had it. Mr. Wolfe has told me to keep the details for later, since Mercer is here and listening, but I have the names and addresses of three people who saw Vassos get into a car at the corner of Graham Street and Avenue A Monday evening a little before nine o'clock. There was only one person in the car, the man driving it, and they can describe him. Then I—"

"Did you describe him for them?"

"No, I'm dry behind the ears, Inspector. Then I wasted an hour trying to pick up the car this side of the river. That was dumb. I got my car and drove to Jersey and spent two hours trying to pick up the car at that end. That wasn't dumb, but I didn't hit. I found a law officer I know, a state man, and he went with me to the cliff. After looking around at the top and finding nothing useful, but it ought to be gone over right, we climbed down to where Vassos's body was found. That should be gone over too, better than it has been, but we found one thing that shouldn't have been missed by a Boy Scout. Vassos hadn't been dead when Mercer pushed him over. He died after he reached the bottom, and before he died he dipped his finger in his blood and printed M, E, R, C, on a rock. It wasn't very distinct, and there was more blood around, but it should have been noticed. It's still there and being protected. The state man is a good officer, and it will be there. I went to a phone and called Mr. Wolfe and he told me to come in. Of course I had already reported what I had found at Graham Street."

Cramer had come forward in his chair. "Did you and the state man climb down together?" he demanded.

Saul smiled. His smile is as tender as he is tough, and it helps to make him the best poker player I know.

"That *would* have been dumb, Inspector. With blood four days old? How could I? Jab myself in the leg and use some of mine, nice and fresh? And it might not match."

"I want the names and addresses of those three people." Cramer stood up. "And I want to use the phone."

"No," Wolfe snapped. "Not until you have taken Mr. Mercer into custody. Look at him. If he is allowed to walk out of here, he might do anything. Besides, I haven't finished. After getting a report from Mr. Durkin this afternoon, I phoned Mrs. Ashby." He looked at her. "Will you tell Mr. Cramer what you told me, madam?"

I didn't turn to see her, back of me on the couch, because that would have taken my eyes away from Mercer. But I heard her. "I told you that my husband hadn't decided whether to leave Mercer's Bobbins or not. He had told Mr. Mercer that he would stay if he got fifty-one per cent of the stock of the corporation, and if he didn't get it he would go to another firm. Just last week he told him he had to know by the end of the month."

"He told me the same thing," Frances Cox said, loud. "He said if he left he wanted to take me with him. I've thought all along that probably Mr. Mercer killed him. She was a real prize, that Cox girl. She was going on. "But I didn't say so because I had no real—"

Mercer stopped her. His idea was to stop her by getting his fingers around her throat, but he didn't quite make it because Saul was there. But he was fast enough and strong enough, in spite of his age, to make a stir. Cramer came on the bound, Joan Ashby let out a scream, Horan scrambled up, knocking his chair over, and of course I was there. And for the first time in my life I saw a man frothing at the mouth, and I wouldn't care to see it again. The line of foam seeping through Mercer's lips, as Saul pinned him from behind, was exactly the color of his hair.

"All right, Panzer," Cramer said. "I'll take him."

I looked away and became aware that we were shy a guest. Andrew Busch had disappeared. He didn't know which room was Elma's, and he would probably barge into Wolfe's room, so I went out to the stairs and on up, two steps at a time. At the first landing a glance showed me that the door of Wolfe's room was closed, so I kept going. At the second landing the door of the South Room was standing open, and I went to it. Elma, over by a window, saw me, but Busch's back was to me. He was talking.

". . . so it's all right, everything's all right, and that Nero Wolfe is the greatest man in the world. I've already asked you if you'll marry me, so I won't ask you again right now, but I just want to say . . ."

I turned and headed for the stairs. He may have been a good office manager, but as a promoter he had a lot to learn. The darned fool was standing ten feet away from her. That is not the way to do it.

Murder Is Corny

I

When the doorbell rang that Tuesday evening in September and I stepped to the hall for a look and through the one-way glass saw Inspector Cramer on the stoop, bearing a fair-sized carton, I proceeded to the door, intending to open it a couple of inches and say through the crack, "Deliveries in the rear." He was uninvited and unexpected, we had no case and no client, and we owed him nothing, so why pretend he was welcome?

But by the time I had reached the door I had changed my mind. Not because of him. He looked perfectly normal—big and burly, round red face with bushy gray eyebrows, broad heavy shoulders straining the sleeve seams of his coat. It was the carton. It was a used one, the right size, the cord around it was the kind McLeod used, and the NERO WOLFE on it in blue crayon was McLeod's style of printing. Having switched the stoop light on, I could observe those details as I approached, so I swung the door open and asked politely, "Where did you get the corn?"

I suppose I should explain a little. Usually Wolfe comes closest to being human after dinner, when we leave the dining room to cross the hall to the office, and he gets his bulk deposited in his favorite chair behind his desk, and Fritz brings coffee; and either Wolfe opens his current book or, if I have no date and am staying in, he starts a conversation. The topic may be anything from women's shoes to the importance of the new moon in Babylonian astrology. But that evening he had taken his cup and crossed to the big globe over by the bookshelves and stood twirling the globe, scowling at it, probably picking a place he would rather be.

For the corn hadn't come. By an arrangement with a farmer named Duncan McLeod up in Putnam County, every Tuesday from July 20 to October 5, sixteen ears of just-picked corn were delivered. They were roasted in the husk, and we did our own shucking as we ate—four ears for me, eight for Wolfe, and four in the kitchen for Fritz. The corn had to arrive no earlier than five-thirty and no later than six-thirty. That day it hadn't arrived at all, and Fritz had had to do some stuffed eggplant, so Wolfe was standing scowling at the globe when the doorbell rang.

And now here was Inspector Cramer with the carton. Could it possibly be it? It was. Handing me his hat to put on the shelf, he tramped down the hall to the office, and when I entered he had put the carton on Wolfe's desk and had his knife out to cut the cord, and Wolfe, cup in hand, was crossing to him. Cramer opened the flaps, took out an ear of corn, held it up, and said, "If you were going to have this for dinner, I guess it's too late."

Wolfe moved to his elbow, turned the flap to see the inscription, his name, grunted, circled around the desk to his chair, and sat. "You have your effect," he said. "I am impressed. Where did you get it?"

"If you don't know, maybe Goodwin does." Cramer shot a glance at me, went to the red leather chair facing the end of Wolfe's desk, and sat. "I've got some questions for you and for him, but of course you want grounds. You would. At a quarter past five, four hours ago, the dead body of a man was found in the alley back of Rusterman's restaurant. He had been hit in the back of the head with a piece of iron pipe which was there on the ground by the body. The station wagon had come in was alongside the receiving platform of the restaurant, and in the station wagon were nine cartons containing ears of corn." Cramer pointed. "That's one of them, your name on it. You get one like it every Tuesday, right?"

Wolfe nodded. "I do. In season. Has the body been identified?"

"Yes. Driver's license and other items in his pockets, including cash, eighty-some dollars. Kenneth Faber, twenty-eight years old. Also men at the restaurant identified him. He had been delivering the corn there the past five weeks, and then he had been coming on here with yours. Right?"

"I don't know."

"The hell you don't. If you're going to start that kind—"

I cut in. "Hold it. Stay in the buggy. As you know, Mr. Wolfe is up in the plant rooms from four to six every day except Sunday. The corn usually comes before six, and either Fritz or I receive it. So Mr. Wolfe doesn't know, but I do. Kenneth Faber has been bringing it the past five weeks. If you want—"

I stopped because Wolfe was moving. Cramer had dropped the ear of corn onto Wolfe's desk, and Wolfe had picked it up and felt it, gripping it in the middle, and now he was shucking it. From where I sat, at my desk, the rows of kernels looked too big, too yellow, and too crowded. Wolfe frowned at it, muttered, "I thought so," put it down, stood up, reached for the carton, said, "You will help, Archie," took an ear, and started shucking it. As I got up Cramer said something but was ignored.

When we finished we had three piles, as assorted by Wolfe. Two ears were too young, six were too old, and eight were just right. He returned to his chair, looked at Cramer, and declared, "This is preposterous."

"So you're stalling," Cramer growled.

"No. Shall I expound it?"

"Yeah. Go ahead."

"Since you have questioned men at the restaurant, you know that the corn comes from a man named Duncan McLeod, who grows it on a farm some sixty miles north of here. He has been supplying it for four years, and he knows precisely what I require. It must be nearly mature, but not quite, and it must be picked not more than three hours before it reaches me. Do you eat sweet corn?"

"Yes. You're stalling."

"No. Who cooks it?"

"My wife. I haven't got a Fritz."

"Does she cook it in water?"

"Sure. Is yours cooked in beer?"

"No. Millions of American women, and some men,

commit that outrage every summer day. They are turning a superb treat into mere provender. Shucked and boiled in water, sweet corn is edible and nutritious; roasted in the husk in the hottest possible oven for forty minutes, shucked at the table, and buttered and salted, nothing else, it is ambrosia. No chef's ingenuity and imagination have ever created a finer dish. American women should themselves be boiled in water. Ideally the corn—"

"I'm not stalling. Ideally the corn should go straight from the stalk to the oven, but of course that's impractical for city dwellers. If it's picked at the right stage of development it is still a treat for the palate after twenty-four hours, or even forty-eight; I have tried it. But look at this." Wolfe pointed to the assorted piles. "This is preposterous. Mr. McLeod knows better. The first year I had him send two dozen ears, and I returned those that were not acceptable. He knows what I require, and he knows how to choose it without opening the husk. He is supposed to be equally meticulous with the supply for the restaurant, but I doubt if he is; they take fifteen to twenty dozen. Are they serving what they got today?"

"Yes. They've admitted that they took it from the station wagon even before they reported the body," Cramer's chin was down, and his eyes were narrowed under the eyebrow hedge. "You're the boss at that restaurant."

Wolfe shook his head. "Not the boss. My trusteeship, under the will of my friend Marko Vukcic when he died, will end next year. You know the arrangement; you investigated the murder; you may remember that I brought the murderer back from Yugoslavia."

"Yeah. Maybe I never thanked you." Cramer's eyes came to me. "You go there fairly often—not to Yugoslavia, to Rusterman's. How often?"

I raised one brow. "That annoys him because he can't do it. "Oh, once a week, sometimes twice. I have privileges, and it's the best restaurant in New York."

"Sure. Were you there today?"

"No."

"Where were you at five-fifteen this afternoon?"

"In the Heron sedan which Mr. Wolfe owns and I drive. Five-fifteen? Grand Concourse, headed for the East River Drive."

"Who was with you?"

"Saul Panzer."

He grunted. "You and Wolfe are the only two men alive Panzer would lie for. Where had you been?"

"Ball game. Yankee Stadium."

"What happened in the ninth inning?" He flipped a hand. "To hell with it. You'd know all right, you'd see to that. How well do you know Max Maslow?"

I raised the brow again. "Connect it, please."

"I'm investigating a murder."

"So I gathered. And apparently I'm a suspect. Connect it."

"One item in Kenneth Faber's pockets was a little notebook. One page had the names of four men written in pencil. Three of the names had checkmarks in front of them. The last one, no checkmark, was Archie Goodwin. The first one was Max Maslow. Will that do?"

"I'd rather see the notebook."

"It's at the laboratory." His voice went up a notch. "Look, Goodwin. You're a licensed private detective."

I nodded. "But that crack about who Saul Panzer would lie for. Okay, I'll file it. I don't know any Max Maslow and have never heard the name before. The other two names with checkmarks?"

"Peter Jay. J-A-Y."

"Don't know him and never heard of him."

"Carl Heydt." He spelled it.

"That's better. Couturier?"

"He makes clothes for women."

"Including a friend of mine, Miss Lily Rowan. I have gone with her a few times to his place to help her decide. His suits and dresses come high, but I suppose he'd turn out a little apron for three Cs."

"How well do you know him?"

"Not well at all. I call him Carl, but you know how that is. We have been fellow weekend guests at Miss Rowan's place in the country a couple of times. I have seen him only when I have been with Miss Rowan."

"Do you know why his name would be in Faber's notebook with a checkmark?"

"I don't know and I couldn't guess."

"Do you want me to connect Susan McLeod before I ask you about her?"

I had supposed that would be coming as soon as I heard the name Carl Heydt, since the cops had had the notebook for four hours and had certainly lost no time making contacts. Saving me for the last, and Cramer himself coming, was of course a compliment, but more for Wolfe than for me.

"No, thanks," I told him. "I'll do the connecting. The first time Kenneth Faber came with the corn, six weeks ago today, the first time I ever saw him, he told me Sue McLeod had got her father to give him a job on the farm. He was very chatty. He said he was a free-lance cartoonist, and the cartoon business was in a slump, and he wanted some sun and air and his muscles needed exercise, and Sue often spent weekends at the farm and that would be nice. You can't beat that for a connection. Go ahead and ask me about Susan McLeod."

Cramer was eying me. "You're never slow, are you, Goodwin?"

I gave him a grin. "Slow as cold honey. But I try hard to keep up."

"Don't overdo. How long have you been intimate with her?"

"Well. There are several definitions for 'intimate.' Which one?"

"You know damn well which one."

My shoulders went up. "If you won't say, I'll have to guess." The shoulders went down. "If you mean the very worst, or the very best, depending on how you look at it, nothing doing. I have known her three years, having met her when she brought the corn one day. Have you seen her?"

"Yes."

"Then you know how she looks, and much obliged for the compliment. She has points. I think she means well, and she can't help it if she can't keep the come-on from showing because she was born with it. She didn't pick her eyes and voice, they came in the package. Her talk is something special. Not only do you never know what she will say next; she doesn't know herself. One evening I kissed her, a good healthy kiss, and when we broke she said, 'I saw a horse kiss a cow once.' But she's a lousy dancer, and after a show or prize fight or ball game I want an hour or two with a band and a partner. So I haven't seen much of her for a year. The last time I saw her was at a party somewhere a couple of weeks ago. I don't know who her escort was, but it wasn't me. As for my being intimate with her, meaning what you mean, what do you expect? I haven't, but even if I had I'm certainly not intimate enough with you to blab it. Anything else?"

"Plenty. You got her a job with that Carl Heydt. You found her a place to live, an apartment that happens to be only six blocks from here."

I cocked my head at him. "Where did you get that? From Carl Heydt?"

"No. From her."

"She didn't mention Miss Rowan?"

"No."

"Then I give her a mark. You were at her about a murder, and she didn't want to drag in Miss Rowan. One day, the second summer she was bringing the corn, two years ago, she said she wanted a job in New York and asked if I could get her one. I doubted if she could hold a job any friend of mine might have open or might make room for, so I consulted Miss Rowan, and she took it on. She got two girls she knew to share their apartment with Sue—it's only five blocks from here, not six—she paid for a course at the Midtown Studio—Sue has paid her back—and she got Carl Heydt to give Sue a tryout at modeling. I understand that Sue is now one of the ten most popular models in New York and her price is a hundred dollars an hour, but that's hearsay. I haven't seen her on a magazine cover. I didn't get her a job or a place to live. I know Miss Rowan better than Sue does; she won't mind my dragging her in. Anything else?"

"Plenty. When and how did you find out that Kenneth Faber had shoved you out and taken Sue over?"

"Nuts," I turned to Wolfe. "Your Honor, I object to the question on the ground that it is insulting, impertinent, and disgusticulous. It assumes not only that I am shovable but also that I can be shoved out of a place I have never been."

"Objection sustained." A corner of Wolfe's mouth was up a little. "You will rephrase the question, Mr. Cramer."

"The hell I will." Cramer's eyes kept at me. "You might as well open up, Goodwin. We have a signed statement from her. What passed between you and Faber when he was here a week ago today?"

"The corn. It passed from him to me."

"So you're a clown. I already know that. A real wit. What else?"

"Well, let's see." I screwed my lips, concentrating. "The bell rang and I went and opened the door and said, quote, 'Greetings. How's things on the farm?' As he handed me the carton he said, 'Lousy, thank you, hot as hell and I've got blisters.' As I took it I said, 'What's a few blisters if you're the backbone of the country?' He said, 'Go soak your head,' and went, and I shut the door and took the carton to the kitchen."

"That's it?"

"That's it."

"Okay," He got up. "You don't wear a hat. You can have one minute to get a toothbrush."

"Now listen," I turned a palm up. "I can throw sliders in a pinch, and do, but this is no pinch. It's close to bedtime. If I don't check with something in Sue McLeod's statement, of course you want to work on me before I can get in touch with her, so go ahead, here I am."

"The minute's up. Come on."

I stayed put. "No, I now have a right to be sore, so I am. You'll have to make it good."

"You think I won't?" At least I had him glaring.

"You're under arrest as a material witness. Move!"

I took my time getting up. "You have no warrant, but I don't want to be fussy," I turned to Wolfe. "If you want me around tomorrow, you might give Parker a ring."

"I shall." He swiveled. "Mr. Cramer. Knowing your considerable talents as I do, I am sometimes dumfounded by your fatuity. You were so bent on baiting Mr. Goodwin that you completely ignored the point I was at pains to make." He pointed at the piles on his desk. "Who picked that corn? Phil!"

"That's *your* point," Cramer rasped. "Mine is who killed Kenneth Faber. Move, Goodwin."

2

At twenty minutes past eleven Wednesday morning, standing at the curb on Leonard Street with Nathaniel Parker, I said, "Of course in a way it's a compliment. Last time the bail was a measly five hundred. Now twenty grand. That's progress."

Parker nodded. "That's one way of looking at it. He argued for fifty thousand, but I got it down to twenty. You know what that means. They actually—Here's one."

A taxi headed in to us and stopped. When we were in and I had told the driver Eighth Avenue and 35th Street, and we were rolling, Parker resumed, leaning to me and keeping his voice down. The legal mind. Hackies are even better listeners than they are talkers, and that one could be a spy sicked on us by the district attorney. "They actually," he said, "think you may have killed that man. This is serious, Archie. I told the judge that bail in the amount that was asked would be justified only if they had enough evidence to charge you with murder, in which case you wouldn't be bailable, and he agreed. As your counsel, I must advise you to be prepared for such a charge at any moment. I didn't like Mandel's attitude. By the way, Wolfe told me to send my bill to you, not him. He said this is your affair and he isn't concerned. I'll make it moderate."

I thanked him. I already knew that Assistant District Attorney Mandel, and maybe Cramer too, regarded me as a real candidate for the big one. Cramer had taken me to his place, Homicide South, and after spending half an hour on me had turned me over to Lieutenant Rowcliff and gone home. Rowcliff had stood me for nearly an hour—I had him stuttering in fourteen minutes, not a record—and had then sent me under convoy to the DA's office, where Mandel had taken me on, obviously expecting to make a night of it.

Which he did, with the help of a pair of dicks from the DA's Homicide Bureau. He had of course been phoned to by both Cramer and Rowcliff, and it was evident from the start that he didn't merely think I was holding out on details that might be useful, to prevent either bother for myself or trouble for someone else; he had me tagged as a real prospect. Naturally I wanted to know why, so I played along. I hadn't with Cramer because he had got me sore in front of Wolfe, and I hadn't with Rowcliff because playing along is impossible with Rowcliff. Of course he was asking the questions, him and the dicks, but the trick is to answer them in such a way that the next question, or maybe one later on, tells you something you want to know, or at least gives you a hint. That takes practice, but I had had plenty, and it makes it simpler when one guy pecks away at you for an hour or so and then backs off, and another guy starts in and goes all over it again.

For instance, the scene of the crime—the alley and receiving platform at the rear of Rusterman's. Since Wolfe was the trustee, there was nothing about that restaurant I wasn't familiar with. From the side street it was only about fifteen yards along the narrow alley to the platform, and the alley ended a few feet farther on at the wall of another building. A car or small truck entering to deliver something had to back out. Knowing, as I had, that Kenneth Faber would come with the corn sometime after five o'clock, I could have walked in and hid under the platform behind a concrete post, with the weapon in my hand, and, when Faber drove in, got out, and came around to open the tailgate, he would never know what hit him. If I could

have done that, who couldn't? I would have had to
know one other thing, that I couldn't be seen from the
windows of the restaurant kitchen because the glass had
been painted on the inside so boys and girls couldn't
climb onto the platform to watch Leo boning a duck
or Felix stirring goose blood into a *Sauce Rouennaise.*
In helping them get it on the record that I knew all
that, I learned only that they had found no one who
had seen the murderer in the alley or entering or leaving it, that Faber had probably been dead five to ten
minutes when someone came from the kitchen to the
platform and found the body, and that the weapon
was a piece of two-inch galvanized iron pipe sixteen and
five-eighths inches long, threaded male at one end and
female at the other, old and battered. Easy to hide under
a coat. Where it came from might be discovered by one
man in ten hours, or by a thousand men in ten years.

Getting those details was nothing, since they would
be in the morning papers, but regarding their slant on
me I got some hints that the papers wouldn't have.
Hints were the best I could get, no facts to check, so
I'll just report how it looked when Parker came to
spring me in the morning. They hadn't let me see Sue's
statement, but it must have been something in it, or
something she had said, or something someone else,
maybe Carl Heydt or Peter Jay or Max Maslow, had
said, either to her or to the cops. Or possibly something
Duncan McLeod, Sue's father, had said. That didn't
seem likely, but I included him because I saw him.
When Parker and I entered the anteroom on our way
out he was there on a chair in the row against the wall,
dressed for town, with a necktie, his square deep-tanned
face shiny with sweat. I crossed over and told him
good morning, and he said it wasn't, it was a bad morning, a day lost and no one to leave to see to things.
It was no place for a talk, with people there on the
chairs, but I might at least have asked him who had
picked the corn if someone hadn't come to take him
inside.

So when I climbed out of the taxi at the corner and
thanked Parker for the lift and told him I'd call him
if and when, and walked the block and a half on 35th

Street to the old brownstone, I was worse off than when I had left, since I hadn't learned anything really useful, and no matter how Parker defined "moderate," the cost of a twenty-grand bond is not peanuts. I couldn't expect to pass the buck to Wolfe, since he had never seen either Kenneth Faber or Sue McLeod, and as I mounted the seven steps to the stoop and put my key in the lock I decided not to try to.

The key wasn't enough. The door opened two inches and stopped. The chain bolt was on. I pushed the button, and Fritz came and slipped the bolt; and his face told me something was stirring before he spoke. If you're not onto the faces you see most of, how can you expect to tell anything from strange ones? As I crossed the sill I said, "Good morning. What's up?"

He turned from closing the door and stared. "But Archie. You look terrible."

"I feel worse. Now what?"

"A woman to see you. Miss Susan McLeod. She used to bring—"

"Yeah. Where is she?"

"In the office."

"Where is he?"

"In the kitchen."

"Has he talked with her?"

"No."

"How long has she been here?"

"Half an hour."

"Excuse my manners. I've had a night." I headed for the end of the hall, the swinging door to the kitchen, pushed it open, and entered. Wolfe was at the center table with a glass of beer in his hand. He grunted. "So. Have you slept?"

"No."

"Have you eaten?"

I got a glass from the cupboard, went to the refrigerator and got milk, filled the glass, and took a sip. "If you could see the bacon and eggs they had brought in for me and I paid two bucks for, let alone taste it, you'd never be the same. You'd be so afraid you might be hauled in as a material witness you'd lose your nerve. They think maybe I killed Faber. For your information,

I didn't," I sipped milk. "This will hold me till lunch. I understand I have a caller. As you told Parker, this is my affair and you are not concerned. May I take her to the front room? I'm not intimate enough with her to take her up to my room." I sipped milk.

"Confound it," he growled. "How much of what you told Mr. Cramer was flummery?"

"None. All straight. But he's on me and so is the DA, and I've got to find out why," I sipped milk.

He was eying me. "You will see Miss McLeod in the office."

"The front room will do. It may be an hour. Two hours."

"You may need the telephone. The office."

If I had been myself I would have given that offer a little attention, but I was somewhat pooped. So I went, taking my half a glass of milk. The door to the office was closed and, entering, I closed it again. She wasn't in the red leather chair. Since she was there for me, not for Wolfe, Fritz had moved up one of the yellow chairs for her, but hearing the door open and seeing me she had sprung up, and by the time I had shut the door and turned she was to me, gripping my arms, her head tilted back to get my eyes. If it hadn't been for the milk I would have used my arms for one of their basic functions, since that's a sensible way to start a good frank talk with a girl. That being impractical, I tilted my head forward and kissed her. Not just a peck. She not only took it, she helped, and her grip on my arms tightened, and I had to keep the glass plumb by feel since I couldn't see it. It wouldn't have been polite for me to quit, so I left it to her.

She let go, backed up a step, and said, "You haven't shaved."

I crossed to my desk, sipped milk, put the glass down, and said, "I spent the night at the district attorney's office, and I'm tired, dirty, and sour. I could shower and shave and change in half an hour."

"You're all right." She plumped onto the chair. "Look at me."

"I am looking at you," I sat. "You'd do fine for a

before-and-after vitamin ad. The before. Did you get to bed?"

"I guess so, I don't know." Her mouth opened to pull air in. Not a yawn, just helping her nose. "It couldn't have been a jail because the windows didn't have bars. They kept me until after midnight asking questions, and one of them took me home. Oh yes, I went to bed, but I didn't sleep, but I must have, because I woke up, Archie, I don't know what you're going to do to me."

"Neither do I." I drank milk, emptying the glass.

"Why, have you done something to me?"

"I didn't mean to."

"Of course not."

"It came out. You remember you explained it for me one night."

I nodded. "I said you have a bypass in your wiring. With ordinary people like me, when words start on their way out they have to go through a checking station for an okay, except when we're too mad or scared or something. You may have a perfectly good checking station, but for some reason, maybe a loose connection, it often gets bypassed."

She was frowning. "But the trouble is, if I haven't got a checking station I'm just plain dumb. If I do have one, it certainly got bypassed when the words came out about my going to meet you there yesterday."

"Meet me where?"

"On Forty-eighth Street. There at the entrance to the alley where I used to turn in to deliver the corn to Rusterman's. I said I was to meet you there at five o'clock and we were going to wait there until Ken came because we wanted to have a talk with him. But I was late, I didn't get there until a quarter past five, and you weren't there, so I left."

"You said that to whom?"

I kept my shirt on. "To several people, I said it to a man who came to the apartment, and in that building he took me to downtown I said it to another man, and then to two more, and it was in a statement they had me sign."

"When did we make the date to meet there? Of course they asked that."

"They asked everything, I said I phoned you yesterday morning and we made it then."

"It's just possible that you *are* dumb. Didn't you realize they would come to me?"

"Why, of course. And you would deny it. But I thought they would think you just didn't want to be involved, and I said you weren't there, and you could probably prove you were somewhere else, so that wouldn't matter, and I had to give them some reason why I went there and then came away without even going in the restaurant to ask if Ken had been there." She leaned forward. "Don't you see, Archie? I couldn't say I had gone there to see Ken, could I?"

"No. Okay, you're not dumb." I crossed my legs and leaned back. "You *had* gone there to see Ken?"

"Yes. There was something—about something."

"You got there at a quarter past five?"

"Yes."

"And came away without even going in the restaurant to ask if Ken had been there?"

"I didn't— Yes, I came away."

I shook my head. "Look, Sue. Maybe you didn't want to get me involved, but you have, and I want to know. If you went there to see Ken and got there at a quarter past five, you *did* see him. Didn't you?"

"I didn't see him alive." Her hands on her lap, very nice hands, were curled into fists. "I saw him dead, I went up the alley and he was there on the ground. I thought he was dead, but, if he wasn't, someone would soon come out and find him, and I was scared. I was scared because I had told him just two days ago that I would like to kill him. I didn't think it out, I didn't stop to think, I was just scared, I didn't realize until I was several blocks away how dumb *that* was."

"Why was it dumb?"

"Because Felix and the doorman had seen me. When I came I passed the front of the restaurant, and they were there on the sidewalk, and we spoke. So I couldn't say I hadn't been there and it was dumb to go away, but I was scared. When I got to the apartment I thought it over and decided what to say, about going there to meet you, and when a man came and started asking questions I told him about it before he asked." She opened a fist to gesture. "I did think about it, Archie. I did think it couldn't matter to you, not much."

That didn't jibe with the bypassing-the-checking-station theory, but there was no point in making an issue of it. "You thought wrong," I said, not complaining, just stating a fact. "Of course they asked you why we were going to meet there to have a talk with Ken, since he would be coming here. Why not here instead of there?"

"Because you didn't want to. You didn't want to talk with him here."

"I see. You really thought it over. Also they asked what we wanted to talk with him about. Had you thought about that?"

"Oh, I didn't have to. About what he had told you, that I thought I was pregnant and he was responsible."

That was a little too much. I goggled at her, and my eyes were in no shape for goggling. "He had told me that?" I demanded. "When?"

"You know when. Last week. Last Tuesday when he brought the corn. He told me about it Saturday—no, Sunday. At the farm."

I uncrossed my legs and straightened up. "I may have heard it wrong. I may be lower than I realized. Ken Faber told you on Sunday that he had told me on Tuesday that you thought you were pregnant and he was responsible? Was that it?"

"Yes. He told Carl too—you know, Carl Heydt. He didn't tell me he had told Carl, but I think he told two other men too—Peter Jay and Max Maslow. I don't think you know them. That was when I told him I would like to kill him, when he told me he had told you."

"And that's what you told the cops we wanted to talk with him about?"

"Yes. I don't see why you say I thought wrong, thinking it wouldn't matter much to you, because you weren't there. Can't you prove you were somewhere else?"

I shut my eyes to look it over. The more I sorted it

out, the messier it got, Mandel hadn't been fooling when he asked the judge to put a fifty-grand tag on me; the wonder was that he hadn't hit me with the big one. I opened my itching eyes and had to blink to get her in focus. "For a frame," I said, "it's close to perfect, but I'm willing to doubt if you meant it. I doubt if you know the ropes well enough, and why pick on me? I am not a patsy. But whether you meant it or not, what are you here for? Why bother to come and tell me about it?"

"Because . . . I thought . . . don't you understand, Archie?"

"I understand plenty, but not why you're here."

"But don't you see, it's my word against yours. They told me last night that you denied that we had arranged to meet there. I wanted to ask you . . . I thought you might change that, you might tell them that you denied it just because you didn't want to be involved, that you had agreed to meet me there but you decided not to go, and they'll have to believe you because of course you were somewhere else. Then they won't have any reason not to believe me." She put out a hand. "Archie . . . will you? Then it will be all right."

"Holy saints. You think so?"

"Of course it will. The way it is now, they think either I'm lying or you're lying, but if you tell them—"

"Shut up!"

She gawked at me; then all of a sudden she broke. Her head went down, and her hands up to cover her face. Her shoulders started to tremble and then she was shaking all over. If she had sobbed or groaned or something I would have merely waited it out, but there was no sound effect at all, and that was dangerous. She might crack. I went to Wolfe's desk and got the vase of orchids, Dendrobium nobile that day, removed the flowers and put them on my desk pad, went to her, got fingers under her chin and forced her head up, and sloshed her good. The vase holds two quarts. Her hands came down and I sloshed her again, and she squealed and grabbed for my arm. I dodged, put the vase on my desk, went to the bathroom, which is over in the corner, and came back with a towel. She was on her feet, dabbing at her front. "Here," I said, "use this."

She took it and wiped her face. "You didn't have to do that," she said.

"The hell I didn't." I got another chair and put it at a dry spot, went to my desk, and sat. "It might help if someone did it to me. Now listen. Whether you meant it or not, I am out on an extremely rickety limb. Ken did not tell me last Tuesday that you thought you were pregnant and he was responsible; he told me nothing whatever, but whether he lied to you or you're lying to the cops and me, they think he did. They also think or suspect that you and I have been what they call intimate. They also expect you to say under oath that I agreed to meet you at the entrance of that alley yesterday at five o'clock, and I can't prove I wasn't there. There's a man who will say he was with me somewhere else, but he's a friend of mine and he often works with me when Mr. Wolfe needs more help, and the cops don't have to believe him and neither would a jury, I don't know what else the cops have or haven't got, but any time now—"

"I didn't lie to you, Archie." She was on the dry chair, gripping the towel. A strand of wet hair dropped over her eye, and she pushed it back. "Everything I told—"

"Skip it. Any time now, any minute, I may be hauled in on a charge of murder, and then where am I? Or suppose I somehow made it stick that I did not agree to meet you there, that you're lying to them, and I wasn't there. Then where will you be? The way it stands, the way you've staged it, today or tomorrow either you or I will be in the jug with no out. So either I—"

"But Archie, you—"

"Don't interrupt. Either I wriggle off by selling them on you—and by the way, I haven't asked you." I got up and went to her. "Stand up. Look at me." I extended my hands at waist level, open, palms up. "Put your hands on mine, palms down. No, don't press, relax, just let them rest there. Damn it, relax! Right. Look at me. Did you kill Ken?"

"No."

"Again. Did you kill him?"

"No, Archie."

I turned and went back to my chair. She came a step forward, backed up, and sat. "That's my private lie detector," I told her. "Not patented. Either I wriggle off by selling them on you, and it would take some wriggling, which is not my style, or I do a job that is my style—I hope. As you know, I work for Nero Wolfe. First I see him and tell him I'm taking a leave of absence—I hope a short one. Then you and I go to some place where we're sure we won't be interrupted, and you tell me things, a lot of things, and no fudging. Where I go from there depends on what you tell me. I'll tell *you* one thing now, if you—"

The door opened and Wolfe was there. He crossed to the corner of his desk, faced her, and spoke. "I'm Nero Wolfe. Will you please move to this chair?" He indicated the red leather chair by a nod, circled around his desk, and sat. He looked at me. "A job that is your style?"

Well. As I remarked when he insisted that I see her in the office, if I hadn't been pooped I would have given that offer a little attention. If I had been myself I would have known, or at least suspected, what he intended, I suppose he and I came as close to trusting each other as any two men can, on matters of joint concern, but as he had told Parker, this was my affair, and I was discussing it with someone in his office, keeping him away from his favorite chair, and I had just told him that nothing of what I had told Cramer was flummery. So he had gone to the hole in the alcove. I looked back at him. "I said I hope. What if I heard the panel open and steered clear?"

"Pfui. Clear of what?"

"Okay. Your trick. But I think she has a right to know."

"I agree." Sue had moved to the red leather chair, and he swiveled. "Miss McLeod, I eavesdropped, without Mr. Goodwin's knowledge. I heard all that was said, and I saw. Do you wish to complain?"

She had fingered her hair back, but it was still a sight. "Why?" she asked.

"Why did I listen? To learn how much of a pickle Mr. Goodwin was in. And I learned. I have intruded because the situation is intolerable. You are either a cockatrice or a witling. Whether by design or stupidity, you have brought Mr. Goodwin to a desperate pass. That is—"

I broke in. "It's my affair. You said so."

He stayed at her. "That is his affair, but now it threatens me. I depend on him. I can't function properly, let alone comfortably, without him. He just told you he would take a leave of absence. That would be inconvenient for me but bearable, even if it were rather prolonged, but it's quite possible that I would lose him for good, and that would be a calamity. I won't have it. Thanks to you, he is in grave jeopardy." He turned. "Archie. This is now our joint affair. By your leave."

I raised both eyebrows. "Retroactive? Parker and my bail?"

He made a face. "Very well. Intimate or not, you have known Miss McLeod three years. Did she kill that man?"

"No and yes."

"That doesn't help."

"I know it doesn't. The 'no' because of a lot of assorted items, including the lie-detector test I just gave her, which of course you would hoot at it if you hooted. The 'yes,' chiefly because she's here. Why did she come? She says, to ask me to change my story and back hers up, that we had a date to meet there. That's a good deal to expect, and I wonder. If she killed him, of course she's scared stiff and she might ask anybody anything, but if she didn't, why come and tell me she went in the alley and saw him dead and scooted? I wonder. On balance, one will get you two that she didn't. One item for 'no,' when a man gets a girl pregnant her normal procedure is to make him marry her, and quick. What she wants most and has got to have is a father for the baby, and not a dead father. She certainly isn't going to kill him unless—"

"That's silly," Sue blurted, "I'm not pregnant."

I stared. "You said Ken told you he told me . . ."

She nodded. "Ken would tell anybody anything."

"But you thought you were?"

"Of course not. How could I? There's only one way a girl can get pregnant, and it couldn't have been that with me because it's never happened."

3

Like everybody else, I like to kid myself that I know why I think this or do that, but sometimes it just won't work, and that was once. I don't mean why I believed her about not being pregnant and how she knew she couldn't be; I do know that; it was the way she said it and the way she looked. I had known her three years. But since, if I believed her on that, I had to scrap the item I had just given Wolfe for 'no' on her money? Why didn't I change the odds to even killing Faber, why didn't I change the odds to even money? I pass. I could cook up a case, for instance if she was straight on one thing, about not being pregnant and why not, she was probably straight on other things too, but who would buy it? It's even possible that every man alive, of whom I am one, has a feeling down below that an unmarried girl who knows she *can't* be pregnant is less apt to commit murder than one who can't be sure. I admit that a good private detective shouldn't have feelings down below, but have you any suggestions?

Since Wolfe pretends to think I could qualify on the witness stand as an expert on attractive young women, of course he turned to me and said, "Archie?" and I nodded yes. An expert shouldn't back and fill, and as I just said, I believed her on the pregnancy issue. Wolfe grunted, told me to take my notebook, gave her a hard eye for five seconds, and started in.

An hour and ten minutes later, when Fritz came to announce lunch, I had filled most of a new notebook and Wolfe was leaning back with his eyes shut and his lips tight. It was evident that he was going to have to work. She had answered all his questions with no apparent tumbling, and it still looked very much as if either I was going to ride the bumps or she was. Or possibly both.

As she told it, she had met Ken Faber eight months ago at a party at the apartment of Peter Jay. Ken had been fast on the follow-up and four months later, in May, she had told him she would marry him some day—say in two or three years, when she was ready to give up modeling—if he had shown that he could support a family. From the notebook: "I was making over eight hundred dollars a week, ten times as much as he was, and of course if I got married I couldn't expect to keep that up. I don't think a married woman should model anyway because if you're married you ought to have babies, and there's no telling what that will do to you, and who looks after the babies?"

In June, at his request, she had got her father to give him a job on the farm, but she had soon regretted it. From the notebook: "Of course he knew I went to the farm weekends in the summer, and the very first week-end it was easy to see what his idea was. He thought it would be different on the farm than in town, it would be easy to get me to do what he wanted, as easy as falling off a log. The second week it was worse, and the third week it was still worse, and I was seeing what he was really like and I wished I hadn't said I would marry him. He accused me of letting other men do what I wouldn't let him do, and he tried to make me promise I wouldn't date any other man, even for dinner or a show. Then the last week in July he seemed to get some sense, and I thought maybe he had just gone through some kind of a phase or something, but last week, Friday evening, he was worse than ever all of a sudden, and Sunday he told me he had told Archie Goodwin that I thought I was pregnant and he was responsible, and of course Archie would pass it on, and if I denied it no one would believe me, and the only thing to do was to get married right away. That was when I told him I'd like to kill him. Then the next day, Monday, Carl—Carl Heydt—told me that Ken had told him the same thing, and I suspected he had told two other men, on account of things they had said, and I decided to go there Tuesday and see him. I was going to tell him he had to tell Archie and Carl it was a lie, and anybody else he had told, and if I had to I'd get a lawyer.'"

If that was straight, and the part about Carl Heydt and Peter Jay and Max Maslow could be checked, that made it more like ten to one that she hadn't killed him. She couldn't have ad-libbed it; she would have had to go there intending to kill him, or at least bruise him, since she couldn't have just happened to have with her a piece of two-inch pipe sixteen inches long. Say twenty to one. But if she hadn't, who had? Better than twenty to one, not some thug. There had been eighty bucks in Ken's pockets, and why would a thug go up that alley with the piece of pipe, much less hide under the platform with it? No. It had to be someone out for Ken specifically who knew that spot, or at least knew about it, and knew he would come there, and when.

Of course it was possible the murderer was someone Sue had never heard of and the motive had no connection with her, but that would make it really tough, and there she was, and Wolfe got all she had—or at least everything she would turn loose of. She didn't know how many different men she had had dates with in the twenty months she had been modeling—maybe thirty. More in the first year than recently; she had thought it would help to get jobs if she knew a lot of men, and it had, but now she turned down as many jobs as she accepted. When she said she didn't know why so many men wanted to date her Wolfe made a face, but I knew she really meant it. It was hard to believe that a girl with so much born come-on actually wasn't aware of it, but I knew her, and so did my friend Lily Rowan, who *is* an expert on women.

She didn't know how many of them had asked her to marry them; maybe ten; she hadn't kept count. Of course you don't like her; to like a girl who says things like that, you'd have to see her and hear her, and if you're a man you wouldn't stop to ask whether you liked her or not. I frankly admit that the fact that she couldn't dance had saved me a lot of wear and tear.

From the time she had met Ken Faber she had let up on dates, and in recent months she had let only three other men take her places. Those three had all asked her to marry them, and they had stuck to it in spite of Ken Faber. Carl Heydt, who had given her her first modeling job, was nearly twice her age, but that wouldn't matter if she wanted to marry him when the time came. Peter Jay, who was something important in a big advertising agency, was younger, and Max Maslow, who was a fashion photographer, was still younger.

She had told Carl Heydt that what Ken had told him wasn't true, but she wasn't sure that he had believed her. She couldn't remember exactly what Peter Jay and Max Maslow had said that made her think that Ken had told them too; she hadn't had the suspicion until Monday, when Carl had told her what Ken had told him. She had told no one that she was going to Rusterman's Tuesday to see Ken. All three of them knew about the corn delivery to Rusterman's and Nero Wolfe; they knew she had made the deliveries for two summers and had kidded her about it; Peter Jay had tried to get her to pose in a cornfield, in an evening gown, for a client of his. They knew Ken was working at the farm and was making the deliveries. From the notebook, Wolfe speaking: "You know those men quite well. You know their temperaments and bents. If one of them, enraged beyond endurance by Mr. Faber's conduct, went there and killed him, which one? Remembering it was not a sudden fit of passion, it was premeditated, planned. From your knowledge of them, which one?"

She was staring. "They didn't."

"Not 'they.' One of them. Which?"

She shook her head. "None of them."

Wolfe wiggled a finger at her. "That's twaddle, Miss McLeod. You may be shocked at the notion that someone close to you is a murderer; anyone would be; but you may not reject it as inconceivable. By your foolish subterfuge you have made it impossible to satisfy the police that neither you nor Mr. Goodwin killed that man except by one procedure: demonstrate that someone else killed him, and identify him. I must see those three men, and, since I never leave my house on business, they must come to me. Will you get them here? At nine o'clock this evening?"

"No," she said, "I won't."

He glared at her. If she had been merely a client, with nothing but a fee at stake, he would have told her to either do as she was told or clear out, but the stake was an errand boy it would be a calamity to lose, me, as he had admitted in my hearing. So he turned the glare off and turned a palm up. "Miss McLeod, I concede that your refusal to think ill of a friend is commendable. I concede that Mr. Faber may have been killed by someone you have never heard of with a motive you can't even conjecture—and by the way, I haven't asked you: do you know of anyone who might have had a ponderable reason for killing him?"

"No."

"But it's possible that Mr. Heydt does, or Mr. Jay or Mr. Maslow. Even accepting your conclusion that none of them killed him, I must see them. I must also see your father, but separately—I'll attend to that. My only possible path to the murderer is the motive, and one or more of those four men, who knew Mr. Faber, may start me on it. I ask you to have those three here this evening. Not you with them."

She was frowning. "But you can't . . . you said identify him. How can you?"

"I don't know. Perhaps I can't, but I must try. Nine o'clock?"

She didn't want to, even after the concessions he had made, but she had to admit that we had to get some kind of information from somebody, and who else was there to start with? So she finally agreed, definitely, and Wolfe leaned back with his eyes shut and his lips tight, and Fritz came to announce lunch. Sue got up to go, and when I returned after seeing her to the door and out, Wolfe had crossed to the dining room and was at the table. Instead of joining him, I stood and said, "Ordinarily I would think I was well worth it, but right now I'm no bargain at any price. Have we a program for the afternoon?"

"No. Except to telephone Mr. McLeod."

"I saw him at the DA's office. Then I'm going up and rinse off before I eat. I think I smell. Tell Fritz to save me a bite in the kitchen."

I went to the hall and mounted the two flights to my room. During the forty minutes it took to do the job I kept telling my brain to lay off until it caught up, but it wouldn't. It insisted on trying to analyze the situation, with the emphasis on Sue McLeod. If I had her figured wrong, if she was it, it would almost certainly be a waste of time to try to get anything from three guys who were absolutely hooked, and if there was no program for the afternoon I had damn well better think one up. If it would be a calamity for Wolfe to lose me for good, what would it be for me? By the time I stepped into the shower the brain had it doped that the main point was the piece of pipe. She had not gone into that alley toting that pipe; that was out. But I hadn't got that point settled conclusively by Cramer or Mandel, and I hadn't seen a morning paper. I would consult the *Times* when I went downstairs. But the brain wanted to know now, and when I left the shower I dried in a hurry, went to the phone on the bedtable, dialed the *Gazette*, got Lon Cohen, and asked him. Of course he knew I had spent the night downtown and he wanted a page or two of facts, but I told him I was naked and would catch cold, and how final was it that whoever had conked Faber had brought the pipe with him? Sewed up, Lon said. Positively. The pipe was at the laboratory, revealing—maybe—its past to the scientists, and three or four dicks with color photos of it were trying to pick up its trail. I thanked him and promised him something for a headline if and when. So that was settled. As I went to a drawer for clean shorts the brain started in on Carl Heydt, but it had darned little to work on, and by the time I tied my tie it was buzzing around trying to find a place to land.

Downstairs, Wolfe was still in the dining room, but I went on by to the kitchen, got at my breakfast table with the *Times*, and was served by Fritz with what do you think? Corn fritters. There had been eight perfectly good ears, and Fritz hates to throw good food away. With bacon and homemade blackberry jam they were ambrosia, and in the *Times* report on the Faber murder Wolfe's name was mentioned twice and mine four times, so it was a fine meal. I had finished the eighth fritter and was deciding whether to take on another one and a third cup of coffee when the doorbell rang, and I got up and went to the hall for a look. Wolfe was back in the office, and I stuck my head in and said, "Mc-Leod."

He let out a growl. True, he had told Sue he must see her father and was even going to phone to ask him to come in from the country, but he always resents an unexpected visitor, no matter who. Ignoring the growl, I went to the front and opened the door, and when Mc-Leod said he wanted to see Mr. Wolfe, with his burr on the r, I invited him in, took his Sunday hat, a dark gray antique fedora in good condition, put it on the shelf, and took him to the office. Wolfe, who is no hand-shaker, told him good afternoon and motioned to the red leather chair.

McLeod stood. "No need to sit," he said. "I've been told about the corn and I came to apologize. I'm to blame, and I'd like to explain how it happened. I didn't pick it; that young man did, Kenneth Faber."

Wolfe grunted. "Wasn't that heedless? I telephoned the restaurant this morning and was told that theirs was as bad as mine. You know what we require."

He nodded. "I ought to by now. You pay a good price, and I want to say it'll never happen again. I'd like to explain it. A man was coming Thursday with a bulldozer to work on a lot I'm clearing, but Monday night he told me he'd have to come Wednesday in-stead, and I had to dynamite a lot of stumps and rock before he came. I got at it by daylight yesterday and I thought I could finish in time to pick the corn, but I had some trouble and I had to leave the corn to that young man. I had showed him and I thought he knew. So I've got to apologize and I'll see it don't happen again. Of course I'm not expecting you to pay for it."

Wolfe grunted. "I'll pay for the eight ears we used. It was vexatious, Mr. McLeod."

"I know it was." He turned and aimed his gray-blue eyes, with their farmer's squint, at me. "Since I'm here I'm going to ask you. What did that young man tell you about my daughter?"

I met his eyes. It was a matter not only of murder, but also of my personal jam that might land me in the jug any minute, and all I really knew of him was that he was Sue's father and he knew how to pick corn. "Not a lot," I said. "Where did you get the idea he told me anything about her?"

"From her. This morning. What he told her he told you. So I'm asking you, to get it straight."

"Mr. McLeod," Wolfe cut in. He nodded at the red leather chair. "Please sit down."

"No need to sit. I just want to know what that young man said about my daughter."

"She has told you what he said he said. She has also told Mr. Goodwin and me. We have spoken with her at length. She came shortly after eleven o'clock this morning to see Mr. Goodwin and stayed two hours."

"My daughter Susan? Came here?"

"Yes."

McLeod moved. In no hurry, he went to the red leather chair, sat, focused on Wolfe, and demanded, "What did she come for?"

Wolfe shook his head. "You have it wrong side up. That tone is for us, not you. We may or may not oblige you later; that will depend. The young man you permitted to pick my corn has been murdered, and because of false statements made by your daughter to the police Mr. Goodwin may be charged with murder. The danger is great and imminent. You say you spent yesterday dynamiting stumps and rocks. Until what hour?"

McLeod's set jaw made his deep-tanned seamed face even squarer. "My daughter doesn't make false statements," he said. "What were they?"

"They were about Mr. Goodwin. Anyone will lie when the alternative is intolerable. She may have been impelled by a desperate need to save herself, but Mr. Goodwin and I do not believe she killed that man, Archie?"

I nodded. "Right. Now any odds you want to name."

"And we're going to learn who did kill him. Did you?"

"No. But I would have, if . . ." He let it hang.

"If what?"

"If I had known what he was saying about my daughter. I told them that, the police. I heard about it from them, and from my daughter, last night and this morning. He was a bad man, an evil man. You say you're going to learn who killed him, but I hope you don't. I told them that too. They asked me what you did, about yesterday, and I told them I was there in the lot working with the stumps until nearly dark and it made me late with the milking. I can tell you this, I don't resent you thinking I might have killed him, because I might."

"Who was helping you with the stumps?"

"Nobody, not in the afternoon. He was with me all morning after he did the chores, but then he had to pick the corn and then he had to go with it."

"You have no other help?"

"No."

"Other children? A wife?"

"My wife died ten years ago. We only had Susan. I told you, I don't resent this, not a bit. I said I would have killed him if I'd known. I didn't want her to come to New York, I knew something like this might happen—the kind of people she got to know and all the pictures of her. I'm an old-fashioned man and I'm a righteous man, only that word righteous may not mean for you what it means for me. You said you might oblige me later. What did my daughter come here for?"

"I don't know." Wolfe's eyes were narrowed at him. "Ask her. Her avowed purpose is open to question. This is futile, Mr. McLeod, since you think a righteous man may wink at murder. I wanted—"

"I didn't say that. I don't wink at murder. But I don't have to want whoever killed Kenneth Faber to get caught and suffer for it. Do I?"

"No, I wanted to see you. I wanted to ask you,

for instance, if you know a man named Carl Heydt, but since—"

"I don't know him. I've never seen him. I've heard his name from my daughter; he was the first one she worked for. What about him?"

"Nothing, since you don't know him. Do you know Max Maslow?"

"No."

"Peter Jay?"

"No. I've heard their names from my daughter. She tells me about people; she tries to tell me they're not as bad as I think they are, only their ideas are different from mine. Now this has happened, and I knew it would, something like this, I don't wink at murder and I don't wink at anything sinful."

"But if you knew who killed that man or had reason to suspect anyone you wouldn't tell me—or the police."

"I would not."

"Then I won't keep you. Good afternoon, sir."

McLeod stayed put. "If you won't tell me what my daughter came here for I can't make you. But you can't tell me she made false statements and not say what they were."

Wolfe grunted. "I can and do. I will tell you nothing." He slapped the desk. "Confound it, after sending me inedible corn you presume to come and make demands on me? Go!"

McLeod's mouth opened and closed again. In no hurry, he got up. "I don't think it's fair," he said, "I don't think it's right." He turned to go and turned back. "Of course you won't be wanting any more corn."

Wolfe was scowling at him. "Why not? It's only the middle of September."

"I mean not from me."

"Then from whom? Mr. Goodwin can't go scouring the countryside with this imbroglio on our hands. I want corn this week. Tomorrow?"

"I don't see . . . There's nobody to bring it."

"Friday, then?"

"I might. I've got a neighbor— Yes, I guess so. The restaurant too?"

Wolfe said yes, he would tell them to expect it, and McLeod turned and went. I stepped to the hall, got to the front ahead of him to hand him his hat, and saw him out. When I returned to the office Wolfe was leaning back, frowning at the ceiling. As I crossed to my desk and sat I felt a yawn coming, and I stopped it. A man expecting to be tagged for murder is in no position to yawn, even if he has had no sleep for thirty hours. I had my nose full the order for more oxygen, swiveled, and said brightly, "That was a big help. Now we know about the corn."

Wolfe straightened up. "Pfui. Call Felix and tell him to expect a delivery on Friday."

"Yes, sir. Good. Then everything's jake."

"That's bad slang. There is good slang and bad slang. How long will it take you to type a full report of our conversation with Miss McLeod, yours and mine, from the beginning?"

"Verbatim?"

"Yes."

"The last half, more than half, is in the notebook. For the first part I'll have to dig, and though my memory is as good as you think it is, that will be a little slower. Altogether, say four hours. But what's the idea? Do you want it to remember me by?"

"No. Two carbons."

I cocked my head. "Your memory is as good as mine—nearly. Are you actually telling me to type all that crap just to keep me off your neck until nine o'clock?"

"No. It may be useful."

"Useful how? As your employee I'm supposed to do what I'm told, and I often do, but this is different. This is our joint affair, you said so, trying to save you from the calamity of losing me. Useful how?"

"I don't know," he bellowed. "I say it *may* be use-ful, if I decide to use it. Can you suggest something that may be more useful?"

"Offhand, no."

"Then if you type it, two carbons."

I got up and went to the kitchen for a glass of milk. I might or might not start on it before four o'clock,

when he would go up to the plant rooms for his afternoon session with the orchids.

4

At five minutes past nine that evening the three
men whose names had had checkmarks in front of them
in Kenneth Faber's little notebook were in the office,
waiting for Wolfe to show. They hadn't come together;
Carl Heydt had arrived first, ten minutes early, then
Peter Jay, on the dot at nine, and then Max Maslow. I
had put Heydt in the red leather chair, and Jay and
Maslow on two of the yellow ones facing Wolfe's desk.
Nearest me was Maslow.

I had seen Heydt before, of course, but you take a
new look at a man when he becomes a homicide candidate. He looked the same as ever—medium height with
a slight bulge in the middle, round face with a wide
mouth, quick dark eyes that kept on the move. Peter
Jay, the something important in the big advertising
agency, tall as me but not as broad, with more than his
share of chin and a thick dark mane that needed a comb,
looked as if he had the regulation ulcer, but it could
have been just the current difficulty. Max Maslow, the
fashion photographer, was a surprise. With the twisted
smile he must have practiced in front of a mirror, the
trick haircut, the string tie dangling, and the jacket with
four buttons buttoned, he was a screwball if I ever saw
one, and I wouldn't have supposed that Sue McLeod
would let such a specimen hang on. I admit it could
have been just that his ideas were different from mine,
but I like mine.

Wolfe came. When there is to be a gathering he
stays in the kitchen until I buzz on the house phone,
and then he doesn't enter, he makes an entrance. Nothing showy, but it's an entrance. A line from the door
to the corner of his desk just misses the red leather chair,
so with Heydt in the chair he would have had to circle
around his feet and also pass between Heydt and the
other two; and he detoured to his right, between the

chair and the wall, to his side of the desk, stood, and shot me a glance. I pronounced their names, indicating who was which, and he gave them a nod, sat, moved his eyes from left to right and back again, and spoke.

"This can be fairly brief," he said, "or it can go on for hours. I think, gentlemen, you would prefer brevity, and so would I. I assume you have all been questioned by the police and by the district attorney or one of his assistants?"

Heydt and Maslow nodded, and Jay said yes. Maslow had his twisted smile on.

"Then you're on record, but I'm not privy to that record. Since you came here to oblige Miss McLeod, you should know our position, Mr. Goodwin's and mine, regarding her. She is not our client; we are under no commitment to her; we are acting solely in our own interest. But as it now stands we are satisfied that she didn't kill Kenneth Faber."

"That's damn nice of you," Maslow said. "So am I."

"Your own interest?" Jay asked. "What's your interest?"

"We're reserving that. We don't know how candid Miss McLeod has been with you, any or all of you, or how devious. I will say only that, because of statements made to the police by Miss McLeod, Mr. Goodwin is under heavy suspicion, and that because she knew the suspicion was unfounded she agreed to ask you gentlemen to come to see me. To lift the suspicion from Mr. Goodwin we must find out where it belongs, and for that we need your help."

"My God," Heydt blurted. "I don't know where it belongs."

The other two looked at him, and he looked back. There had been a feel in the atmosphere and the looks made it more than a feel. Evidently each of them had ideas about the other two, but of course it wasn't as simple as that if one of them had killed Faber, since he would be faking it. Anyhow, they all had ideas and they were itching.

"Quite possibly," Wolfe conceded, "none of you knows. But it is not mere conjecture that one of you has good reason to know. All of you knew he would be there that day at that hour, and you could have gone there at some previous time to reconnoiter. All of you had an adequate motive—adequate, at least, for the one it moved; Mr. Faber had either debased or grossly slandered the woman you wanted to marry. All of you had some special significance in his private thoughts or plans; your names were in his notebook, with checkmarks. You are not targets chosen at random for want of better ones; you are plainly marked by circumstances. Do you dispute that?"

Maslow said, "All right, that's our bad luck." Heydt, biting his lip, said nothing. Jay said, "It's no news that we're targets. Go on from there."

Wolfe nodded. "That's the rub. The police have questioned you, but I doubt if they have been important; they have been set at Mr. Goodwin by Miss McLeod, I don't know—"

"That's your interest," Jay said, "To get Goodwin from under."

"Certainly, I said so. I—"

"He has known Miss McLeod longer than we have," Maslow said. "He's the hero type. He rescued her from the sticks and started her on the path of glory. He's her hero. I asked her once why she didn't marry him if he was such a prize, and she said he hadn't asked her. Now you say she has set the police on him. Permit me to say I don't believe it. If they're on him they have a damn good reason. Also permit me to say I hope he *does* get from under, but not by making me the goat. I'm no hero."

Wolfe shook his head. "As I said, I'm reserving what Miss McLeod has told the police. She may tell you if you ask her. As for you gentlemen, I don't know how curious the police have been about you. Have they tried seriously to find someone who saw one of you in that neighborhood Tuesday afternoon? Of course they have asked you where you were that afternoon, that's mere routine, but have they properly checked your accounts? Are you under surveillance? I doubt it; and I haven't the resources for those procedures. I invite you to eliminate yourselves from con-

sideration if you can. The man who killed Kenneth Faber was in that alley, concealed under that platform,
shortly after five o'clock yesterday afternoon. Mr.
Heydt. Can you furnish incontestable evidence that
you weren't there?"

Heydt cleared his throat. "If I could, I don't have to
furnish it to you. It seems to me—oh, what the hell.
No, I can't."

"Mr. Jay?"

"Incontestable, no." Jay leaned forward, his chin
out. "I came here because Miss McLeod asked me
to, but if I understand what you're after I might as
well go. You intend to find out who killed Faber and
pin it on him. To prove it wasn't Archie Goodwin. Is
that it?"

"Yes."

"Then count me out. I don't want Goodwin to get
it, but neither do I want anyone else to. Not even
Max Maslow."

"That's damn nice of you, Pete," Maslow said. "A
real pal."

Wolfe turned to him. "You, sir. Can you eliminate
yourself?"

"Not by proving I wasn't there." Maslow flipped a
hand. "I must say, Wolfe, I'm surprised at you. I
thought you were very tough and cagey, but you've
swallowed something. You said we all wanted to marry
Miss McLeod. Who fed you that? I admit I do, and as
far as I know Carl Heydt does, but not my pal Pete.
He's the pay-as-you-go type. I wouldn't exactly call
him a Casanova, because Casanova never tried to score
by talking up marriage, and that's Pete's favorite gam-
bit. I could name—"

"Stand up." It was his pal Pete, on his feet, with fists,
glaring down at him.

Maslow tilted his head back. "I wouldn't, Pete. I was
merely—"

"Stand up or I'll slap you out of the chair."

Of course I had plenty of time to get there and in
between them, but I was curious. It was likely that Jay,
not caring about his knuckles, would go for the jaw,
and I wanted to see what effect it would have on the

twisted smile. My curiosity didn't get satisfied. As Maslow came up out of the chair he sidestepped, and Jay had to turn, hauling his right back. He started it for Maslow's jaw by the longest route, and Maslow ducked, came on in, and landed with his right at the very best spot for a bare fist. A beautiful kidney punch. As Jay started to bend Maslow delivered another one to the same spot, harder, and Jay went down. He didn't tumble, he just wilted. By then I was there. Maslow went to his chair, sat, breathed, and fingered his string tie. The smile was intact, maybe twisted a little more. He spoke to Wolfe. "I hope you didn't misunderstand me. I wasn't suggesting that I think he killed Faber. Even if he did I wouldn't want him to get it. On that point we're pals. I was only saying I don't see how you got your reputation if you— You all right, Pete?"

I was helping Jay up. A kidney punch doesn't daze you, it just makes you sick. I asked him if he wanted a bathroom, and he shook his head, and I steered him to his chair. He turned his face to Maslow, muttered a couple of extremely vulgar words, and belched.

Wolfe spoke. "Will you have brandy, Mr. Jay? Whisky? Coffee?"

Jay shook his head and belched again.

Wolfe turned. "Mr. Heydt. The others have made it clear that if they have information that would help to expose the murderer they won't divulge it. How about you?"

Heydt cleared his throat. "I'm glad I don't have to answer that," he said. "I don't have to answer it because I have no information that would help. I know Archie Goodwin and I might say we're friends. If he's really in a jam I would want to help if I could. You say Miss McLeod has said something to the police that set them on him, but you won't tell us what she said."

"Ask her. You can give me no information whatever?"

"No."

Wolfe's eyes moved right, to the other two, and back again. "I doubt if it's worth the trouble," he said. "Assuming that one of you killed that man, I doubt if I can get at him from the front; I must go around. But

I may have given you a false impression, and if so I wish to correct it. I said that to lift the suspicion from Mr. Goodwin we must find out where it belongs, but that isn't vital, for we have an alternative. We can merely shift the suspicion to Miss McLeod. That will be simple, and it will relieve Mr. Goodwin of further annoyance. We'll discuss it after you leave, and decide. You gentlemen may view the matter differently when Miss McLeod is in custody, charged with murder, without bail, but that is your—"

"You're a goddam liar," Peter Jay.

"Amazing," Max Maslow. "Where did you get your reputation? What do you expect us to do, kick and scream or go down on our knees?"

"Of course you don't mean it," Carl Heydt. "You said you're satisfied that she didn't kill him."

Wolfe nodded. "I doubt if she would be convicted. She might not even go to trial; the police are not blockheads. It will be an ordeal for her, but it will also be a lesson; her implication of Mr. Goodwin may not have been willful, but it was inexcusable." His eyes went to Maslow. "You have mentioned my reputation. I made it and I don't risk it rashly. If tomorrow you learn that Miss McLeod has been arrested and is inaccessible, you may—"

"If," That crooked smile.

"Yes. It is contingent not on our power but on our preference. I am inviting you gentlemen to have a voice in our decision. You have told me nothing whatever, and I do not believe that you have nothing whatever to tell. Do you want to talk now, to me, or later, to the police, when that woman is in a pickle?"

"You're bluffing," Maslow said. "I call." He got up and headed for the hall. I got up and followed him out, got his hat from the shelf, and opened the front door; and as I closed it behind him and started back down the hall here came the other two. I opened the door again, and Jay, who had no hat, went by and on out, but Heydt stood there. I got his hat and he took it and put it on. "Look, Archie," he said. "You've got to do something."

"Check," I said. "What, for instance?"

"I don't know. But about Sue—my God, he doesn't mean it, does he?"

"It isn't just a question of what he means, it's also what I mean. Damn it, I'm short on sleep, and I may soon be short on life, liberty, and the pursuit of happiness. Get the news every hour on the hour. Pleasant dreams."

"What did Sue tell the police about you?"

"No comment. My resistance is low and with the door open I might catch cold. If you don't mind?"

He went. I shut the door, put the chain bolt on, returned to the office, sat at my desk, and said, "So you thought it might be useful."

He grunted. "Have you finished it?"

"Yes. Twelve pages."

"May I see it?"

Not an order, a request. At least he was remembering that it was a joint affair. I opened a drawer, got the original, and took it to him. He inspected the heading and the first page, flipped through the sheets, took a look at the end, dropped it on his desk, and said, "Your notebook, please." I sat and got my notebook and pen.

"There will be two," he said, "one for you and one for me. First mine. Heading in caps, affidavit by Nero Wolfe. The usual State of New York, County of New York. The text: I hereby depose that the twelve foregoing typewritten pages attached hereto, comma, each page initialed by me, comma, are a full and accurate record of a conversation that took place in my office on October thirteenth, nineteen sixty-one, by Susan McLeod, comma, Archie Goodwin, comma, and myself, semicolon; that nothing of consequence has been omitted or added in this typewritten record, semicolon; and that the conversation was wholly impromptu, comma, with no prior preparation or arrangement. A space for my signature, and below, the conventional formula for notarizing. The one for you, on the same sheet if there is room, will be the same with the appropriate changes."

I looked up. "All right, it wasn't just to keep me off your neck. Okay on the power. But there's still the if on the preference. She didn't kill him. She came to me and opened the bag. I'm her hero. She as good as told Maslow that she'd marry me if I asked her. Maybe she could learn how to dance if she tried hard, though I admit that's doubtful. She makes a lot more than you pay me, and we could postpone the babies. You said you doubt if she would be convicted, but that's not good enough. Before I sign that affidavit I would need to know that you won't chuck the joint affair as soon as the heat is off of me."

"Rrrhh," he said.

"I agree," I said, "it's a goddam nuisance. It's entirely her fault, she dragged me in without even telling me, and if a girl pushes a man in a hole he has a right to wiggle out, but you must remember that I am now a hero. Heroes don't wiggle. Will you say that it will be our joint affair to make sure that she doesn't go to trial?"

"I wouldn't say that I will make sure of anything whatever."

"Correction. That you will be concerned?"

He took air in, all the way, through his nose, and let it out through his mouth. "Very well, I'll be concerned." He glanced at the twelve pages on his desk. "Will you bring Miss Pinelli to my room at five minutes to nine in the morning?"

"No. She doesn't get to her office until nine-thirty."

"Then bring her to the plant rooms at nine-forty with the affidavit." He looked at the wall clock. "You can type it in the morning. You've had no sleep for forty hours. Go to bed."

That was quite a compliment, and I was appreciating it as I mounted the stairs to my room. Except for a real emergency he will permit no interruptions from nine to eleven in the morning, when he is in the plant rooms, but he wasn't going to wait until he came down to the office to get the affidavit notarized. As I got into bed and turned the light off I was considering whether to ask for a raise now or wait till the end of the year, but before I made up my mind I didn't have a mind. It was gone.

I never did actually make up my mind about passing the buck to Sue. I was still on the fence after breakfast Thursday morning, when I dialed the number of Lila Pinelli, who adds maybe two bucks a week to the take of her secretarial service in a building on Eighth Avenue by doubling as a notary public. Doing the affidavits didn't commit me to anything; the question was, what then? So I asked her to come, and she came, and I took her up to the plant rooms. She was in a hurry to get back, but she had never seen the orchids, and no one alive could just breeze on by those benches, with everything from the neat little Oncidiums to the big show-offs like the Laeliocattleyas. So it was after ten o'clock when we came back down and I paid her and let her out, and I went to the office and put the document in the safe.

As I say, I never did actually make up my mind; it just happened. At ten minutes past eleven Wolfe, having come down at eleven as usual, was at his desk looking over the morning crop of mail, and I was at mine sorting the germination slips he had brought, when the doorbell rang. I stepped to the hall for a look, turned, and said, "Cramer. I'll go hide in the cellar."

"Confound it," he growled. "I wanted— Very well."

"There's no law about answering doorbells."

"No. We'll see."

I went to the front, opened up, said good morning, and gave him room. He crossed the sill, took a folded paper from a pocket, and handed it to me. I unfolded it, and a glance was enough, but I read it through. "At least my name's spelled right," I said. I extended my hands, the wrists together. "Okay, do it right. You never know."

"You'd clown in the chair," he said. "I want to see Wolfe." He marched down the hall and into the office. Very careless. I could have scooted on out and away, and for half a second I considered it, but I wouldn't have been there to see the look on his face when he found I was gone. When I entered the office he was lowering his fanny onto the red leather chair and putting his hat on the stand beside it. Also he was speaking. "I have just handed Goodwin a warrant for his arrest," he was saying, "and this time he'll stay."

I stood. "It's an honor," I said. "Anyone can be banged by a bull or a dick. It takes me to be pinched by an inspector, and twice in one week."

His eyes stayed at Wolfe. "I came myself," he said, "because I want to tell you how it stands. A police officer with a warrant to serve is not only allowed to use his discretion, he's supposed to. I know damn well what Goodwin will do, he'll clam up, and a crowbar wouldn't pry him open. Give me that warrant, Goodwin."

"It's mine. You've served it."

"I have not. I just showed it to you." He stretched an arm and took it. "When I was here Tuesday night," he told Wolfe, "you were dumfounded by my fatuity. So you said in your fancy way. All you cared about was who picked that corn. I came myself to see how you feel now. Goodwin will talk if you tell him to. Do you want me to wait in the front room while you discuss it? Not all day, say ten minutes. I'm giving you a—"

He stopped to glare. Wolfe had pushed his chair back and was rising, and of course Cramer thought he was walking out. It wouldn't have been the first time. But Wolfe headed for the safe, not the hall. As he turned the handle and pulled the door open, there I was. If he had told me to bring it instead of going for it himself, I could have stalled while I made up my mind, even with Cramer there, but as I have said twice before I never did actually make up my mind. I merely went to my desk and sat. I owed Sue McLeod nothing. If either she or I was going to be cooped, there were two good reasons why it should be her: she had made the soup herself, and I wouldn't be much help in the joint affair if I was salted down. So I sat, and Wolfe got it from the safe, went and handed it to Cramer, and spoke. "I suggest that you look at the affidavits first. The last two sheets."

Over the years I have made a large assortment of cracks about Inspector Cramer, but I admit he has his points. Having inspected the affidavits, he went through the twelve pages fast, and then he went back and started over and took his time. Altogether, more than half an hour; and not once did he ask a question or even look up. And when he finished, even then no questions. Lieutenant Rowcliff or Sergeant Purley Stebbins would have kept at us for an hour. Cramer merely gave each of us a five-second straight hard look, folded the document and put it in his inside breast pocket, rose and came to my desk, picked up the phone, and dialed. In a moment he spoke.

"Donovan? Inspector Cramer. Give me Sergeant Stebbins." In another moment: "Purley? Get Susan McLeod. Don't call her, get her. Go yourself. I'll be there in ten minutes and I want her there fast. Take a man along. If she balks, wrap her up and carry her."

He cradled the phone, went to the stand and got his hat, and marched out.

5

Of all the thousand or more times I have felt like putting vinegar in Wolfe's beer, I believe the closest I ever came to doing it was that Thursday evening when the doorbell rang at a quarter past nine, and after a look at the front I told him that Carl Heydt, Max Maslow, and Peter Jay were on the stoop, and he said they were not to be admitted.

In the nine and a half hours that had passed since Cramer had used my phone to call Purley Stebbins I had let it lie. I couldn't expect Wolfe to start any further until there was a reaction, or there wasn't, say by tomorrow noon, to what had happened to Sue. However, I had made a move on my own. When Wolfe had left the office at four o'clock to go up to the plant rooms, I had told him I would be out on an errand for an hour or so, and I had taken a walk, to Ruster-man's, thinking I might pick up some little hint. I didn't. First I went out back for a look at the plat-form and the alley, which might seem screwy, since two days and nights had passed and the city scientists had combed it, but you never know. I once got an idea just running my eye around a hotel room where a woman had spent a night six months earlier. But I got nothing from the platform or alley except a scraped ear from squeezing under the platform and out again, and after talking with Felix and Joe and some of the kitchen staff I crossed it off. No one had seen or heard anyone or anything until Zoltan had stepped out for a cigarette (no smoking is allowed in the kitchen) and had seen the station wagon and the body on the ground.

I would have let it ride that evening, no needling until tomorrow noon. When Lily Rowan phoned around seven o'clock and said Sue had phoned her from the DA's office that she was under arrest and had to have a lawyer and would Lily send her one, and Lily wanted me to come and tell her what was what, I would have gone if I hadn't wanted to be on hand if there was a development. But when the development came Wolfe told me not to let it in.

I straight-eyed him. "You said you'd be concerned."

"I am concerned."

"Then here they are. You tossed her to the wolves to open them up, and here——"

"No, I did that to keep you out of jail. I am considering how to deal with the problem, and until I decide there is no point in seeing them. Tell them they'll hear from us."

The doorbell rang again. "Then I'll see them. In the front room."

"No. Not in my house." He went back to his book. Either put vinegar in his beer or get the Marley .32 from my desk drawer and shoot him dead, but that would have to wait; they were on the stoop. I went and opened the door enough for me to slip through, did so, bumping into Carl Heydt, and pulled the door shut. "Good evening," I said. "Mr. Wolfe is busy on an important matter and can't be disturbed. Do you want to disturb me instead?"

They all spoke at once. The general idea seemed to

be that I would open the door and they would handle the disturbing.

"You don't seem to realize," I told them, "that you're up against a genius. So am I, only I'm used to it. You were damn fools to think he was bluffing. You might have known he would do exactly what he said."

"Then he did?" Peter Jay. "He did it?"

"We did. I share the glory. We did."

"Glory hell," Max Maslow. "You know Sue didn't kill Ken Faber. He said so."

"He said we were satisfied that she didn't. We still are. He also said that we doubt if she'll be convicted. He also said that our interest was to get me from under, and we had alternatives. We could either find out who killed Faber, for which we needed your help; or, if you refused to help, we could switch it to Sue. You refused, and we switched it, and I am in the clear, and here you are. Why? Why should he waste time on you now? He is busy on an important matter; he's reading a book entitled My Life in Court, by Louis Nizer. Why should he put it down for you?"

"I can't believe it, Archie." Carl Heydt had hold of my arm. "I can't believe you'd do a thing like this to Sue—when you say she didn't—"

"You never can tell, Carl. There was that woman who went to the park every day to feed the pigeons, but she fed her husband arsenic. I have a suggestion. This is Mr. Wolfe's house and he doesn't want you in it, but if you guys have changed your minds, at least two of you, about helping to find out who killed Faber, I'm a licensed detective too and I could spare a couple of hours. We can sit here on the steps, or we can go somewhere—"

"And you can tell us," Maslow said, "what Sue told the cops that got them on you. I may believe that when I hear it."

"You won't hear it from me. That's not the idea. You tell me things. I ask questions and you answer them. If I don't ask them, who will? I doubt if the cops or the DA will; they've got too good a line on Sue. I'll tell you this much, they know she was there

Tuesday at the right time, and they know that she lied to them about what she was there for and what she saw. I can spare an hour or two."

They exchanged glances, and they were not the glances of buddies with a common interest. They also exchanged words and found they agreed on one point: if one of them took me up they all would. Peter Jay said we could go to his place and they agreed on that too, and we descended to the sidewalk and headed east. At Eighth Avenue we flagged a taxi with room for four. It was ten minutes to ten when it rolled to the curb at a marquee on Park Avenue in the Seventies.

Jay's apartment, on the fifteenth floor, was quite a perch for a bachelor. The living room was high, wide, and handsome, and it would have been an appropriate spot for our talk, since it was there that Sue McLeod and Ken Faber had first met, but Jay took us on through to a room smaller but also handsome, with chairs and carpet of matching green, a desk, bookshelves, and a TV-player cabinet. He asked us what we would drink but got no orders, and we sat.

"All right, ask your questions," Maslow said. The twisted smile.

He was blocking my view of Heydt, and I shifted my chair. "I've changed my mind," I said, "I looked it over on the way, and I decided to take another tack. Sue told the police, and it was in her signed statement, that she and I had arranged to meet there at the alley at five o'clock, and she was late, she didn't get there until five-fifteen, and I wasn't there, so she left. She had to tell them she was there because she had been seen in front of the restaurant, just around the corner, by two of the staff, who know her."

Their eyes were glued on me. "So you weren't there at five-fifteen," Jay said. "The body was found at five-fifteen. So you had been and gone?"

"No. Sue also told the police that Faber had told her on Sunday that he had told me on Tuesday that she thought she was pregnant and he was responsible. He had told you that, all three of you. She said that was why she and I were going to meet there, to make Faber swallow his lies. So it's fair to say she set the cops on me, and it's no wonder they turned on the heat. The trouble—"

"Why not?" Maslow demanded. "Why isn't it still on?"

"Don't interrupt. The trouble was, she lied. Not about what Faber had told her on Sunday he had told me on Tuesday; that was probably his lie, he probably had told her that, but it wasn't true; he had told me nothing on Tuesday. That's why your names in his notebook had checkmarks but mine didn't; he was going to feed us that to put the pressure on Sue, and he had fed it to you but not me. So that was his lie, not Sue's. Hers was about our arranging to meet there Tuesday afternoon to have it out with Faber. We hadn't. We hadn't arranged anything. She also—"

"So you say," Peter Jay.

"Don't interrupt. She also lied about what she did when she got there at five-fifteen. She said she saw I wasn't there and left. Actually she went down the alley, saw Faber's body there on the ground with his skull smashed, panicked, and blew. The time thing—"

"So you say," Peter Jay.

"Shut up. The time thing is only a matter of seconds. Sue says she got there at five-fifteen, and the record says that a man coming from the kitchen discovered the body at five-fifteen. Sue may be off half a minute, or the man may. Evidently she had just been and gone when the man came from the kitchen."

"Look, pal," Maslow had his head cocked and his eyes narrowed. "Shut up? Go soak your head. Who's lying, Sue or you?"

I nodded. "That's a fair question. Until noon today, a little before noon, they thought I was. Then they found out I wasn't. They didn't just guess again, they found out, and that's why they took her down and they're going to keep her. Which—"

"How did they find out?"

"Ask them. You can be sure it was good. They were liking it fine, having me on a hook, and they hated to see me flop off. It had to be good, and it was. Which brings me to the point. I think Sue's lie was part truth. I think she had arranged with someone to meet her there at five o'clock. She got there fifteen minutes late and he wasn't there, and she went down the alley and saw Faber dead, and what would she think? That's obvious. No wonder she panicked. She went home and looked it over. She couldn't deny she had been there because she had been seen. If she said she had gone there on her own to see Faber, alone, they wouldn't believe she hadn't gone in the alley, and they certainly *would* believe she had killed him. So she decided to tell the truth, part of it, that she had arranged to meet someone and she got there late and he wasn't there and she had left—leaving out that she had gone in the alley and seen the body. But since she thought that the man she had arranged to meet had killed Faber she couldn't name him; but they would insist on her naming him. So she decided to name me. It wasn't so dirty really; she thought I could prove I was somewhere else, having decided not to meet her. I couldn't, but she didn't know that." I turned a palm up. "So the point is, who had agreed to meet her there?"

Heydt said, "That took a lot of cutting and fitting, Archie."

"You were going to ask questions," Maslow said. "Ask one we can answer."

"I'll settle for that one," I said. "Say it was one of you, which of course I *am* saying, I don't expect him to answer it. If Sue stands pat and doesn't name him and it gets to where he has to choose between letting her go to trial and unloading, he might come across, but not here and now. But I do expect the other two to consider it. Put it another way: if Sue decided to jump on Faber for the lies he was spreading around and to ask one of you to help, which one would she pick? Or still another: which one of you would be most likely to decide to jump Faber and ask Sue to join in? I like the first one better because it was probably her idea." I looked at Heydt. "What about it, Carl? Just a plain answer to a plain question. Which one would she pick? You?"

"No, Maslow."

"Why?"

"He's articulate and he's tough. I'm not tough, and Sue knows it."

"How about Jay?"

"My God, no. I hope not. She must know that nobody can depend on him for anything that takes guts." Jay left his chair, and his hands were fists as he moved. Guts or not, he certainly believed in making contact. Thinking that Heydt probably wasn't as well educated as Maslow, I got up and blocked Jay off, and damned if he didn't swing at me, or start to. I got his arm and whirled him and shoved, and he stumbled but managed to stay on his feet. As he turned, Maslow spoke.

"Hold it, Pete. I have an idea. There's no love lost among us three, but we all feel the same about this Goodwin. He's a persona non grata if I ever saw one." He got up. "Let's bounce him. Not just a nudge, the bum's rush. Care to help, Carl?"

Heydt shook his head. "No, thanks. I'll watch."

"Okay. It'll be simpler if you just relax, Goodwin."

I couldn't turn and go, leaving my rear open, "I hope you won't tickle," I said, backing up a step.

"Come in behind, Pete," Maslow said, and started, slow, his elbows out a little and his open hands extended and up some. Since he had been so neat with the kidney punch he probably knew a few tricks, maybe the armpit or the apple, and with Jay on my back I would have been a setup, so I doubled up and whirled, came up bumping Jay, and gave him the edge of my hand, as sharp as I could make it, on the side of his neck, the tendon below the ear. It got exactly the right spot and so much for him, but Maslow had my left wrist and was getting his shoulder in for the lock, and in another tenth of a second I would have been meat. The only way to go was down, and I went, sliding off his shoulder and bending my elbow into his belly, and he made a mistake. Having lost the lock, he reached for my other wrist. That opened him up, and I rolled into him, brought my right arm around, and had his neck with a knee in his back.

"Do you want to hear it crack?" I asked him, which was bad manners, since he couldn't answer. I loosened my arm a little. "I admit I was lucky. If Jay had been sideways you would have had me." I looked at Jay, who was on a chair, rubbing his neck. "If you want to play games you ought to take lessons. Maslow would be a good teacher." I unwound my arm and got erect. "Don't bother to see me out," I said and headed for the front.

I was still breathing a little fast when I emerged to the sidewalk, having straightened my tie and run my comb through my hair in the elevator. My watch said twenty past ten. Also in the elevator I had decided to make a phone call, so I walked to Madison Avenue, found a booth, and dialed one of the numbers I knew best. Miss Lily Rowan was in and would be pleased to have me come and tell her things, and I walked the twelve blocks to the number on 63rd Street where her penthouse occupies the roof.

Since it wasn't one of Wolfe's cases with a client involved, but a joint affair, and since it was Lily who had started Sue on her way at my request, I gave her the whole picture. Her chief reactions were a) that she didn't blame Sue and I had no right to, I should feel flattered; b) that I had to somehow get Sue out of it without involving whoever had removed such a louse as Kenneth Faber from circulation; and c) that if I did have to involve him she hoped to heaven it wasn't Carl Heydt because there was no one else around who could make clothes that were fit to wear, especially suits. She had sent a lawyer to Sue, Bernard Ross, and he had seen her and had phoned an hour before I came to report that she was being held without bail and he would decide in the morning whether to apply for a writ.

It was after one o'clock when I climbed out of a cab in front of the old brownstone on West 35th Street, mounted the stoop, used my key, went down the hall to the office and switched the light on, and got a surprise. Under a paperweight on my desk was a note in Wolfe's handwriting. It said:

AG: *Saul will take the car in the morning, probably for most of the day. His car is not presently available.*

NW

I went to the safe, manipulated the knob, opened the door, got the petty-cash book from the drawer, flipped to the current page, and saw an entry:

10/14 SP exp AG 100

I put it back, shut the door, twirled the knob, and considered. Wolfe had summoned Saul, and he had come and had been given an errand for which he needed a car. What errand, for God's sake? Not to drive to Putnam County to get the corn that had been ordered for Friday; for that he wouldn't need to start in the morning, he wouldn't need a hundred bucks for possible expenses, and the entry wouldn't say "exp AG." It shouldn't say that anyway since I wasn't a paying client; it should say "exp JA" for joint affair. And if we were going to split the outlay I should damn well have been consulted beforehand. But up in my room, as I took off and put on, what was biting me was the errand. In the name of the Almighty Lord or J. Edgar Hoover, whichever you prefer, what and where was the errand?

Wolfe eats breakfast in his room from a tray taken up by Fritz, and ordinarily I don't see him until he comes down from the plant rooms at eleven o'clock. If he has something important or complicated for me he sends word by Fritz for me to go up to his room; for something trivial he gets me on the house phone. That Friday morning there was neither word by Fritz nor the buzzer, and after a late and leisurely breakfast in the kitchen, having learned nothing new from the report of developments in the morning papers on the Sweet Corn Murder, as the *Gazette* called it, I went to the office and opened the mail. If Wolfe saw fit to keep Saul's errand strictly private, he could eat wormy old corn boiled in water before I'd ask him. I decided to go out for a walk and was starting for the kitchen to tell Fritz when the phone rang. I got it, and a woman said she was the secretary of Mr. Bernard Ross, counsel for Miss Susan McLeod, and Mr. Ross would like very much to talk with Mr. Wolfe and Mr. Goodwin at their earliest convenience. He would greatly appreclate it if they would call at his office today, this morning if possible.

I would have enjoyed telling Wolfe that Bernard Ross, the celebrated attorney, didn't know that Nero Wolfe, the celebrated detective, never left his house to call on anyone whoever, but since I wasn't on speaking terms with him I had to skip it. I told the secretary that Wolfe couldn't but I could and would, went and told Fritz I would probably be back for lunch, put a carbon copy of the twelve-page conversation with affidavits in my pocket, and departed.

I did get back for lunch, just barely. Including the time he took to study the document I had brought, Ross kept me a solid two hours and a half. When I left he knew nearly everything I did, but not quite; I omitted a few items that were immaterial as far as he was concerned—for instance, that Wolfe had sent Saul Panzer somewhere to do something. Since I couldn't tell him where, to do what, there was no point in mentioning it.

I would have preferred to buy my lunch somewhere, say at Rusterman's, rather than sit through a meal with Wolfe, but he would be the one to gripe, not me, if he didn't know where I was. Entering his house, and hearing him in the dining room speaking to Fritz, I went first to the office, and there on my desk under a paperweight were four sawbucks. Leaving them there, I went to the dining room and said good morning, though it wasn't.

He nodded and went on dishing shrimps from a steaming casserole. "Good afternoon. That forty dollars on your desk can be returned to the safe. Saul had no expenses and I gave him sixty dollars for his six hours."

"His daily minimum is eighty."

"He wouldn't take eighty. He didn't want to take anything, since this is our personal affair, but I insisted. This shrimp Bordelaise is without onions but has some garlic. I think an improvement, but Fritz and I invite your opinion."

"I'll be glad to give it. It smells good." I sat. That was by no means the first time the question had arisen whether he was more pigheaded than I was strong-minded. I was supposed to explode. I was supposed to demand to know where and how Saul had spent the six hours, and he would then be good enough to explain that he had got an idea last night in my absence, and, not knowing where I was, he had had to call Saul. So I wouldn't explode. I would eat shrimp Bordelaise without onions but with garlic and like it. Obviously, whatever Saul's errand had been, it had been a wash-out, since he had returned and reported and been paid off. So it was Wolfe's move, since he had refused to see the three candidates when they came and rang the bell, and I would not explode. Nor would I report on last night or this morning unless and until he asked for it. Back in the office after lunch, he got settled in his favorite chair with *My Life in Court,* and I brought a file of cards from the cabinet and got busy with the germination records. At one minute to four he put his book down and went to keep his date with the orchids. It would have been a pleasure to take the Marley .32 from the drawer and plug him in the back.

I was at my desk, looking through the evening edition of the *Gazette* that had just been delivered, when I heard a noise I couldn't believe. The elevator. I looked at my watch: half past five. That was unprecedented. He never did that. Once in the plant rooms he stuck there for the two hours, no matter what. If he had a notion that couldn't wait he buzzed me on the house phone, or Fritz if I wasn't there. I dropped the paper and got up and stepped to the hall. The elevator jolted to a stop at the bottom, the door opened, and he emerged.

"The corn," he said. "Has it come?"

For Pete's sake. Being finicky about grub is all right up to a point, but there's a limit. "No," I said. "Unless Saul brought it."

He grunted. "A possibility occurred to me. When it comes—if it comes—no. I'll see for myself. The possibility is remote, but it would be—"

"Here it is," I said. "Good timing." A man with a carton had appeared on the stoop. As I started to the front the door bell rang, and as I opened the door

Wolfe was there beside me. The man, a skinny little guy in pants too big for him and a bright green shirt, spoke. "Nero Wolfe?"

"I'm Nero Wolfe." He was on the sill. "You have my corn?"

"Right here." He put the carton down and let go of the cord.

"May I have your name, sir?"

"My name's Palmer. Delbert Palmer. Why?"

"I like to know the names of men who render me a service. Did you pick the corn?"

"Hell, no. McLeod picked it."

"Did you pack it in the carton?"

"No, he did. Look here, I know you're a detective. You just ask questions from habit, huh?"

"No, Mr. Palmer. I merely want to be sure about the corn. I'm obliged to you. Good day, sir." He bent over to slip his fingers under the cord, lifted the carton, and headed for the office. Palmer told me distinctly, "It takes all kinds," turned, and started down the steps, and I shut the door. In the office, Wolfe was standing eying the carton, which he had put on the seat of the red leather chair. As I crossed over he said without looking up, "Get Mr. Cramer."

It's nice to have a man around who obeys orders no matter how batty they are and saves the questions for later. That time the questions got answered before they were asked. I went to my desk, dialed Homicide South, and got Cramer, and Wolfe, who had gone to his chair, took his phone.

"Mr. Cramer? I must ask a favor. I have here in my office a carton which has just been delivered to me. It is supposed to contain corn, and perhaps it does, but it is conceivable that it contains dynamite and a contraption that will detonate it when the cord is cut and the flaps raised. My suspicion may be groundless, but I have it. I know this is not your department, but you will know how to proceed. Will you please notify the proper person without delay? . . . That can wait until we know what's in the carton. . . . Certainly. Even if it contains only corn I'll give you all relevant information. . . . No, there is no ticking sound. If it does contain explosive there is almost certainly no danger until the carton is opened. . . . Yes, I'll make sure."

He hung up, swiveled, and glared at the carton. "Confound it," he growled, "again. We'll get some somewhere before the season ends."

6

The first city employee to arrive, four or five minutes after Wolfe hung up, was one in uniform. Wolfe was telling me what Saul's errand had been when the doorbell rang, and since I resented the interruption I trotted to the front, opened the door, saw a prowl car at the curb, and demanded rudely, "Well?"

"Where's that carton?" he demanded back.

"Where it will stay until someone comes who knows something." I was shutting the door but his foot was there.

"You're Archie Goodwin," he said. "I know about you. I'm coming in. Did you yell for help or didn't you?"

He had a point. An officer of the law doesn't have to bring a search warrant to enter a house whose owner has asked the police to come and get a carton of maybe dynamite. I gave him room to enter, shut the door, took him to the office, pointed to the carton, and said, "If you touch it and it goes off we can sue you for damages."

"You couldn't pay me to touch it," he said. "I'm here to see that nobody does." He glanced around, went over by the big globe, and stood, a good fifteen feet away from the carton. With him there, the rest of the explanation of Saul's errand had to wait, but I had something to look at to pass the time—a carbon copy, one sheet, which Wolfe had taken from his desk drawer and handed me, of something Saul had typed on my machine during my absence Thursday evening.

The second city employee to arrive, at ten minutes

to six, was Inspector Cramer. When the bell rang and I went to let him in the look on his face was one I had seen before. He knew Wolfe had something fancy by the tail, and he would have given a month's pay before taxes to know what. He tramped to the office, saw the carton, turned to the cop, got a salute but didn't acknowledge it, and said, "You can go, Schwab."

"Yes, sir. Stay out front?"

"No. You won't be needed."

Fully as rude as I had been, but he was a superior officer. Schwab saluted again and went. Cramer looked at the red leather chair. He always sat there, but the carton was on it. I moved up one of the yellow ones, and he sat, took his hat off and dropped it on the floor, and asked Wolfe, "What is this, a gag?"

Wolfe shook his head. "It may be a bugaboo, but I'm not crying wolf. I can tell you nothing until we know what's in the carton."

"The hell you can't. When did it come?"

"One minute before I telephoned you."

"Who brought it?"

"A stranger. A man I had never seen before."

"Why do you think it's dynamite?"

"I think it may be. I reserve further information until—"

I missed the rest because the doorbell rang and I went. It was the bomb squad, two of them. They were in uniform, but one look and you knew they weren't flatties—if nothing else, their eyes. When I opened the door I saw another one down on the sidewalk, and their special bus, with its made-to-order enclosed body, was double-parked in front. I asked, "Bomb squad?" and the shorter one said, "Right," and I convoyed them to the office. Cramer, on his feet, returned their salute, pointed to the carton, and said, "It may be just corn. I mean the kind of corn you eat. Or it may not. Nero Wolfe thinks not. He also thinks it's safe until the flaps are opened, but you're the experts. As soon as you know, phone me here. How long will it take?"

"That depends, Inspector. It could be an hour, or ten hours—or it could be never."

"I hope not never. Will you call me here as soon as you know?"

"Yes, sir."

The other one, the taller one, had stooped to press his ear against the carton and kept it there. He raised his head, said, "No comment," eased his fingers under the carton's bottom, a hand at each side, and came up with it. I said, "The man who brought it carried it by the cord," and got ignored. They went, the one with the carton in front, and I followed to the stoop, watched them put it in the bus, and returned to the office. Cramer was in the red leather chair, and Wolfe was speaking.

". . . But if you insist, very well. My reason for thinking it may contain an explosive is that it was brought by a stranger. My name printed on it was unusual, but naturally such a detail would not be over-looked. There are a number of people in the metropol-itan area who have reason to wish me ill, and it would be imprudent—"

"My God, you can lie."

Wolfe tapped the desk with a fingertip. "Mr. Cramer. If you insist on lies you'll get them. Until I know what's in that carton. Then we'll see." He picked up his book, opened to his place, and swiveled to get the light right.

Cramer was stuck. He looked at me, started to say something, and vetoed it. He couldn't get up and go because he had told the Bomb Squad to call him there, but an inspector couldn't just sit. He took a cigar from a pocket, looked at it, put it back, arose, came to me, and said, "I've got some calls to make." Meaning he wanted my chair, which was a good dodge since it got him some action; I had to move. He stayed at the phone nearly half an hour, making four or five calls, none of which sounded important, then got up and went over to the big globe and started studying geography. Ten minutes was enough for that, and he switched to the bookshelves. Back at my desk, leaning back with my legs crossed, my hands clasped behind my head, I noted which books he took out and looked at. Now that I knew who had killed Ken Faber, little things like that were interesting. The one he looked at longest was *The Coming Fury*, by Bruce Catton. He was still at that when the phone rang. I turned to get it, but by the time I had it to my ear he was there. A man asked for Inspector Cramer and I handed it to him and permitted myself a grin as I saw Wolfe put his book down and reach for his phone. He wasn't going to take hearsay, even from an inspector.

It was a short conversation; Cramer's end of it wasn't more than twenty words. He hung up and went to the red leather chair. "Okay," he growled. "If you had opened that carton they wouldn't have found all the pieces. You didn't think it was dynamite, you knew it was. Talk."

Wolfe, his lips tight, was breathing deep. "Not me," he said. "It would have been Archie or Fritz, or both of them. And of course my house. The possibility occurred to me, and I came down, barely in time. Three minutes later . . . Pfui. That man is a blackguard." He shook his head, as if getting rid of a fly. "Well. Shortly after ten o'clock last evening I decided how to proceed, and I sent for Saul Panzer. When he came—"

"Who put that dynamite in that carton?"

"I'm telling you. When he came I had him type something on a sheet of paper and told him to drive to Duncan McLeod's farm this morning and give it to Mr. McLeod, Archie. You have the copy."

I took it from my pocket and went and handed it to Cramer. He kept it, but this is what it said:

MEMORANDUM FROM NERO WOLFE
TO DUNCAN McLEOD

I suggest that you should have in readiness acceptable answers to the following questions if and when they are asked:

1. When did Kenneth Faber tell you that your daughter was pregnant and he was responsible?

2. Where did you go when you drove away from your farm Tuesday afternoon around two

o'clock—perhaps a little later—and returned around seven o'clock, late for milking?

3. Where did you get the piece of pipe? Was it on your premises?

4. Do you know that your daughter saw you leaving the alley Tuesday afternoon? Did you see her?

5. Is it true that the man with the bulldozer told you Monday night that he would have to come Wednesday instead of Thursday?

There are many questions you may be asked; these are only samples. If competent investigators are moved to start inquiries of this nature, you will of course be in a difficult position, and it would be well to anticipate it.

Cramer looked up and aimed beady eyes at Wolfe.

"You knew last night that McLeod killed Faber."

"Not certain knowledge. A reasoned conclusion."

"You knew he left his farm Tuesday afternoon. You knew his daughter saw him at the alley. You knew—"

"No. Those were conclusions." Wolfe turned a palm up. "Mr. Cramer. You sat there yesterday morning and read a document sworn to by Mr. Goodwin and me. When you finished it you knew everything that I knew, and I have learned nothing since then. From the knowledge we shared I had concluded that McLeod had killed Faber. You haven't. Shall I detail it?"

"Yes."

"First, the corn. I presume McLeod told you, as he did me, that he had Faber pick the corn because he had to dynamite some stumps and rocks."

"Yes."

"That seemed to me unlikely. He knows how extremely particular I am, and also the restaurant. We pay him well, more than well; it must be a substantial portion of his income. He knew that young man couldn't possibly do that job. It must have been something more urgent than stumps and rocks that led him to risk losing such desirable customers. Second, the pipe. It was chiefly on account of the pipe that I wanted to see Mr. Heydt, Mr. Maslow, and Mr. Jay, Any man——"

"When did you see them?"

"They came here Wednesday evening, at Miss McLeod's request. Any man, sufficiently provoked, might plan to kill, but very few men would choose a massive iron bludgeon for a weapon to carry through the streets. Seeing those three I thought it highly improbable that any of them would. But a countryman might, a man who does rough work with rough and heavy tools."

"You came to a conclusion on stuff like that?"

"No. Those details were merely corroborative. The conclusive item came from Miss McLeod. You read that document. I asked her—I'll quote it from memory. I said to her, 'You know those men quite well. You know their temperaments. If one of them, enraged beyond endurance by Mr. Faber's conduct, went there and killed him, which one? It wasn't a sudden fit of passion, it was premeditated and planned. From your knowledge of them, which one? How did she answer me?'"

"She said, 'They didn't.'"

"Yes. Didn't you think that significant? Of course I had the advantage of seeing and hearing her."

"Sure it was significant. It wasn't the reaction you always get to the idea that some close friend has committed murder. It wasn't shock. She just stated a fact. She knew they hadn't."

Wolfe nodded. "Precisely. And I saw and heard her. And there was only one way she could know they hadn't, with such certainty in her words and voice and manner: She knew who had. Did you form that conclusion?"

"Yes."

"Then why didn't you go on? If she hadn't killed him herself but knew who had, and it wasn't one of those three men——isn't it obvious?"

"You slipped that in, if she hadn't killed him herself. Why hadn't she?"

A corner of Wolfe's mouth went up. "There it is, your one major flaw: a distorted conception of the impossible. You will reject as inconceivable such a phenomenon as a man being at two different spots simultaneously, though any adroit trickster could easily contrive it; but you consider it credible that that young woman—even after you had studied her conversation with Mr. Goodwin and me—that she concealed that piece of pipe on her person and took it there with the intention of crushing a man's skull with it. Preposterous. That *is* inconceivable." He waved it away. "Of course that's academic, now that that wretch has betrayed himself by sending me dynamite instead of corn, and the last step to my conclusion was inevitable. Since she knew who had killed Faber but wouldn't name him, and it wasn't one of those three, it was her father; and since she was certain—I heard and saw her say, 'They didn't'—she had seen him there. I doubt if he knew it, because—but that's immaterial. So much for—"

He stopped because Cramer was up, coming to my desk. He picked up the phone, dialed, and in a moment said, "Irwin? Inspector Cramer. I want Sergeant Stebbins." After another moment: "Purley? Get Carmel, the sheriff's office. Ask him to get Duncan McLeod and hold him, and no mistake. . . . Yes, Susan McLeod's father. Send two men to Carmel and tell them to call in as soon as they arrive. Tell Carmel to watch it, McLeod is down for murder and he may be rough. . . . No, that can wait. I'll be there soon—half an hour, maybe less."

He hung up, about-faced to Wolfe, and growled, "You knew all this Wednesday afternoon, two days ago."

Wolfe nodded. "And you have known it since yesterday morning. It's a question of interpretation, not of knowledge. Will you please sit? As you know, I like eyes at my level. Thank you. Yes, as early as Wednesday afternoon, when Miss McLeod left, I was all but certain of the identity of the murderer, but I took the precaution of seeing those three men that evening because it was just possible that one of them would disclose something cogent. They didn't. When you came yesterday morning with that warrant, I gave you that document for two reasons: to keep Mr. Goodwin out of jail, and to share my knowledge with you. I wasn't obliged to share also my interpretation of it. Any moment since yesterday noon I have rather expected to hear that Mr. McLeod had been taken into custody, but no."

"So you decided to share your interpretation with him instead of me."

"I like that," Wolfe said approvingly. "That was neat. I prefer to put it that I decided not to decide. Having given you all the facts I had, I had met my obligation as a citizen and a licensed private detective. I was under no compulsion, legal or moral, to assume the role of a nemesis. It was only conjecture that Faber had told Mr. McLeod that he had debauched his daughter, but he had told others, and McLeod must have had a potent motive, so it was highly probable. If so, the question of moral turpitude was moot, and I would not rule on it. Since I had given you the facts, I thought it only fair to inform Mr. McLeod that he was menaced by a logical conclusion from those facts; and I did so. I used Mr. Panzer as my messenger because I chose not to involve Mr. Goodwin. He was unaware of the conclusion I had reached, and if I had told him there might have been disagreement regarding the course to take. He can be—uh—difficult."

Cramer grunted. "Yeah. He can. So you deliberately warned a murderer. Telling him to have answers ready. Nuts. You expected him to lam."

"No. I had no specific expectation. It would have been idle to speculate, but if I had, I doubt if I would have expected him to scoot. He couldn't take his farm along, and he would be leaving his daughter in mortal jeopardy. I didn't consciously speculate, but my subconscious must have, for suddenly, when I was busy at the potting bench, it struck me. Saul Panzer's description of McLeod's stony face as he read the memorandum; the stubborn ego of a self-righteous man; dynamite for stumps and rocks; corn; a closed carton. Most improbable. I resumed the potting. But conceivable. I dropped the trowel and went to the elevator, and within thirty seconds after I emerged in the hall the carton came."

"Luck," Cramer said. "Your goddam incredible luck. If it had made mincemeat of Goodwin you might have been willing to admit for once— Okay, it didn't." He got up. "Stick around, Goodwin. They'll want you at the DA's office, probably in the morning." To Wolfe: "What if that phone call had said the carton held corn, just corn? You think you could have talked me off, don't you?"

"I could have tried."

"By God. Talk about stubborn egos." Cramer shook his head. "That break you got on the carton. You know, any normal man, if he got a break like that, coming down just in the nick of time, what any normal man would do, he would go down on his knees and thank God. Do you know what you'll do? You'll thank *you*. I admit it would be a job for you to get down on your knees, but—"

The phone rang. I swiveled and got it, and a voice I recognized asked for Inspector Cramer. I turned and told him, "Purley Stebbins," and he came and took it. The conversation was even shorter than the one about the carton, and Cramer's part was only a dozen words and a couple of growls. He hung up, went and got his hat, and headed for the hall, but a step short of the door he stopped and turned.

"I might as well tell you," he said. "It'll give you a better appetite for dinner, even if it's not corn. About an hour ago Duncan McLeod sat or stood or lay on a pile of dynamite and it went off. They've got his head and some other pieces. They'll want to decide whether it was an accident or he did it. Maybe you can help them interpret the facts."

He turned and went.

7

One day last week there was a party at Lily Rowan's penthouse. She never invites more than six to dinner—eight counting her and me—but that was a dancing party and around coffee time a dozen more came and three musicians got set in the alcove and started up. After rounds with Lily and three or four others, I approached Sue McLeod and offered a hand. She gave me a look. "You know you don't want to. Let's go outside."

I said it was cold, and she said she knew it and headed for the foyer. We got her wrap, a fur thing which she probably didn't own, since top-flight models are offered loans of everything from socks to sable, went back in, on through, and out to the terrace. There were evergreens in tubs, and we crossed to them for shelter from the wind.

"You told Lily I hate you," she said. "I don't."

"Not 'hate,'" I said. "She misquoted me or you're misquoting her. She said I should dance with you and I said when I tried it a month ago you froze."

"I know I did." She put a hand on my arm. "Archie. It was hard, you know it was. If I hadn't got my father to let him work on the farm . . . it was my fault, I know it was . . . but I couldn't help thinking if you hadn't sent him that . . . letting him know you knew . . ."

"I didn't send it, Mr. Wolfe did. But I would have. Okay, he was your father, so it was hard. But no matter whose father he was, I'm not wearing an arm band for the guy who packed dynamite in that carton."

"Of course not. I know. Of course not. I tell myself I'll have to forget it . . . but it's not easy . . ."

She shivered. "Anyway I wanted to say I don't hate you. You don't have to dance with me, and you know I'm not going to get married until I can stop working and have babies, and I know you never are, and even if you do it will be Lily, but you don't have to stand there and let me *really* freeze, do you?"

"I didn't. You don't have to be rude, even with a girl who can't dance, and it was cold out there.

Blood Will Tell

Naturally most of the items in the mail that is delivered to the old brownstone on West 35th Street are addressed to Nero Wolfe, but since I both work and live there eight or ten out of a hundred are addressed to me. It is my custom to let my share wait until after I have opened Wolfe's, looked it over, and put it on his desk, but sometimes curiosity butts in. As it did that Tuesday morning when I came to an elegant cream-colored envelope, outsize, addressed to me on a typewriter, with the return address in the corner engraved in dark brown:

JAMES NEVILLE VANCE
Two Nineteen Horn Street
New York 12   New York

Never heard of him. It wasn't flat; it bulged with something soft inside. Like everybody else, I occasionally get envelopes containing samples of something that bulges them, but not expensive envelopes with engraving that isn't phony. So I slit it open and removed the contents. A folded sheet of paper that matched the envelope, including the engraved name and address, had a message typed in the center:

ARCHIE GOODWIN—KEEP THIS UNTIL YOU HEAR FROM ME.
JNV

"This" was a necktie, a four-in-hand, neatly folded to go in the envelope. I stretched it out—long, narrow, maybe silk, light tan, almost the same color as the stationery, with thin brown diagonal lines. A Sutcliffe label, so certainly silk, say twenty bucks. But he should have sent it to the cleaners instead of me, because it had a spot, a big one two inches long, near one end, about the same tone of brown as the thin lines; but the lines' brown was clean and live and the spot's brown was dirty and dead. I sniffed at it, but I am not a beagle. Having seen a few dried blood-stains here and there, I knew the dirty color was right, but that's no phenolphthalin test. Even so, I told myself as I dropped the tie in a drawer, supposing that James Neville Vance worked in a butcher shop and forgot his bib, why pick on me? As I closed the drawer I shrugged.

That's the way to take it when you get a blood-stained (maybe) necktie in the mail from a stranger, just shrug, but I admit that in the next couple of hours I did something and didn't do something else. What I did do was ring Lon Cohen at the *Gazette* to ask a question, and an hour later he called back to say that James Neville Vance, now in his late fifties, still owned all the real estate he had inherited from his father, still spent winters on the Riviera, and was still a bachelor; and what did he want of a private detective? I reserved that. What I didn't do was take a walk. When nothing is stirring and Wolfe has given me no program I usual-ly go out after the routine morning chores to work my legs and have a look at the town and my fellow men, not to mention women, but that morning I skipped it because JNV might come or phone. It had been an honest shrug, but you can't shrug all day.

I might as well have had my walk because the phone call didn't come until a quarter past eleven, after Wolfe had come down to the office from his two-hour morning session with the orchids up in the plant rooms on the roof. He had put a spray of *Cymbidium Doris* in the vase on his desk and got his personal seventh of a ton disposed in his oversize custom-made chair, and was scowling at the dust jacket of a book, one of the items that had been addressed to him, when the phone rang and I got it.

"Nero Wolfe's office, Archie Goodwin speaking."

"Is this Archie Goodwin?"

Three people out of ten will do that. I am always tempted to say no, it's a trained dog, and see what comes next, but I might get barked at. So I said, "It is. In person."

"This is James Neville Vance. Did you receive something in the mail from me?"

His voice couldn't decide whether to be a squeak or a falsetto and had the worst features of both. "Yes, presumably," I said. "Your envelope and letterhead."

"And an enclosure."

"Right."

"Please destroy it. Burn it. I intended—But what I intended doesn't matter now. . . . I was mistaken. Burn it. I'm sorry to have bothered you."

He hung up.

I cradled the phone and swiveled. Wolfe had opened the book to the title page and was eying it with the same kind of look a man I know has for a pretty girl he has just met.

"If I may interrupt," I said. "Since there's nothing urgent in the mail I have an errand, personal or professional, I don't know which." I got the envelope, letterhead, and enclosure from the drawer, rose, and handed them to him. "If that spot on the tie is blood, my theory was that someone stabbed or shot James Neville Vance and got rid of the corpse all right but didn't know what to do with the tie, so he sent it to me, but that phone call was a bagpipe saying he was James Neville Vance, and he had been mistaken, and I would please burn what he had sent me by mail. So evidently—"

"A bagpipe?"

"I merely meant he squeaked. So evidently he couldn't burn it himself because he didn't have a match, and now he's impersonating James Neville Vance, who owns—or owned—various gobs of real estate, and it is my duty as a citizen and a licensed private detective to expose and denounce—"

"Pfui. Some floundering numskull."

"Okay, I'll go out back to burn it. It'll smell."

He grunted. "It may not be blood."

I nodded. "Sure. But if it's ketchup and tobacco juice I can tell him how to get it out and charge him two bucks. That will be a bigger fee than any you've collected for nearly a month."

Another grunt. "Where is Horn Street?"

"In the Village. Thirty-minute walk. I've had no walk."

"Very well." He opened the book.

2

Most of the houses on Horn Street, which is only three blocks long, could stand a coat of paint, but Number 219, a four-story brick, was all dressed up—the brick cream-colored and the trim dark brown; and the venetian blinds at the windows matched the bricks. Since Vance was in clover I supposed it was just for him, but in the vestibule there were three names in a panel on the wall with buttons. The bottom one was Fougere, the middle one was Kirk, and the top one was James Neville Vance. I pushed the top one, and after a wait a voice came from a grill. "Who is it?"

I stooped a little to put my mouth on a level with the lower grill and said, "My name is Archie Goodwin. I'd like to see Mr. Vance."

"This is Vance. What do you want?"

It was a baritone, no trace of a squeak. I told the grill, "I have something that belongs to you and I want to return it."

"You have something that belongs to me?"

"Right."

"What is it and where did you get it?"

"Correction. I *think* it belongs to you. It's a four-in-hand silk tie, Sutcliffe label, the same color as this house, with diagonal lines the same color as the trim. Cream and brown."

"Who are you and where did you get it?"

I got impatient. "Here's a suggestion," I said. "Install closed-circuit television so you can see the vestibule from up there, and phone me at the office of Nero Wolfe, where I work, and I'll come back. It will take

a week or so and set you back ten grand, but it'll
be worth it to see the tie without letting me in. After
you've identified it I'll tell you where I got it. If you
don't—"

"Did you say Nero Wolfe? The detective?"

"Yes."

"But what— This is ridiculous."

"I agree. Completely. Give me a ring when you're
ready."

"But I— All right. Use the elevator. I'm in the studio, the top floor—four."

There was a click at the door, and on the third click
I pushed it open and entered. To my surprise the small
hall was not more cream and brown but a deep rich
red with black panel-borders, and the door of the do-
it-yourself elevator was stainless steel. When I pushed
the button and the door opened, and, inside, pushed
the 4 button and was lifted, there was practically no
noise or vibration—very different from the one in the
old brownstone which Wolfe always used and I never
did.

Stepping out when the door opened, I got another
surprise. Since he had called it the studio I was expecting to smell turpentine and see a clutter of vintage
Vances, but at first glance it was a piano warehouse.
There were three of them in the big room, which was
the length and width of the house.

The man standing there waited to speak until my
glance got to him. Undersized, with too much chin
for his neat smooth face, no wrinkles, he wasn't as im-
pressive as his stationery, but his clothes were—
cream-colored silk shirt and brown made-to-fit slacks.
He cocked his head, nodded, and said, "I recognize
you. I've seen you at the Flamingo." He came a step.
"What's this about a tie? Let me see it."

"It's the one you sent me," I said.

He frowned. "The one I sent you?"

"There seems to be a gap," I said. "Are you James
Neville Vance?"

"I am. Certainly."

I got the envelope and letterhead from my breast
pocket and showed them for inspection. "Then that's

your stationery?" He was going to take them, but I held on. He examined the address on the envelope and the message on the letterhead, frowning, lifted the frown to me, and demanded, "What kind of a game is this?"

"I've walked two miles to find out." I got the tie from my side pocket. "This was in the envelope. Is it yours?"

I let him take it, and he looked it over front and back. "What's this spot?"

"I don't know. Is it yours?"

"Yes, I mean it must be. That pattern, the colors—they reserve it for me, or they're supposed to."

"Did you mail it to me in this envelope?"

"I did not. Why would—"

"Did you phone me this morning and tell me to burn it?"

"I did not. You got it in the mail this morning?"

I nodded. "And a phone call at a quarter past eleven from a man who squeaked and told me to burn it. Have you got a photograph of yourself handy?"

"Why . . . yes. Why?"

"You have recognized me, but I haven't recognized you. You ask what kind of a game this is, and so do I. What if you're not Vance?"

"That's ridiculous!"

"Sure, but why not humor me?"

He was going to say why not, changed his mind, and moved. Crossing the room, detouring around a piano, to a bank of cabinets and shelves at the wall, he took something from a shelf and came and handed it to me. It was a thin book with a leather binding that had stamped on it in gold: THE MUSIC OF THE FUTURE by James Neville Vance. Inside, the first two pages were blank; the third had just two words at the bottom: PRIVATELY PRINTED; and the fourth had a picture of the author.

A glance was enough. I put it on a nearby table. "Okay. Nice picture. Any ideas or suggestions?"

"How could I haver?" He was peevish. "It's crazy!" He gave the tie another look. "It must be mine. I can settle that. Come along."

He headed for the rear and I followed, back beyond the second piano, and then down spiral stairs, wide for a spiral, with carpeted steps and a polished wooden rail. At the bottom, the rear end of a good-sized living room, he turned right through an open door and we were in a bedroom. He crossed to another door and opened it, and I stopped two steps off. It was a walk-in closet. A friend of mine once told me that a woman's clothes closet will tell you more about her than any other room in the house, and if that goes for a man too there was my chance to get the lowdown on James Neville Vance, but I was interested only in his neckties. They were on a rack at the right, three rows of them, quite an assortment, some cream and brown but by no means all. He fingered through part of one row, repeated it, turned and emerged, and said, "It's mine. I had nine and gave one to somebody, and there are only seven." He shook his head. "I can't imagine . . ." He let it hang. "What on earth . . ." He let that hang too.

"And your stationery," I said.

"Yes. Of course."

"And the phone call telling me to burn it. With a squeak."

"Yes. You asked if I had any ideas or suggestions. Have you?"

"I could have, but they would be expensive. I work for Nero Wolfe and it would be on his time, and the bill would be bad news. You must know who has access to your stationery and that closet, and you ought to be able to make some kind of a guess about who and why. And you won't need the tie. It came to me in the mail, so actually and legally it's in my possession, and I ought to keep it." I put a hand out. "If you don't mind?"

"Of course." He handed it over. "But I might— You're not going to burn it?"

"No indeed." I stuck it in my side pocket. The envelope and letterhead were back in my breast pocket. "I have a little collection of souvenirs. If and when you have occasion to produce it for—"

A bell tinkled somewhere, a soft music tinkle, possibly music of the future. He frowned and turned and started for the front, and I followed, back through the open door, and across the living room to another door, which he opened. Two men were there in a little foyer —one a square little guy in shirt sleeves and brown denim pants, and the other, also square but big, a harness bull.

"Yes, Bert?" Vance said.

"This cop," the little guy said. "He wants in to Mrs. Kirk's apartment."

"What for?"

The bull spoke. "Just to look, Mr. Vance. I'm on patrol and I got a call. Probably nothing, it usually isn't, but I've got to look. Sorry to bother you."

"Look at what?"

"I don't know. Probably nothing, as I say. Just to see that all's in order. Law and order."

"Why shouldn't it be in order? This is my house, officer."

"Yeah, I know it is. And this is my job. I get a call, I do as I'm told. When I pushed the Kirk button there was no answer, so I got the janitor. Routine. I said I'm sorry to bother you."

"Very well. You have the key, Bert?"

"Yes, sir."

"Ring before you— I'd better come." He crossed the sill and when I was out closed the door. Four of us in the elevator didn't leave much room. When it stopped at 2 and they stepped out I stepped out too, into another small foyer. Vance pressed a button on a doorjamb, waited half a minute, pressed it again, kept his finger on it for five seconds, and waited some more. "All right, Bert," he said and moved aside. Bert put a key in the lock—a Rabson, I noticed—turned it, turned the knob, pushed the door open, and made room for Vance to enter. Then the cop, and then me. Two steps in, Vance stopped, faced the rear, and raised his baritone. "Bonny! It's Jim!"

I saw it first, a blue slipper on its side on the floor with a foot in it, extending beyond the edge of a couch. I moved automatically but stopped short. Let the cop do his own discovering. He did; he saw it too and went; and when he had passed the end of the couch he had stopped shorter than I had, growled, "God-almighty," and stood looking down. Then I moved, and so did Vance. When Vance saw it, all of it, he went stiff, gawking, then he made a sort of choking noise, and then he crumpled. It wasn't a faint; his knees just quit on him and he went down, and no wonder. Even live blood on a live face makes an impression, and when the face is dead and the blood has dried all over one side and the ear, plenty of it, you do need knees.

I don't say I wasn't impressed, but my problem wasn't knees. It took me maybe six seconds to decide. Bert had joined us and was reacting. Vance had grabbed the back of the couch to pull himself up. The cop was squatting for a close-up of the dead face. No one knew if I was there or not, and in another six seconds I went to the door, easy, let myself out, took the elevator down, and on out to the sidewalk. A police car was double-parked right in front, and the cop at the wheel, seeing me emerge from that house, gave me an eye but let it go at that as I headed west.

Approaching Sixth Avenue, I felt sweat trickling down onto my cheek and got out my handkerchief. The sun was at the top on a warm August day, but I don't sweat when I'm walking, and besides, why didn't I know it before it collected enough to trickle? There you are. One man's knees buckle immediately and another man starts sweating five minutes later and doesn't know it.

It was a quarter to one when I climbed out of a taxi in front of the old brownstone on West 35th Street, mounted the seven steps of the stoop, and used my key. Before proceeding down the hall to the office I used my handkerchief thoroughly; Wolfe, who misses nothing, had never seen me sweat and wouldn't now. When I entered he was at his desk with the new book, and he took his eyes from it barely enough for a side-wise glance at me as I crossed to my desk. I sat and said, "I don't like to interrupt, but I have a report."

He grunted. "Is it necessary?"

"It's desirable. There's nearly half an hour till lunch,"

and if someone comes, for instance an officer of the law, it would be better if you knew about it."

He let the book down a little. "What the devil are you into now?"

"That's the report. Ten minutes will do it, fifteen at the outside, even verbatim."

He inserted a bookmark and put the book on the desk. "Well?"

I started in, verbatim, and by the time I was telling Vance he should install closed-circuit television he was leaning back with his eyes closed. Merely force of habit. When I mentioned the title of the privately printed book he made a noise—he says all music is a vestige of barbarism—and when I came to the end he snorted and opened his eyes.

"I don't believe it," he said flatly. "You've omitted something. A death by violence, and, not involved and with no commitment, you left? Nonsense." He straightened up.

I nodded. "You're not interested and you don't intend to be, so you didn't bother to look at it. I was present at the discovery of a dead body, obviously murdered. If I had hung around I would have been stuck. In another minute the cop would have ordered us to stay put, and he would have taken my name and recognized it. When Homicide came, probably Stebbins but no matter who, he would have learned why I was there, if not from me, then from Vance, and he would have taken the envelope and letterhead and necktie, and I wanted them for souvenirs. As I told Vance, they are actually and legally in my possession."

"Pfui."

"I disagree. Of course I would have liked to stay long enough to get a sample of that blood to have it compared with the spot on the tie. If it was the same I would be the first to know it and it's nice to be first. Also of course, Vance will tell them about me, and the question is can I be hooked for obstructing justice if I refuse to hand over the tie? I don't see how. There's nothing to connect it with the homicide until and unless her blood is compared with the spot."

Wolfe grunted. "Flummery. Provoking the police is permissible only when it serves a purpose."

"Certainly. And if James Neville Vance comes or calls to say that he expects to be charged with the murder of Mrs. Kirk, if that's who she was, partly because of the tie he didn't send me, and he wants to hire you, wouldn't it be convenient to have the tie? And the envelope and letterhead?"

"I have no expectation of being engaged by Mr. Vance. Nor desire."

"Sure. Because you would have to work. I remarked yesterday that the gross take for the first seven months of nineteen sixty-two is nine grand behind nineteen sixty-one. I am performing one of the main functions you pay me for."

"Not brilliantly," he said and picked up the book. Merely a childish gesture, since Fritz would enter in eight minutes to announce lunch. I went and opened the safe and stashed my souvenirs on a shelf in the inner compartment.

3

Inspector Cramer of Homicide South came at ten minutes past six.

I had been functioning all afternoon, I don't say brilliantly. During lunch, in the dining room across the hall, while listening to Wolfe's table talk with one ear, I decided to make myself scarce while I considered the matter. There was no sense in getting out on a limb just for the hell of it, and a homicide dick might show any minute, so as we left the table I told Wolfe that since we had no expectations or desires I was going out on some personal chores. He gave me a sharp glance, made a face, and headed for the office. As I was turning to the front the phone rang and I went in and got it. If it it was the DA's office inviting me to call, I would make up my mind on the way down-town.

It was Lon Cohen. He had compliments. "No question about it, Archie," he said, "you'd be worth your weight in blood rubies to any newspaper in town, especially the *Gazette*. At nine-thirty you phone for dope on James Neville Vance. At twelve-twenty, less than three hours later, a cop finds a body in his house and both you and he are present. Marvelous. Any leg man can find out what happened, but knowing what's going to happen—you're one in ten million. What's on the program for tomorrow? I only want a day at a time."

I was a little short with him because my problem was the program for today.

I was out of the house and halfway to Eighth Avenue, no destination in mind, when I realized I was ignoring the main point—no, two main points. One, if a dick came before Wolfe went up to the plant rooms at four o'clock, Wolfe might possibly give him the souvenirs, to keep me out of trouble. Two, if the spot on the tie wasn't blood and its being sent to me was just some kind of a gag, and it had no connection with a murder, I was stewing about nothing. So I turned and went back. Wolfe, at his desk with his book, apparently paid no attention as I opened the safe and took out the souvenirs, but of course he saw. I pocketed them and left.

Twenty minutes later I was seated in a room on the tenth floor of a building on 43rd Street, telling a man at a desk, "This is for me personally, Mr. Hirsh, not for Mr. Wolfe, but it's possible that he may have a use for it before long," I put the tie on the desk and pointed to the spot. "How long will it take to tell what that is?"

He bent his head for a look without touching it.

"Maybe ten minutes, maybe a week."

"How long will it take to tell if it's blood?"

He got a glass from a drawer and took another look. "It's a fairly fresh stain. That it isn't blood, negative for hemoglobin, ten minutes. That it is blood, thirty or forty minutes. That it is or isn't human blood, up to ninety minutes, maybe less. To type it with certainty if it's human, at least five hours."

"I only need yes or no on the human. Would you have to ruin the whole spot?"

"Oh, no. Just a few threads."

"Okay, I'll wait. As I say, it's not for Mr. Wolfe, but I'll appreciate it very much. I'll be in the anteroom."

"You might as well wait here." He rose, with the tie. "I'll have to do it myself. It's vacation time and we're shorthanded."

An hour and a half later, at twenty minutes to five, I was in a down elevator, the tie back in my pocket minus only a few threads. It was human blood, and the stain was less than a week old, probably much less. So I wasn't in a stew for nothing, but now what? Of course I could go back to the office and try for fingerprints on the envelope and letterhead, but that would have been just passing time since I had nothing to compare them with. Or I could phone James Neville Vance, tell him what the spot was, and ask if he now had any ideas or suggestions, but that would have been pushing it, since I didn't know whether he had told the cops why I was there.

Considering, as I emerged to the sidewalk, how little I did know, next to nothing, that it was either go home and sit on it or learn something somehow, and that the *Gazette* building was only a five-minute walk, I turned east at 44th Street. Lon Cohen's room is on the twentieth floor, two doors down the hall from the corner office of the publisher. When I walked in, having been announced, he was at one of the three phones on his desk, and I sat. When he hung up he swiveled and said, "No welcome. If you were a real pal you would have told me this morning and we could have had a photographer there."

"Next time." I crossed my legs to show that we had all day. "You will now please tell me whose body I helped discover and go on from there. I've got amnesia."

"The twilight edition will be on the stands in half an hour and costs a dime."

"Sure, but I want it all, not only what's fit to print."

Before I left, nearly an hour later, he had two journalists up from downstairs. The crop that can be brought in on a hot one, including pictures, in less than five hours, makes you proud to be an American. For instance, there was a photo of Mrs. Martin Kirk, then Miss Bonny Sommers, in a bikini on a beach in 1958.

I'll stick to the essentials. Bonny Sommers had been a secretary in a prominent firm of architects, and a year ago, at the age of twenty-five, she had married one of its not-yet-prominent young men, Martin Kirk, age thirty-three. There were contradictions as to how soon it had started to sour, but none on the fact that Kirk had moved out two weeks ago, to a hotel room. If he had developed a conflicting interest, its object hadn't been spotted, but efforts to find and identify it were in process. As for Bonny, it was established that she was inclined to experiments, but the details needed further inquiry and were getting it. Four names were mentioned in that connection. One of them was James Neville Vance, and another was Paul Fougere, the tenant, with his wife, of the ground floor of Vance's house. Fougere was an electronics technician and vice-president of Audivideo, Inc.

As for today, Kirk had phoned police headquarters a little before noon, saying that he had dialed his wife's number six times in eighteen hours and got no answer; that he had gone to the house around eleven o'clock, got no response to his ring from the vestibule, used his key to get in, pushed the button at the apartment door repeatedly and heard the bell, without result, and departed without entering; and that he wanted the police to take a look. He had been asked to be there to let a cop use his key but had declined.

Bonny Kirk had last been seen alive, to present knowledge, by a man from a package store who had delivered a bottle of vodka to her at the apartment door, and been paid by her, a little before one o'clock Monday afternoon. The unopened vodka bottle, found under the couch with blood on it, had been used to smash Bonny Kirk's skull sometime between one P.M. and eight P.M. Monday, the latter limit having been supplied by the medical examiner.

Among those who had been summoned or escorted

to the DA's office were Martin Kirk, James Neville Vance, Mr. and Mrs. Paul Fougere, and Bert Odom, the janitor. Presumably some of them, perhaps all, were still there.

For all that and a lot more I'm leaving out I didn't owe Lon anything, since on our give-and-take record to date I had a credit balance, and I didn't mention the necktie. Of course he wanted to know who Wolfe's client was and what about Vance, and it never hurts to have Wolfe's name in the paper, not to mention mine, but since the whole point was that Wolfe was short on clients I decided to save it. Naturally he didn't believe it, that Wolfe had no client, and when I got up to go he said, "No welcome and no fare you well either."

I took a taxi because Wolfe likes to find me in the office when he comes down from the plant rooms at six o'clock, and he pays me and I had spent the day on personal chores, but with the traffic at that hour I might as well have walked, and it was ten past six when the hackie finally made it. As I was climbing out, a car I recognized pulled up just behind, and as I stood a man I also recognized got out of it—a big solid specimen with a big red face topped by an old felt hat even on a hot August day. As he approached I greeted him, "I'll be damned. You yourself?"

Ignoring me, he called to my hackie, "Where did you get this fare?" Apparently the hackie recognized Inspector Cramer of Homicide South, for he called back, "Forty-second and Lexington, Inspector."

"All right, move on." To me: "We'll go in."

I shook my head. "I'll save you the trouble. Mr. Wolfe has a new book and there's no point in annoying him. The tie was mailed to me, not him, and he knows nothing about it and doesn't want to."

"I'd rather get that from him. Come on."

"Nothing doing. He's sore enough as it is, and so am I. I've wasted a day. I've learned that the spot on the tie is human blood, but what—"

"How did you learn that?"

"I had it tested at a laboratory."

"You did." His face got redder. "You left the scene

of a crime, withholding information. Then you tampered with evidence. If you think—"

"Nuts. Evidence of what? Even with blood it's not evidence if it isn't the same type as the victim's. As for leaving the scene, I wasn't concerned and no one told me to stay. As for tampering, it's still a perfectly good spot with just a few threads gone. I had to know if it was blood because if it wasn't I was going to keep it, and if a court ordered me to fork it over I would have fought it. I wanted to find out who had sent it to me and why, and I still do. But since it's blood I couldn't fight an order." I got the souvenirs from my pockets. "Here. When you're through with them I want them back."

"You do." He took them and looked them over. "There's a typewriter in Vance's place. Did you take a sample from it for comparison?"

"You know damn well I didn't, since he has told you what I said and did."

"He could forget. Is this the tie you got in the mail this morning and is this the envelope it came in?"

"Yes. Now that's an idea. I could have got another set from Vance. I wish I'd thought of it."

"You could have. I know you. I'm taking you down, but we'll go in first. I want to ask Wolfe a question."

"I'm *not* going in, and one will get you ten you won't get in. He's not interested and doesn't intend to be. I could come down after dinner. We're having lobsters, simmered in white wine with tarragon, and a white wine sauce with the tomalley and coral—"

"I'm taking you." He aimed a thumb at the car. "Get in."

4

I got home well after midnight and before going up two flights to bed hit the refrigerator for leftover lobster and a glass of milk, to remove both hunger and the taste of the excuse for bread and stringy corned beef I had been supplied with at the DA's office.

Since my connection with their homicide had been short and simple, the twenty seconds I had spent in the Kirk apartment, and my connection with Vance hadn't been a lot longer, an hour of me should have been more than enough, including typing the statement for me to sign, and it wasn't until after nine o'clock that I realized, from a question by Assistant DA Mandel, what the idea was. They actually thought that the tie thing might be some kind of dodge that I had been in on, and they were keeping me until they got a report on the stain. So I cooled down and took it easy, got on speaking terms with a dick who was put in a room with me to see that I didn't jump out a window, got him to produce a deck for some friendly gin, and in two hours managed to lose $4.70. I called time at that point and paid him because he was getting sleepy and it would have been next to impossible to keep him ahead.

I got my money's worth. Around midnight someone came and called him out, and when he returned ten minutes later and said I was no longer needed I gave him a friendly grin, a good loser, no hard feelings, and said, "So the blood's the same type, huh?" And he nodded and said, "Yeah, modern science is wonderful."

So, I told myself as I got the lobster out, I got not only my money's worth but my time's worth, and by the time I was upstairs and in my pajamas I had decided that if Wolfe wasn't interested I certainly was, and I was going to find out who had sent me that tie even if I had to take a month's leave of absence.

Except in emergencies I get a full eight hours' sleep, and that was merely a project, not an emergency, so I didn't get down for breakfast, which I eat in the kitchen, until after ten o'clock. As I got orange juice from the refrigerator and Fritz started the burner under the cake griddle he asked where I had dined, and I said he knew darned well I hadn't dined at all, since I had phoned that I was at the DA's office, and he nodded and said, "These clients in trouble."

"Look, Fritz," I told him, "you're a chef, not a diplomat, so why do you keep that up? You know we've had no client for a month and you want to know if we've hooked one, so why don't you just ask? Repeat after me, 'Have we got a client?' Try it."

"Archie." He turned a palm up. "You would have to say yes or no. The way I do it, you can *biaiser* if you wish."

I had to ask him how to spell it so I could look it up when I went to the office. Sitting, I picked up the *Times,* and my brow went up when I saw that it had made the front page. Probably on account of Martin Kirk; the *Times* loves architects as much as it hates disk jockeys and private detectives. It had nothing useful to add to what I had got from Lon, but it mentioned that Mrs. Kirk had been born in Manhattan, Kansas. Any other paper which had dug up that detail would have had a feature piece about born in Manhattan and died in Manhattan.

After three griddle cakes with homemade sausage and one with thyme honey, and two cups of coffee, I made it to the office in time to have the desks dusted, fresh water in the vase, *biaiser* looked up, and the mail opened, when Wolfe came down from the plant rooms. I waited until the orchids were in the vase and he had sat and glanced through the mail to tell him that it now looked as if someone had sent me a hot piece of evidence in a homicide, and I intended to find out why, of course on my own time, and anyway he wouldn't be needing me since apparently there was nobody that needed him.

His lips tightened. "Evidence? Merely a conjecture."

"No, sir. I took it to Ludlow and it's human blood. So I gave it to Cramer. Of course you've read the *Times?*"

"Yes."

"The blood is the same type as Mrs. Kirk's. If it was or is a floundering numskull, obviously I'd better see—"

The doorbell rang.

I got up and went, telling myself it was even money it was James Neville Vance, but it wasn't. A glance at the one-way glass panel in the front door settled that. It was a panhandler who had run out of luck and started ringing doorbells—a tall, lanky one pretending he had to lean against the jamb to keep himself upright. Opening the door, I said politely, "It's a hard life. Good morning."

He got me in focus with bleary eyes and said, "I would like to see Nero Wolfe. My name is Martin Kirk."

If you think I should have recognized him from the pictures Lon had shown me, I don't agree. You should have seen him. I told him Mr. Wolfe saw people only by appointment, but I'd ask. "You're the Martin Kirk who lives at Two-nineteen Horn Street?"

He said he was, and I invited him in, ushered him into the front room and to a seat, which he evidently needed, went to the office by way of the connecting door, closed the door, and crossed to Wolfe's desk. "I'm on my own time now," I told him. "It's Martin Kirk. He asked to see you, but of course you're not interested. May I use the front room?"

He took a deep breath, in through his nose and out through his mouth, then glared at me for five seconds and growled, "Bring him in."

"But you don't—"

"Bring him."

Unheard of. Absolutely contrary to nature—his nature. The Nero Wolfe I thought I knew would at least have wanted me to pump him first. With a genius you never know. As I returned to the front room and told Kirk to come, I decided that the idea must be to show me that I would be a sap to waste my time. He would make short work of Martin Kirk. So as Kirk flopped into the red leather chair near the end of Wolfe's desk he snapped at him, "Well, sir? I have read the morning paper. Why do you come to me?"

Kirk pressed the heels of his palms against his eyes. He groaned. He lowered his hands and the bleary eyes blinked a dozen times. "You'll have to make allowances," he said. "I just left the district attorney's office. I was there all night and no sleep."

"Have you eaten?"

"My God no."

Wolfe made a face. That complicated it. The mere thought of a man going without food was disagreeable, and to have one there in his house was intolerable. He had to either get him out in a hurry or feed him. "Why should I make allowances?" he demanded.

Kirk actually tried to smile, and it made me want to feed him myself. "I know about you," he said. "You're hard. And you charge high fees. I can pay you, don't worry about that. They think I killed my wife. They let me go, but they—"

"Did you kill your wife?"

"No. But they think I did, and they think they can prove it. I haven't got a lawyer, and I don't know any lawyer I want to go to. I came to you because I know about you—partly that, and partly because they asked me a lot of questions about you—about you and Archie Goodwin." He looked at me, blinking to manage the change of focus. "You're Archie Goodwin, aren't you?"

I told him yes and he went back to Wolfe. "They asked if I knew you or Goodwin, if I had ever met you, and they seemed to think I had—no, they *did* think I had. It seemed to have some connection with something that was mailed to Goodwin, and something about a necktie, and something about a phone call he got yesterday. I'm sorry to be so vague, but I said you'd have to make allowances, I'm not myself. I haven't been myself since—I found—" His jaw had started to work and he stopped to control it. "My wife," he said. "They kept at me that she wasn't much of a wife, and all right, she wasn't, but if a woman —I mean if a man—"

He stopped again to handle his jaw. In a moment he went on, "So I came to you partly because I thought you might know about a necktie and a phone call and something that was mailed to Goodwin. Do you?"

"Possibly." Wolfe was regarding him. "Mr. Kirk. You said you can pay me, but I don't sell information; I sell only services."

"That's what I want, your services."

"You want to hire me to investigate this affair?"

"Yes. That's why I'm here."

"And you can pay me without undue strain?"

"Yes. I have— Yes. Do you want a check now?"

"A thousand dollars will do as a retainer."

I had to shut my eyes a second to keep from gawking. That wasn't only unheard of, it was unbelievable. Taking on a job, which meant that he would have to work, without the usual dodging and stalling—that could be on account of the lag in receipts; but taking a murder suspect for a client offhand, no questions asked but the routine did you kill her and can you pay me, without the faintest notion whether he was guilty or not and how much the cops had on him—that simply wasn't done, not by anybody, let alone Nero Wolfe. I had to clamp my teeth on my lip to sit and take it. As Kirk got out a checkfold and a pen Wolfe pushed a button on his desk, and in a moment Fritz came.

"A tray, please," Wolfe told him. "The *madrilène* is ready?"

"Yes, sir."

"And the pudding?"

"Yes, sir."

"A bowl of each, cheese with water cress, and hot tea."

When Fritz turned and went I would have liked to go along, to tell him that there could be something worse than having no client.

5

An hour later, when the doorbell rang again, Kirk was still there and still the client, and I would still have had to toss a coin to decide where I stood on the question, did he or didn't he?

Wolfe had of course refused to either talk or listen until the tray had come and gone. Kirk had said he couldn't eat, but when Wolfe insisted he tried, and if a man can swallow anything he can swallow Fritz's *madrilène* with beet juice, and after one spoonful of his lemon sherry pudding with brown sugar sauce there's no argument. The cheese and water cress were still on the tray when I took it to the kitchen, but the bowls were empty.

When I returned Wolfe had started in. ". . . so I'll reverse the process," he was saying. "I'll tell you and then ask you. Are you sufficiently yourself to comprehend?"

"I'm better. I didn't think I could eat. I'm glad you made me." He didn't look any better.

Wolfe nodded. "The brain can be hoodwinked but not the stomach. First, then, your statement that you didn't kill your wife is of course of no weight. I have assumed that you didn't for reasons of my own, which I reserve. Do you know or suspect who did kill her?"

"No. There are— No."

"Then attend. An item in yesterday's mail to this house was an envelope addressed to Mr. Goodwin, typewritten. A paper inside had a typewritten note saying, 'Archie Goodwin, keep this until you hear from me, JNV.' The envelope and paper were the engraved stationery of James Neville Vance. Also in the envelope was a four-in-hand necktie, cream-colored with brown diagonal stripes, and it had a spot on it, a large brown stain."

Kirk was squinting, concentrating. "So that's how it was. They never told me exactly . . ."

"They wouldn't. Neither would I if I weren't engaged in your interest. At a quarter past eleven yesterday morning Mr. Goodwin got a phone call, and a voice that squeaked, presumably for disguise, said it was James Neville Vance and asked him to burn what he had received in the mail. Mr. Goodwin, provoked, went to Two-nineteen Horn Street and was admitted by Vance, who identified the tie as one of his but denied that he had sent it. As Mr. Goodwin was about to go a policeman arrived who wanted access to your apartment, and he was with Mr. Vance and the policeman when your wife's body was discovered, but he left immediately. Later he took—"

"But what—"

"Don't interrupt. He took the tie to a laboratory and learned that the spot was human blood. He gave the tie, and the envelope and letterhead, to a law officer who had been told of the tie episode by Mr. Vance, and the police have established that the blood is the same type as your wife's. You say they think they can prove that you killed your wife. Did they take your fingerprints?"

"Yes. They— I let them."

"Could your fingerprints be on that envelope and letterhead?"

"Of course not. How could they? I don't understand—"

"If you please, Mr. Vance told Mr. Goodwin that he had nine ties of that pattern and gave one to somebody. Did he give it to you? Cream with brown stripes."

Kirk's mouth opened and stayed open. The question was answered.

"When did he give it to you?"

"About two months ago."

"Where is it now?"

"I suppose—I don't know."

"When you moved to a hotel room two weeks ago you took personal effects, including that tie?"

"I don't know. I didn't notice. I took all my clothes, but I wasn't noticing things like ties. I'll see if it's there."

"It isn't." Wolfe took a deep breath, leaned back, and closed his eyes. Kirk looked at me, blinking, and was going to say something, but I shook my head. He had said enough already to make me think it might have been better all around if I had burned the damned souvenirs and crossed it off. He put his palms to his temples and massaged.

Wolfe opened his eyes and straightened up. He regarded Kirk, not cordially. "It's a mess," he stated. "I have questions of course, but you'll answer them more to the point if I first expound this necktie tangle. Are your wits up to it? Should you sleep first?"

"No. If I don't— I'm all right."

"Pfui. You can't even focus your eyes properly. I'll merely describe it and ignore the intricacies. Assuming that the blood on the tie is in fact your wife's blood, there are three obvious theories. The police theory must be that when you killed your wife the blood got on the tie, either inadvertently or by your deliberate act, and to implicate Vance you used his stationery to mail it to Mr. Goodwin. It was probably premeditated, since you had the stationery at hand. I don't ask if that was possible; the police must know it was. You had been in his apartment, hadn't you?"

"Yes."

"Frequently?"

"Yes. Both my wife and I—yes."

"Is there a typewriter in his apartment?"

"There's one in his studio."

"You could have used it. Is there one in your apartment?"

"Yes."

"More subtly, you could have used that, thinking it would be assumed—but that's one of the intricacies I'll ignore for the moment. So much for the police theory. Rejecting it because you didn't kill your wife, I need an alternative, and there are two. One: Vance killed her. It would take an hour or more to talk that out, all its twists respecting the tie. He had it on and blood got on it, and he used it to call attention to himself in so preposterous a manner that it would inevitably be shifted to you; but in that case he had previously retrieved the tie he had given you, so it had been premeditated for at least two weeks. If the tie he gave you is in your hotel room, that will be another twist. Still another: he thought it possible that Mr. Goodwin would burn it as requested on the phone, and if so he would admit he had sent it, since it would no longer be available for inspection, saying he had found it somewhere on his premises and intended to get Mr. Goodwin to investigate, but changed his mind."

"But why? I don't see . . ."

"Neither do I. I said it's a mess. The other alternative; X killed your wife and undertook to involve both Vance and you. Before considering him, what about Vance? If he killed her, why? Did he have a why?"

Kirk shook his head. "If he did—No. Not Vance."

"She wasn't much of a wife. Your phrase. Granting

that no woman is much of a wife, did she have distinctive flaws?"

He shut his eyes for a long moment, opened them, and said, "She's dead."

"And you're here because the police think you killed her, and they are digging up every fact about her that's accessible. Decorum is pointless. At your trial, if it comes to that, her defects will become public property. What were they?"

"They were already public property—our little public." He swallowed. "I knew when I married her that she was promis—no, she wasn't promiscuous, she was too sensitive for that. She was incredibly beautiful. You know that?"

"No."

"She was, I thought then that she was simply curious about men, and impetuous—and a little reckless. I didn't know until after we had been married a few months that she had no moral sense about sexual relations—not just no moral sense, no *sense*. She was sensitive, very sensitive, but that's different. But I was stuck. I don't mean I was stuck just because I was married to her, that's simple enough nowadays, I mean I was really *stuck*. Do you know what it's like to have all your feelings and desires, all the desires that really matter, to have them all centered on a woman, one woman?"

"No."

"I do." He shook his head, jerked it from side to side several times. "What got me started?"

He could have meant either what got him started on that woman or what got him started talking about her. Wolfe, assuming the latter, said, "I asked you about Mr. Vance. Was he one of the objects of her curiosity?"

"Good Lord, no."

"You can't be sure of that."

"Oh yes I can. She never bothered to pretend. I tell you, she had no *sense*. I did some work for Vance on a couple of buildings, and I had that apartment before I was married. For her he was a nice old guy, rather a bore, who let her use one of his pianos when she felt like it. I *am* sure."

Wolfe grunted. "Then X. He must meet certain specifications. It would be fatuous not to assume, tentatively at least, that whoever killed your wife sent the necktie to Mr. Goodwin, either to involve Mr. Vance or with some design more artful. So he had access to Vance's stationery and either to his tie rack or to yours; and he had had enough association with your wife to want her dead. That narrows it, and you should be able to suggest candidates."

Kirk was squinting, concentrating. "I don't think I can," he said, "I could name men who have been . . . associated with my wife, but none of them has ever met Vance as far as I know. Or I could name men I have seen at Vance's place, but none of them has—"

He stopped abruptly. Wolfe eyed him. "His name?"

"No. He didn't want her dead."

"You can't know that. His name?"

"I'm not going to accuse him."

"Preserve your scruples by all means, I won't accuse him either without sufficient cause. His name?"

"Paul Fougère."

Wolfe nodded. "The tenant on the ground floor. As I said, I have read the morning paper. He was an object of your wife's curiosity?"

"Yes."

"Had the curiosity been satisfied?"

"If you mean was she through with him, I don't know. I don't think so, I'm not sure."

"Had he had opportunities to get some of Vance's stationery?"

"Yes. Plenty of them."

"We'll return to him later." Wolfe glanced up at the clock and shifted his bulk in the chair. "Now you. Not to try you; to learn the extent of your peril. I want the answers you have given the police. I don't ask where you were Monday afternoon because if you were excluded by an alibi you wouldn't be here. Why did you move to a hotel room two weeks ago? What you have told the police."

"I told them the truth. I had to decide what to do. Seeing my wife and hearing her, having her touch me —it had become impossible."

"Did you decide what to do?"

"Yes, I decided to try to persuade her to have a baby, I thought that might make her . . . might change her. I realized I couldn't be sure the baby was mine, but there was no way out of that. That's what I told the police, but it wasn't true. The baby idea was only one of many that I thought of, and I knew it was no good, I knew I couldn't take it, not knowing if I was its father, I didn't actually decide anything."

"But you dialed her phone number six times between four o'clock Monday afternoon and ten o'clock Tuesday morning. What for?"

"What I told the police? To say I wanted to see her, to persuade her to have a baby."

"Actually what for?"

"To hear her voice." Kirk made fists and pressed them on his knees. "Mr. Wolfe, you don't know. I was stuck. You could pity me or you could sneer at me, but I wouldn't give a damn, it wouldn't mean a thing. Say I was obsessed, and what does that mean? I still had my faculties, I could do my work pretty well, and I could even think straight about her, as far as think-ing went. One of the ideas I had, I realized that the one thing I could do that would settle it was to kill her, I knew I couldn't do it, but I realized that that was the one sure thing, and I wished I could do it."

He opened the fists and closed them again. "I hadn't seen her or heard her voice for two weeks, and I dialed the number, and when there was still no answer the sixth time I went there. When there was no answer to my ring from the vestibule and I went in and took the elevator I intended to use my key upstairs too, but I didn't, I simply couldn't. She might be there and—and not alone. I left and went to a bar and bought a drink but didn't drink it, I wanted to know if her things were there, and I thought of phoning Jimmy Vance, but finally decided to phone police headquarters in-stead. Even if they found her there and someone with her, that might—"

The doorbell rang, and I went, again giving myself even money that it was Vance, and losing again. It was a girl, or woman, and she had a kind of eyes that I had met only twice before, once a woman and once a man. I have a habit, when it's a stranger on the stoop, of taking a five-second look through the one-way glass and tagging him or her, to see how close I can come. From inside, the view through the glass is practically clear, but from the outside it might as well be wood. But she could see through. Of course she couldn't, but she was face-to-face with me, and her eyes, slanted up, had exactly the look they would have if she were seeing me. They were nice enough hazel eyes, but I hadn't liked it the other two times it had happened, and I didn't like it then. Not trying to tag her, I opened the door.

"I beg your pardon," she said. "I believe Mr. Kirk is here? Martin Kirk?"

It wasn't possible. They wouldn't put a female dick on his tail, and even if they did she wouldn't be it, with that attractive little face and soft little voice. But there she was. "I beg *your* pardon," I said, "but what makes you think so?"

"He must be. I saw him come in and I haven't seen him come out."

"Then he's here. And?"

"Would you mind telling me whose house—who lives here?"

"Nero Wolfe. It's his house and he lives here."

"That's an odd name. Nero Wolfe? What does he— Is he a lawyer?"

Either she meant it or she was extremely good. If the former, it would be a pleasure to tell Wolfe and see him grunt. "No," I said. Let her work for it.

"Is Mr. Kirk all right?"

"We haven't been introduced," I said. "My name is Archie Goodwin and I live here. Your turn."

Her mouth opened and closed again. She considered it, her eyes meeting mine exactly as they had when she couldn't see me. "I'm Rita Fougere," she said. "Mrs. Paul Fougere. Will you tell Mr. Kirk I'm here and would like to see him?"

It was my turn to consider. The rule didn't apply— the rule that I am to take no one in to Wolfe without consulting him; she wanted to see Kirk, not Wolfe. And

I was riled. The tie had been mailed to me, not him, but he hadn't even glanced at me before taking Kirk on and feeding him. I was by no means satisfied that Kirk was straight, and I wanted to see how he took it when Paul Fougere's wife suddenly appeared.

"You might as well tell him yourself," I said. "Also you might as well know that Nero Wolfe is a private detective, and so am I. Come in."

I made room for her and she entered, and after shutting the door I preceded her down the hall and into the office. As I approached Wolfe's desk I said, "Someone to see Mr. Kirk," and I was right there when he twisted around and saw her, said "Rita!" and left the chair. She offered both hands, and he took them. "Martin, Martin," she said, low, with those eyes at him.

"But how . . ." He let her hands go. "How did you know I was here?"

"I followed you."

"Followed me?"

She nodded. "From down there. I was there too, and when I left and had got into a taxi you came out. I called to you but you didn't hear me, and when you got another taxi I told my driver to follow. I saw you come in here, and I waited outside, and when you didn't come out, a whole hour—"

"But what— You shouldn't, Rita. You can't— There's nothing you can do. Were you there all night too?"

"No, just this morning. I was afraid—your face, the way you looked. I was terribly afraid. I know I can't—or maybe I can. If you'll come— Have you eaten anything?"

"Yes, I thought I couldn't, but Nero Wolfe—" He stopped and turned. "I'm sorry, Mr. Wolfe, Mrs. Fougere." Back to her: "They think I killed Bonny, but I didn't, and Mr. Wolfe is going to—uh—investigate. That's a swell word, that is—'investigate.' There's nothing you can do, Rita, absolutely nothing, but I—you're a real friend."

She started a hand to touch him but let it drop. "I'll wait for you," she said. "I'll be outside."

"If you please." It was Wolfe. His eyes were at the client. "You have a chore, Mr. Kirk. I need to know if that article is among your belongings in your room, and you will please go and find out and phone me. Meanwhile I'll talk with Mrs. Fougere. If you will, madam? I'm working for Mr. Kirk."

"Why . . ." She looked at Kirk. Those eyes. "If he's working for you . . ."

"I've told him," Kirk blurted. "About Bonny and Paul. He asked and I told him. But you stay out of it."

"Nonsense," Wolfe snapped. "She has been questioned by the police. And she's your friend?"

Her hand went out again, and that time reached him. "You go, Martin," she said. "Whatever it is he wants. But you'll come back?"

He said he would and headed for the hall, and I went to see him out. When I returned Mrs. Fougere was in the red leather chair, which would have held two of her, and Wolfe, leaning back, was regarding her without enthusiasm. He would rather tackle almost any man than any woman on earth.

"Let's get a basis," he growled. "Do you think Mr. Kirk killed his wife?"

She was sitting straight, her hands curled over the ends of the chair arms, her eyes meeting his. "You're working for him," she said.

"Yes. I think he didn't. What do you think?"

"I don't know. I don't care. I know how that sounds, but I don't care. I'm very—well, say very practical. You're not a lawyer?"

"I'm a licensed private detective. Allowing for the strain you're under, you look twenty. Are you older?"

She did not look twenty. I would have guessed twenty-eight, but I didn't allow enough for the strain, for she said, "I'm twenty-four."

"Since you're practical you won't mind blunt questions. How long have you lived in that house?"

"Since my marriage. Nearly three years."

"Where were you Monday afternoon from one o'clock to eight?"

"Of course the police asked that. I had lunch with Martin Kirk and walked to his office building with him about half past two. Then I went to the Metropolitan Museum of Art to look at costumes. I do some stage costumes. I was there about two hours. Then I—"

"That will do. What did you say when the police asked if you were in the habit of lunching with Mr. Kirk?"

"It wasn't a habit. He had left his wife and he—he needed friends."

"You're strongly attached to him?"

"Yes."

"Is he attached to you?"

"No."

Wolfe grunted. "If this were a hostile examination your answers would be admirable, but for me they're a little curt. Do you know how your husband spent Monday afternoon?"

"I know how he says he did. He went to Long Island City to look at some equipment and got back too late to go to the office. He went to a bar and had drinks and came home a little before seven, and we went out to a restaurant for dinner." She made a little gesture. "Mr. Wolfe, I don't want to be curt. If I thought I knew anything that would help Martin, anything at all, I'd tell you."

"Then we'll see what you know. What if I establish that your husband killed Mrs. Kirk?"

She took a moment. "Do you mean if you proved it? If you got him arrested for it?"

Wolfe nodded. "That would probably be necessary to clear Mr. Kirk."

"Then I would be glad for Martin, but sorry for my husband. No matter who killed Bonny Kirk, I would be sorry for him. She deserved— No, I won't say that. I believe it, but I won't say it."

"Pfui. More people saying what they believe would be a great improvement. Because I often do I am unfit for common intercourse. You were aware of your husband's intimacy with Mrs. Kirk?"

"Yes."

"They knew you were?"

"Yes."

"You were complacent about it?"

"No." It came out a whisper, and she repeated it. "No." Her mouth began working, and she clamped her jaw to stop it. "Of course," she said, "you think I might have killed her. If I had it would have been on account of Martin, not my husband. She was ruining Martin's life, making it impossible for him. But she couldn't ruin my husband's life because he's too—well, too shallow."

She stopped, breathed, and went on, "I wouldn't have dreamed that I would ever be saying things like this, to anyone, but I said some of them even to the police. Now I would say anything if it would help Martin. I wasn't complacent about Paul and Bonny; it just didn't matter, because nothing mattered but Martin. I was an ignorant little fool when I married Paul, I thought I might as well because I had never been in love and I thought I never would be. When they began asking me questions yesterday I decided I wouldn't try to hide how I feel about Martin, and anyway, I don't think I could, now. I did before."

Wolfe looked at the clock. Twenty to one. Thirty-five minutes till lunch. "You say she couldn't have ruined your husband's life because he's too shallow. Do you utterly reject the possibility that he killed her?"

She took a breath. "I don't"—That's too strong. If he was there with her and she said something or did something . . . I don't know."

"Do you know if he had in his possession some of the personal stationery of James Neville Vance? A letterhead, an envelope?"

Her eyes widened. "What? Jimmy Vance?"

"Yes. That's relevant because of a circumstance you don't know about, but Mr. Kirk does. It's a simple question. Did you ever see a blank unused letterhead or envelope, Mr. Vance's, in your apartment?"

"No. Not a blank one. One he had written on, yes." You have been in his apartment."

"Certainly."

"Do you know where he keeps his stationery?"

"Yes, in a desk in his studio. In a drawer. You say this is relevant?"

"Yes, Mr. Kirk may explain if you ask him. How well do you know Mr. Vance?"

"Why . . . he owns that house. We see him some socially. There's a recital in his studio about every month."

"Did he kill Mrs. Kirk?"

"No. Of course I've asked myself that. I've asked myself everything. But Jimmy Vance—if you knew him—why would he? Why did you ask about his stationery?"

"Ask Mr. Kirk. I am covering some random points. Did Mrs. Kirk drink vodka?"

"No. If she did I never saw her. She didn't drink much of anything, but when she did it was always gin and tonic in the summer and Bacardis in the winter."

"Does your husband drink vodka?"

"Yes. Now, nearly always."

"Does Mr. Kirk?"

"No, never. He drinks scotch."

"Does Mr. Vance?"

"Yes. He got my husband started on it. The police asked me all this."

"Naturally. Do you drink vodka?"

"No. I drink sherry." She shook her head. "I don't understand—maybe you'll tell me. All the questions the police asked me—they seem to be sure it was one of us, Martin or Paul or Jimmy Vance or me. Now you too. But it could have been some other man that Bonny . . . or someone, a burglar or something—couldn't it?"

"Not impossible," Wolfe conceded, "but more than doubtful. Because of the circumstance that prompted my question about Mr. Vance's stationery, and now this question: What kind of a housekeeper are you? Do you concern yourself with the condition of your husband's clothing?"

She nearly smiled. "You ask the strangest questions. Yes, I do. Even though we're not—Yes, I sew on buttons."

"Then you know what he has, or had. Have you ever seen among his things a cream-colored necktie with diagonal brown stripes, narrow stripes?"

She frowned. "That's Jimmy Vance again, those are his colors. He has a tie like that, more than one proba-bly."

"He had nine. Again a simple question. Have you ever seen one of them in your husband's possession? Not necessarily in his hands or on his person; say in one of his drawers?"

"No, Mr. Wolfe, this circumstance—what is it? You say Martin knows about it, but I'm answering your questions, and I—"

The phone rang. I swiveled and got it, used my formula, and the client's voice came. "This is Martin Kirk. Tell Mr. Wolfe the tie's not here. It's gone."

"Of course you made sure."

"Yes. Positive."

"Hold the wire," I turned. "Kirk. The article isn't there."

He nodded. "As expected."

"Any instructions?"

He pursed his lips, and Rita, on her feet, beat him to it. Asking, "May I speak to him?" she came with her hand out for the phone. Wolfe nodded. I pointed to the phone on his desk and told her to use that one, and she went and got it. I stayed on.

"Martin?"

"Yes, Rita?"

"Yes. Where are you?"

"In my room at the hotel. You're still there?"

"Yes. What are you going to do? Are you going to your officer?"

"Good Lord no. I'm going to see Jimmy Vance. Then I'm going to see Nero Wolfe again. Someone has—"

I cut in. "Hold it. I've told Mr. Wolfe and he'll have instructions. Hold the wire." I turned. "He says he's going to see Vance. Shall I tell him to lay off or will you?"

"Neither. He's had no sleep and not much to eat. Tell him to come this evening, say nine o'clock, if he's awake, and report on his talk with Mr. Vance."

"You tell him," I said and hung up. Being a salaried employee, I should of course keep my place in the presence of company, and that's exactly what I was doing; keeping my place. I had had enough and then some, and Wolfe's glare, which of course came automatically, was wasted because my head was turned and he had my profile, including the set of my jaw. When Rita was through with the phone he took it, spoke briefly with his client, cradled it, and looked at the clock. Six minutes to lunch.

"Do you want me any more?" she asked him. "I'd like to go."

"Later perhaps," he said. "If you'll phone a little after six?"

I got up and spoke. "If you don't mind, Mrs. Fougere." I crossed to the door to the front room and opened it. "If you'll wait in here just a few minutes?"

She looked at Wolfe, saw that he had no comment, and came. When she had crossed the sill I closed the door, which is as soundproof as the wall, went to Wolfe's desk, and said, "If it blows up in your face you're not going to blame it on me. I merely called your attention a couple of times to the fact that a fee would be welcome. I didn't say it was desperate, that you should grab a measly grand from a character who is probably going to be tagged for the big one. And now when he says he is going to see Vance, to handle the tie question on his own—and the tie was sent to me, not you—you not only don't veto it, you don't even tell me to go and sit in. Also she's going there too, that's obvious, and you merely tell her to phone you later. I admit you're a genius, but when you took his check you couldn't possibly have had the faintest idea whether he was guilty or not, and even now you don't know the score. They may have him absolutely wrapped up. The tie was mailed to me and I gave it to Cramer, and I'm asking, not respectfully."

He nodded. "Well said. A good speech."

"Thank you. And?"

"I didn't tell you to go because it's lunchtime. Also I doubt if you would get anything useful. Naturally I'll have to see Mr. Vance—and Mr. Fougere. As for desperation, when I took Mr. Kirk's check I knew it was extremely improbable that he had killed his wife, and I—"

"How?"

He shook his head. "You call me to account? You know everything that I know; ponder it yourself. If instead of lunch you choose to be present at a futile conversation, do so by all means. I will not be hectored into an explanation you shouldn't need."

Fritz entered to announce lunch, saw what the atmosphere was, and stood. I went and opened the door to the front room, passed through, and told Rita, "All right, Mrs. Fougere. I'm going along."

6

When you're good and sore at someone it's simple. You cuss him out, to his face if he's available and privately if he isn't, and you take steps if and as you can. When you're sore at yourself it's even simpler; the subject is right there and can't skip. But when you're sore at yourself and someone else at the same time you're in a fix. If you try to concentrate on one the other one horns in and gets you off balance, and that was the state I was in as I stood aside in the vestibule of Two-nineteen Horn Street while Rita Fougere used her key on the door. In the taxi on the way down I had told her about the necktie problem. She might as well get it from me as later from Kirk, and she might as well understand why Kirk wanted to see Vance.

I supposed she would want to go first to her own apartment on the ground floor; surely any woman would whose face needed attention as much as hers— but no. Straight to the elevator and up, and out at the third floor, and she pressed the button at Vance's door. It opened, and Vance was there. His face wasn't as neat and smooth as it had been the day before, and he had on a different outfit—a conservative gray suit, a white shirt, and a plain gray tie. Of course the DA's office had had him down too. He said "Rita!" and put out a hand, then saw me, but I can't say what kind of a welcome I would have got because Kirk interrupted, stepping over and telling Rita she shouldn't have come.

She said something, but he wasn't listening because he had noticed me.

"I'm glad you're here," he said. "It's not very clear in my mind, what Nero Wolfe told me about the tie. I was just going to tell Vance about him. Rita, please! You can't—this is *my* trouble."

"Listen, Martin," she said, "you shouldn't be here. I know now why they think it was one of us, so it's *our* trouble. You should leave it to him—Nero Wolfe. You shouldn't be talking about it with anybody, not even me. Isn't that right, Mr. Goodwin?"

"Mr. Wolfe knew he was coming," I said. I have mentioned that I was sore. "Mr. Wolfe has been called a wizard by various people, and with a wizard you never know. Of course he had me come." I had to force my tongue to let that through, but a private scrap should be kept private.

Vance was frowning at me. "Nero Wolfe had you come? Here?"

"I went to him," Kirk said. "He told me about the necktie. That's what I want to ask you about. You remember you gave me one, one of those—"

A bell tinkled. I was between Vance and the door, and I moved to let him by. He opened the door and a man stepped in, darted a glance around, and squeaked, "What, a party? A hell of a time for a party, Jimmy."

I say he squeaked because he did, but it was obviously his natural squeak, not the kind on the phone that had told me to burn the tie, though it didn't fit his six feet and broad shoulders and handsome, manly face. "It's no party, Paul," Vance told him, but Paul ignored him and was at Rita. "My pet, you're a perfect fright. You look godawful." He wheeled to Kirk. "And look at you, Martin my boy. Only why not? Why are you still loose?" He looked at me. "Are you a cop?"

I shook my head. "I don't count. Skip me."

"With pleasure." To Vance: "I came to ask you something, and now I can ask everybody. Do you know that the cops have got one of your neckties with a spot on it?"

Vance nodded. "Yes, I know."

"Where did they get it? Why are they riding me about it? Why did they ask me if I had taken it or one like it out of your closet? Did you tell them I had?"

"Certainly not. I told them one was missing, that's all."

Kirk blurted, "And you told them you gave one like it to me."

Vance frowned at him. "Damn it, Martin, I had to, didn't I? They would have found out anyway. Other people knew about it."

"Of course you had to," Kirk said. "I know that. But that one is missing too. I just looked for it and it's gone. It was taken from my room here before I left, because I took everything with me and it's not there. I came to ask you if you know—"

"Can it," Paul cut in. "You've got a nerve to ask anybody anything. Why are you loose? Okay, you killed her, she's dead. What kind of a dodge are you trying with one of Jimmy's neckties with a spot on it?"

"No," Kirk said. "I didn't kill her."

"Oh, can it. I was thinking maybe you do have some guts after all. She decorated you with one of the finest pairs of horns on record, and you never moved a finger. You just took it lying down—or I should say standing up. I thought it would be hard to find a poorer excuse for a man, but yesterday when I heard what had happened—"

Of course I had heard and read of a man slapping another man, but that was the first time I had ever actually seen it—a smack with an open palm on the side of the head. Kirk said nothing, he merely slapped him, and Paul Fougere said nothing either, he merely started a fist for Kirk's jaw. I didn't move. Since Fougere was four inches broader and twenty pounds heavier, I fully expected to see Kirk go down, and in any situation I am supposed to take any necessary steps to protect the interests of a client, but if Wolfe wanted that client protected he could come and do it himself.

But I got a surprise and so did Fougere. He landed once, a glancing blow on the shoulder as Kirk twisted and jerked his head back, but that was all. Not that

Kirk had any technique. I would guess that the point was that at last he was doing something he had really wanted to do for a long time, and while spirit isn't all, it's a lot. He clipped Fougere at least twenty times, just anywhere—face, neck, chest, ribs—never with enough steam to floor him or even stagger him. But one of the wild pokes got the nose fair and square, and the blood started. It was up to me because Vance was busy keeping Rita off, and when the blood had Fougere's mouth and chin pretty well covered I got Kirk from behind and yanked him back and then stepped in between.

"You're going to drip," I told Fougere. "I suppose you know where the bathroom is."

He was panting. He put his hand to his mouth, took it away, saw the blood, and turned and headed for the rear. I pivoted. Kirk, also panting, was on a chair, head down, inspecting his knuckles. They probably had no skin left. Vance was staring at him, apparently as surprised as Fougere had been. Rita was positively glowing. With color in her face she was more than attractive. "Should I go?" she asked me. "Does he need help?"

That's true love. Martin the Great had hit him, so he must be in a bad way. It would have been a shame to tell her it had been just pecks. I said no, he'd probably make it, and went to help Kirk examine his knuckles. They weren't so bad.

"Why didn't you stop them?" Vance demanded.

"I thought I did," I said. "With a mauler like Kirk you have to time it."

"I wouldn't have thought . . ." He let it go. "Did you say he went to Nero Wolfe?"

"No, he did. But I can confirm it, I was present. He has hired Nero Wolfe. That's why I'm here. I am collecting information that will establish the innocence of Mr. Wolfe's client. Have you got any?"

"I'm afraid I haven't." He was frowning. "But of course he is innocent. What Paul Fougere said, that's ridiculous. I hope he didn't tell the police that. But with their experience, I don't suppose—"

The bell tinkled. Vance went to the door and opened

it, and in came the law. Anyone with half an eye would know it was the law even if they had never seen or heard of Sergeant Purley Stebbins. Two steps in he stopped for a look and saw me.

"Yeah," he said, "I thought so. You and Wolfe are going to be good and sick of this one. I hope you try to hang on." His eyes went right. Fougere had appeared at the rear of the room. "Everybody, huh? I'm sorry to interrupt, Mr. Vance."

He moved. "You're wanted downtown for more questions, Mr. Kirk. I'll take you."

Rita made a noise. Kirk tilted his head to look up at the tough, rough face. "My God, I've answered all the questions there are."

"We've got some new ones. I might as well ask one of them now. Did you buy a typewriter at the Midtown Office Equipment Company on July nineteenth and trade in your old one?"

"Yes. I don't know—July nineteenth—about then, yes."

"Okay. We want you to identify the one you traded in. Come along."

"Are you arresting me?"

"If you prefer it that way I can. Material witness. Or if you balk I'll phone for a warrant and keep you company till it comes, maybe an hour. With Goodwin here I've got to toe the line. He's hell on wheels, Goodwin is."

Kirk made it to his feet. "All right," he mumbled. He had been without sleep for thirty hours and maybe more. Rita Fougere aimed those eyes at me.

I bowed out. Being hell on wheels is fine and dandy if you have anywhere to steer for, but I hadn't. I went and opened the door and on out, took the elevator down, exchanged no greeting with the driver of the police car out front, though we had met, walked till I found a taxi, and told the hackie 618 West 35th Street; and when he said that was Nero Wolfe's house I actually said such is fame. That's the shape I was in.

Wolfe was at table in the dining room, putting a gob of his favorite cheese on a wafer. When I entered he looked up and said politely, "Fritz is keeping the kidneys warm."

I stopped three steps in. "Many thanks," I said even more politely. "You were right as usual; the conversation was futile. They had a tail on Kirk, here and to the hotel and on to Horn Street. When Purley Stebbins arrived at Vance's apartment he knew Kirk was there and he wasn't surprised to see me. He had come for your client and took him. They have found the typewriter that addressed that envelope to me and the message. It belonged to Kirk, but on July nineteenth he traded it in on another one. Since you don't talk business at meals, I'll eat in the kitchen."

I wheeled, hell on wheels, and went to the kitchen.

7

Nearly four hours later, at six o'clock, Mr. and Mrs. Paul Fougere were in the office, waiting for Wolfe to come down from the plant rooms—she in the red leather chair and he in one of the yellow ones in front of Wolfe's desk. To my surprise he had two marks, a red slightly puffed nose and a little bruise under his left eye. I hadn't thought Kirk had shown that much power, but of course with bare knuckles it doesn't take much.

Nothing had happened to change my attitude or opinion. When I went to the office after finishing with the kept-warm kidneys and accessories Wolfe permitted me to report on the conversation and slugging match at Vance's apartment, leaning back and closing his eyes to show he was listening, but he didn't even grunt when I told the Stebbins part, though ordinarily it gets under his skin, way under, when a client is hauled in. When I was through I said it was a good thing he knew Kirk was innocent since otherwise the typewriter development might make him wonder.

His eyes opened. "I didn't say I knew it. I said it was extremely improbable that he had killed his wife, and it still is. Any of the others could have managed access to his typewriter for a few minutes, in his absence."

"Sure. And when his wife told him she had let someone use it, it made him so mad he got rid of it the next day. She could confirm it, but she's dead. Tough. Or his getting rid of it just then could have been coincidence, but that would be even tougher. Judges and juries hate coincidence, and I've heard you make remarks about it."

"Only when it's in my way, not when it serves me." He straightened up and reached for his book. "Can Mrs. Fougere have her husband here at six o'clock?"

"I haven't asked her. I doubt it. They're not chummy, and he's the wrong end of the horse."

"Perhaps . . ." He considered it. He shook his head. "No. I must see him. Tell her to tell him, or you tell him, that he has slandered my client before witnesses, and he will either sign a retraction and apology or defend a suit for defamation of character. I'll expect him at six o'clock." He picked up the book and opened it.

Cut. I hadn't expected him to open up, since he is as pigheaded as I am steadfast, but he could have made some little comment. As I looked up the Fougere number and dialed it, I was actually considering something I had never done and thought I never would: retract, apologize, and ask him please to tell me, as a favor to an old associate and loyal assistant, what the hell was in his mind, if anything. But of course I didn't. When I hung up after getting no answer from the Fougere number, I had an idea: I would ask him if he wanted me to phone Parker. With a client collared as a material witness and probably headed for the coop on a murder charge, it should be not only routine but automatic for him to get Parker. But I looked at his face as he sat, comfortable, his eyes on the book, and vetoed it. He would merely say no and go on reading. It would have improved my feelings to pick up something and throw it at him, but not the situation, so I arose, went to the hall and up two flights to my room, stood at the window, and reviewed the past thirty hours, trying to spot the catch I had missed, granting there had been one. The trouble was I was sore. You can work when you're sore, or eat or sleep or fight, but you can't think straight.

My next sight of Wolfe was at two minutes past six when the elevator brought him down from the plant rooms and he entered the office. The slander approach had got results. The fifth time I tried the Fougere number, a little after four, Paul had answered, and I poured it on. On the phone his squeak sounded more like the one that had told me to burn the tie, but of course it would. A voice on a phone, unless it's one you know well, is tricky. He said he'd come. An hour later Rita phoned. She was too frantic to be practical. She wanted to know if we had heard from Kirk, and were we doing anything and if so what, and shouldn't Kirk have a lawyer. Being sore, I told her Wolfe was responsible to his client, not to her, that Kirk would of course need a lawyer, if and when he was charged with something, and that we were expecting her husband at six o'clock. When she said she knew that and she was coming along, I said she might as well have saved the dime. I am rude to people only when I am being rude to myself, or they have asked for it. I admit she hadn't asked for it.

For Wolfe, being rude is no problem at all. When he entered he detoured around the red leather chair to his desk, gave Rita a nod, sat, narrowed his eyes at the husband, and snapped, "You're Paul Fougere?"

It's hard to snap back with a squeak, but Fougere did the best he could with what he had. "You're Nero Wolfe?"

"I am. Did you kill that woman?"

I had known when I let them in that Fougere had decided on his line. It's easy to see when a man's all set. So the unexpected question flustered him. "You know damn well I didn't," he said. "You know who did, or you ought to."

"Possibly I don't. Do you?"

Fougere looked at his wife, at me, and back at Wolfe. He was adjusting. "You'd like that, wouldn't you?" he said. "With witnesses. All right, I can't prove it, and anyway that's not up to me, it's up to the cops. But I'm not going to sign anything. I've told Vance I shouldn't have said it, and I've told my wife. Ask her." He turned to me. "You were the only other one that heard me. I'm telling you now, I can't prove it and I shouldn't have said it." Back to Wolfe: "That covers it. Now try hooking me for defamation of character."

"Pfui." Wolfe flipped a hand to dismiss it. "I never intended to. That was only to get you here. I wanted to tell you something and ask you something. First, you're a blatherskite. You may perhaps know that Mr. Kirk didn't kill his wife, but you can't possibly know that he did. Manifestly you're either a jackass or a murderer, and conceivably both." He turned his head. "Archie. A twenty-dollar bill, please."

I went to the safe and got a twenty from the petty cash drawer and came back and offered it, but he shook his head. "Give it to Mrs. Fougere." To Paul: "I assume your wife is an acceptable stakeholder. Give her a dollar. Twenty to one Mr. Kirk did *not* kill his wife."

"You've got a bet." Fougere got out his wallet, extracted a bill, and handed it to me. "You keep it, Goodwin. My wife might spend it. I suppose his conviction decides it? Do I have to wait until after the appeals and all the horsing around?"

Obviously Rita wasn't hearing him. Probably she had had a lot of practice at not hearing him. She was gazing at Wolfe. "You really mean that, don't you?" she asked. "You mean it?"

"I expect to win that dollar, madam." His eyes stayed at Fougere. "As for you, sir, let's see how sure you are. I would like to ask some questions which may give you a hint of my expectations. If you don't care to hear them you are of course at liberty to go."

Fougere laughed. It would be fair to say that he giggled, but I'll give him a break. He laughed. "Hell, I've got a bet down," he said. "Go right ahead. You've already asked me if *I* killed her. I've answered that."

Wolfe nodded. "But you're not a mere onlooker. You're not in the audience; you're on the stage. Do you know about the envelope Mr. Goodwin received in the mail yesterday morning and its contents?"

"Yes, I do now. From Vance and my wife."

"Then you know why attention is centered on you four, both the police's attention and mine. You all had opportunity; any of you could have been admitted to that apartment Monday afternoon by Mrs. Kirk, and Mr. Kirk had a key. The means, the vodka bottle, was at hand. What about motive? Let's consider that. That's what I want to discuss with you. You are well acquainted with those three people and their relationships, both with one another and with Mrs. Kirk. Your adroit handling of my charge of slander showed that you have a facile and ingenious mind. I invite you to exercise it. Start with yourself. If you killed Mrs. Kirk, what was your motive?"

Fougere pronounced a word that isn't supposed to be used with a lady present, and since some lady may read this I'll skip it. He added, "I didn't."

"I know. I'll rephrase it. If you had killed Mrs. Kirk, what would have been your motive? You're staying to hear my questions because you're curious. I'm curious too. What would have been your motive? Is it inconceivable that you could have had one? You need not be reserved because your wife is here; she has informed me of your intimacy with Mrs. Kirk. When I suggested to her the possibility that you had killed her, she said no, you were too shallow. Are you?"

Fougere looked at Rita. "That's a new one, my pet. Shallow. You should have told me." To Wolfe: "Certainly I could have had a motive for killing her. I could name four men that could—counting Kirk, five."

"What would yours have been?"

"That would depend on when. Two months ago it would have been for my—well, for my health."

"And Monday? I'm not just prattling. Monday?"

"It's prattle to me. Monday, that would have been different. It would still have been for my health, but in a different way. Very different. Do you want me to spell it out?"

"I think not. So much for you. If your wife killed her, what was her motive?"

"Now that's a thought." He grinned. "That appeals

to me. We hadn't touched each other for nearly a year and she wanted me back. I'm shallow, but I've got charm. I'm not using it right now, but I've got it, don't think I haven't."

I was looking at Rita because I had had enough of looking at him, and from the expression on her face I would have given twenty to one that she was thinking what I was: that he was one in a million. He actually had no idea of how she felt about Kirk. Not that he would necessarily have brought it in, but his tone, even more than his words, made it obvious. I took another look at him. A man that dumb could batter a woman's skull with a vodka bottle and mosey to the nearest bar and order a vodka and tonic.

Wolfe had had the thought too, for he asked, "Have you no other motive to suggest for your wife?"

"No. Isn't that enough? A jealous wife?"

"There are precedents. I assume Mr. Kirk presents no difficulty. Since you think you know he killed her, you must know why."

"So do you."

"Correct. Since like the others it's an if. He could no longer abide her infidelities, he couldn't break loose because he was infatuated, and he couldn't change her, so he took the only way out, since he wanted to live. You agree?"

"Sure. That has precedents too."

"It has indeed. That leaves only Mr. Vance, and I suppose he does present difficulties, but call on your ingenuity. If he killed her, why?"

Fougere shook his head. "That would take more than ingenuity. You might as well pass Jimmy Vance. He was still hoping."

"Hoping for what?"

"For her. She had poor Jimmy on a string, and he was still hoping."

"Mr. Kirk told me that she regarded him as a nice old guy—his phrase—and rather a bore."

Fougere grinned. I had decided the first time he grinned that I would never grin again. "Martin wouldn't know," he said, "She told me all about it. She had a lot of fun with Jimmy. Bore, my eye. When she was bored she would go up and use one of his pianos, that was just an excuse, and dangle him. Of course it wasn't only fun. He had started it, reaching for her, and he owned the house and she liked it there, so she played him."

"But he was still hoping."

"Oh sure, for her that was easy. If you had known Bonny— Hell, she could have played you and kept you hoping. Bonny could play any man alive."

"Have you told the police this?"

"You mean about Vance? No. Why would I? I don't know why I'm telling you."

"I invited it. I worked for it." Wolfe leaned back and took a deep breath, then another one. "I am obliged to you, sir, and I don't like to be in debt. I'll save you a dollar. We'll call the bet off."

"We will not," Fougere squeaked. "You want to welsh?"

"No, I want to show my appreciation. Very well; it can be returned to you." Wolfe swiveled. "Madam, it's fortunate that you came with your husband. There will be three of us to refresh his memory on what he has told me if at some future time he is inclined to forget. I suggest that you should write it down and . . ."

I was listening with only one ear. Now that I knew which target he was aiming at, I should certainly be able to spot what had made him pick it, and I shut my eyes to concentrate. If you had already spotted it, as you probably had, and are thinking I'm thick, you will please consider that all four points went back to before the body was discovered. I got one point in half a minute, but that wasn't enough, and by the time I opened my eyes Fougere had gone and Rita was on her feet, prattling. Wolfe looked at me. I am expected—by him—both to understand women and to know how to handle them, which is ridiculous. I'll skip how I handled her and got her out because I was rude again, making twice in less than two hours.

When I returned to the office after shutting the door behind her I had things to say, but Wolfe was leaning back with his eyes closed, and his lips were working, so I went to my desk and sat. When we're alone I'll interrupt him no matter what he's doing, with only one exception, the lip exercise. When he's pushing his lips out and then pulling them in, out and in, he's working so hard that if I spoke he wouldn't hear me. It may take only seconds or it may go on and on. That time it was a good three minutes.

He opened his eyes, sat up, and growled, "We're going to need Mrs. Fougere."

I stood up. "I might possibly catch her. Is it urgent?"

"No. After dinner will do. Confound it."

"I agree." I sat down. "I'm up with you. There were two things. Right?"

"Four."

"Then I'm shy a couple. I have his phoning and his letting me have the tie. What else?"

"Only *seven* ties. Why?"

"Oh." I looked at it. "Okay. And?"

"Well . . . take you. What have you that is a part of you? Say the relics you keep in a locked drawer. Would you give one of them to someone casually?"

"No." I gave that a longer look. "Uhuh," I conceded. "Check. But all four points wouldn't convince a jury that he's a murderer, and I doubt if they would convince Cramer or the DA that he ought to be jugged."

"Certainly not. We have a job before we're ready for Mr. Cramer, and not an easy one. Phenomena needed for proof may not exist, and even if they do they may be undiscoverable. Our only recourse—"

The doorbell rang. I got up and went to the hall, took a look, stepped back into the office, and said, "Nuts. Cramer."

"No," he snapped.

"Do you want to count ten?"

"No."

I admit it's a pleasure to slip the bolt in, open the door the two inches the chain permits, and through the crack tell a police inspector that Mr. Wolfe is engaged and can't be disturbed. The simple pleasures of a private detective. But that time I didn't have it. I was still a step short of the door when a bellow came from the office, my name, and I turned and went back.

"Bring him," Wolfe commanded.

The doorbell rang. "Maybe this time you *should* count ten," I suggested.

"No, Bring him."

I went. From my long acquaintance with Cramer's face I can tell with one glance through the glass if he's on the warpath, so I knew he wasn't before I opened the door. He even greeted me as if it didn't hurt. Of course he didn't let me take his hat, that would have been going too far, but he removed it on his way down the hall. When he's boiling he leaves it on. From the way he greeted Wolfe it seemed likely that he would have offered a hand to shake if he hadn't known that Wolfe never did.

"Another hot day," he said and sat in the red leather chair, not settling back, and hanging on to his hat. "I just stopped in on my way home. You're never on your way home, because you're always home."

I stared at him. Unbelievable. He was chatting! Wolfe grunted. "I go out now and then. Will you have some beer?" That was logical. If Cramer acted like a guest, he had to act like a host.

"No, thanks." Pals. "A couple of questions and I'll go. The district attorney has about decided to hold Martin Kirk on a homicide charge. Kirk was here today for over an hour. Are you working for him?"

"Yes."

Cramer put his hat on the stand at his elbow. "I'm not going to pretend that I'm here to hand you something—like a chance to cut loose from a murderer. The fact is, frankly, I think it's possible the DA's office is moving a little too fast. There are several reasons why I think that. The fact that you have taken Kirk on as a client isn't the most important one, but I admit it is one. You don't take on a murder suspect, no matter what he can pay, unless you think you can clear him. I said a couple of questions, and here's the second one. If I go back downtown instead of home to supper, to persuade the DA to go slow, have you got anything I can use?"

One corner of Wolfe's mouth went up a sixteenth of an inch, his kind of a smile. "A new approach, Mr. Cramer. Rather transparent."

"The hell it is. It's a compliment. I wouldn't use it with any other private dick alive, and you know it. I'm not shoving, I'm just asking."

"Well, it's barely possible . . ." Wolfe focused narrowed eyes on a corner of his desk and rubbed his nose with a fingertip. Pure fake. He had had his idea, whatever it was, when he bellowed me back to the office. He held the pose for ten seconds and then moved his eyes to Cramer and said, "I know who killed Mrs. Kirk."

"Uhuh. The DA thinks he does."

"He's wrong. I have a proposal. I suppose you have spoken with Mr. Vance, James Neville Vance. If you will send a man to his apartment at ten o'clock this evening to take him to you, and you keep him until you hear from me or Mr. Goodwin, and then send or bring him to me, I'll give you enough to persuade the district attorney that he shouldn't hold Mr. Kirk on any charge at all."

Cramer had his chin up. "Vance? Vance?"

"Yes, sir."

"My God." He looked at me but saw only a manly, open face. He took a cigar from his pocket, slow motion, stuck it in his mouth, clamped his teeth on it, and took it out again. "You know damn well I won't. Connive at illegal entry? Of course that's why you want him away."

"Merely your conjecture. I give you the fullest assurance, in good faith without reservation, that there will be no illegal entry or any other illegal act."

"Then I don't see . . ." Moving back in the chair, he lost the cigar. It dropped to the floor. He ignored it. "No, Vance is a respectable citizen in good standing. You'd have to open up."

Wolfe nodded. "I'm prepared to. Not to give you facts, for you already have them; I'll merely expound.

You shouldn't need it, but you have been centered on Mr. Kirk. Do you know all the details of the necktie episode? Mr. Goodwin getting it in the mail, the phone call he received, and his visit to Mr. Vance?"

"Yes."

"Then attend. Four points. First the phone call. It came at a quarter past eleven. You assume that Mr. Kirk made it, pretending he was Vance. That's untenable, or at least implausible. How would he dare? For all he knew, Mr. Goodwin had phoned Vance or gone to see him immediately after opening the envelope. For him to phone and say he was Vance would have been asinine."

Cramer grunted. "He was off his hinges. The shape he was in, he wouldn't see that."

"I concede the possibility. The second point. When Mr. Goodwin went to see Vance he showed him the envelope and letterhead and let him take the tie to examine it. Vance was completely mystified. You know what was said and done. He inspected the ties in his closet and said that the one that had been mailed to Mr. Goodwin was his. But when Mr. Goodwin asked for it he handed it over without hesitation. Preposterous."

Cramer shook his head. "I don't think so. The body hadn't been discovered. He thought it was just some screwy gag."

"Pfui. One of his ties taken from his closet, his stationery used to mail it to a private detective with a message ostensibly from him, and the phone call; and he was so devoid of curiosity or annoyance that he let Mr. Goodwin take the tie, and the envelope and letterhead, with no sign of reluctance? Nonsense."

"But he did. If he killed her, why isn't it still nonsense?"

"Because it was part of his devious and crackbrained plan." Wolfe looked at the clock. "It's too close to dinnertime to go into that now. It was ill-conceived and ill-executed, and it was infantile, but it wasn't nonsense. The third point, and the most significant: *two* missing neckties. He had nine and had given one to

Mr. Kirk, and there were only seven left. Of course you have accounted for that in your theory. How?"

"That's obvious. Kirk took it from Vance's closet. Part of *his* plan to implicate Vance."

Wolfe nodded. "As Vance intended you to. But have you examined that assumption thoroughly?"

"Yes. I don't like it. That's one reason I think the DA is moving too fast. Kirk would have been a sap to do that. Someone else could have taken it to implicate Kirk. For instance, Fougere."

"Why not Vance himself?"

"Because a man doesn't smash a woman's skull unless he has a damn good reason and Vance had no reason at all."

Wolfe grunted. "I challenge that, but first the fourth point. Those neckties were an integral item of James Neville Vance's projection of his selfhood. Made exclusively for him, they were more than merely distinctive and personal; they were morsels of his ego. Conceivably he might have given one of them to someone close and dear to him, but not to Martin Kirk—not unless it was an essential step in an undertaking of vital importance. So it was."

"Damn it," Cramer growled, "his *reason!*"

A corner of Wolfe's mouth went up. "Your new approach is an improvement, Mr. Cramer. You know I wouldn't fix on a man as a murderer without a motive, so I must have one for Mr. Vance, and you want it. Not now. You would get up and go. That would be enough for you to take to the district attorney, and while it would postpone a murder charge against my client it would by no means clear him permanently, because I strongly doubt if you can get enough evidence against Vance to hold him, let alone convict him. My knowledge of Vance's motive is by hearsay, so don't bother to warn me about withholding evidence; I have none that you don't have. If I get some I'll be glad to share it. I need to know with certainty where Mr. Vance will be this evening from ten o'clock on, and when Mr. Goodwin told me that you were at the door it occurred to me that the surest way would be for you to have him with you. Do you want it in writing, signed by both of us, that there will be no illegal act—under penalty of losing our licenses?"

Cramer uttered a word about the same flavor as the one Fougere had used, but of course there was no lady present. He followed it up. "I suppose I'd send it to the Commissioner so he could frame it?" He flattened his palms on the chair arms. "Look, Wolfe. I know you. I know you've got something. I admit your four points taken together add up. I'll take your word that you won't send Goodwin to break and enter. I know I can't pry any more out of you even if it wasn't time for you to eat, and anyway I eat too. But you say I'm to keep Vance until I hear from you or Goodwin, and that might mean all night, and he's not just some bum. Nothing doing. Make it tomorrow morning, say ten o'clock, and limit it to six hours if I *don't* hear from you or Goodwin, and I'll buy it."

Wolfe grinned. "That's better anyway. I was rushing it. I said send a man to get him."

"I heard you."

"Very well." Wolfe turned. "Archie. Mr. Cramer and I need a few minutes to make sure of details. Tell Fritz. And use the phone in the kitchen to get Mrs. Fougere. I must see her this evening. Also get Saul and Fred and Orrie. I want them either this evening or at eight in the morning."

I rose. "Does it matter which?"

"No."

I beat it to the kitchen.

8

If you ever need an operative and only the best will do, get Saul Panzer if you can. If Saul isn't available, get Fred Durkin or Orrie Cather. That was the trio who entered James Neville Vance's apartment with me at a quarter past ten Thursday morning.

What made the entry legal was that when I rang

the bells, both downstairs and upstairs, the doors were opened from the inside. Who opened them was Rita Fougere. Upstairs she held it open until we were in and then closed it. I preferred not to touch the door—not that it mattered, but I like things neat.

The door shut, Rita turned to me. She still had those eyes, but the lids were puffy, and her face had had no attention at all. "Where's Martin?" she asked. Her soft little voice was more like a croak. "Have you heard from him?"

I shook my head. "As Mr. Wolfe told you last evening, he's being held as a material witness. Getting a lawyer to arrange for bail would cost money—his money. This will be cheaper and better if it works. Mr. Wolfe told you that."

"I know, but . . . what if it doesn't?"

"That's his department." I turned. "This is Mr. Panzer, Mr. Durkin. Mr. Cather. They know who you are. As you know, you're to stay put, and if you'd like to help you might make some coffee. If the phone rings answer it. If the doorbell rings *don't* answer it. Right?"

"Yes."

"Okay. Gentlemen, sic 'em."

The way you prowl a place depends on what you're after. If you're looking for one large item, say a stolen elephant, of course it's simple. The toughest is when you're just looking. We did want one specific item, a necktie, but also we wanted anything whatever that might help, no matter what, and Saul and Fred and Orrie had been thoroughly briefed. So we were just looking after Saul found the necktie, and that means things like inspecting the seams of a mattress and unfolding handkerchiefs and flipping through the pages of books. It takes a lot longer when you are leaving everything exactly as it was.

We had been at it over an hour when Saul found the tie. I had shown them the seven on the rack in the closet so they would know what it looked like. Saul and Orrie were up in the studio, and when I heard them coming down the spiral stair I knew they had something and met them at the foot, and Saul handed it to me. It was folded, and pinned to it was one of Vance's engraved letterheads, on which Saul had written: "Found by me at 11:25 A.M. on August 9, 1962, inside a piano score of Scriabin's *Vers la Flamme* which was in a cabinet in the studio of James Neville Vance at 219 Horn Street, Manhattan, New York City." He had signed it with his little twirl on the tail of the z.

"You're my hero," I told him. "It would be an honor to tie your shoestrings and I want your autograph. But you know how Orrie is on gags and so do I. We'll take a look."

I entered the bedroom, with them following, and went to the closet. The seven were still on the rack; I counted them twice. "Okay," I told Saul, "it's it. I'll vote for you for President." I took the seven from the rack and handed them to him. "Here, we'll take them along."

After that it was just looking, both in the apartment and in the studio, and that gets tedious. By two o'clock it was damn tedious because we were hungry and we had decided not to take time out to eat, but Cramer had agreed to keep Vance for six hours, and while we had Exhibit A and that was all Wolfe really expected, an Exhibit X would be deeply appreciated. So we kept at it.

A little before three o'clock I was standing in the middle of the living room frowning around. Rita was lying on a couch with her eyes closed. Fred was up in the studio with Saul and Orrie. I was trying to remember some little something that had been in my mind an hour ago, and finally I did. When Fred had taken a pile of gloves from a drawer he had looked in each glove but hadn't felt in it, and he hadn't taken them to the light. I went to the bedroom, got the gloves from the drawer, took them to the window, and really looked; and in the fifth glove, a pigskin hand-sewed number, there was Exhibit X. When I saw it inside the glove I thought it was just a gob of some kind of junk, but when I pulled it out and saw what it was I felt something I hadn't felt very often, a hot spot at the base of my spine. I don't often talk to myself either, but I said aloud, "Believe it or not, that's exactly what it is. It has to be." I put it back in the glove, put the glove in my pocket, returned the other gloves to the drawer, went to the phone on the bedstand, and dialed a number.

Wolfe's voice came: "Yes?" I've been trying for years to get him to answer the phone properly.

"Me," I said. "We'll be there in less than half an hour. Saul found the tie. It was in a piano score in a cabinet in the studio. I just found Exhibit X. I can tell you what he did. After he killed her he cut off a lock of her hair with blood on it, plenty of blood, and took it for a keepsake. After the blood was dry he put it inside one of his gloves in a drawer, which is where I found it. That has to be it. You may not believe it till you see it, but you will then."

"Indeed." A pause. "Satisfactory. Very satisfactory. Bring the glove."

"Certainly. A suggestion—or call it a request. Tell Cramer to have him there at a quarter after four, or half past. We're starving, including Mrs. Fougere, and we need time—"

"You know my schedule. I'll tell Mr. Cramer six o'clock. Fritz will—"

"No." I was emphatic. "For once you'll have to skip it. The six hours is up at four o'clock, and if you put it off until six Cramer may let him go home, with or without an escort, and he might find that both the tie and the keepsake are gone. Would that be satisfactory?"

Silence. "No." More silence. "Confound it." Still more. "Very well. Fritz will have something ready."

"Better make it half past and—"

He had hung up.

9

Inspector Cramer settled back in the red leather chair, narrowed his eyes at Wolfe, and rasped, "I've told Mr. Vance that this won't be on any official record and he can answer your questions or not as he pleases."

He wouldn't have settled back if he had been the only city employee present, since he knew that almost certainly some fur was going to fly. Sergeant Purley Stebbins was there at his right on a chair against the wall. Purley never sits with his back to anyone, even his superior officer, if he can help it. James Neville Vance was on a chair facing Wolfe's desk, between Cramer and me. Rita Fougere was on the couch at the left of my desk, and Saul and Fred and Orrie were grouped over by the big globe.

"There won't be many questions," Wolfe told Cramer. "Nothing remains to be satisfied but my curiosity on a point or two." His head turned. "Mr. Vance, only you can satisfy it." To me: "Archie?"

I regretted having to take my eyes away from Vance. Not that I thought he needed watching; it was just that I wanted to. You can learn things, or you think you can, from the face of a man who knows something is headed for him but doesn't know exactly what and is trying to be ready to meet it. Up to that point Vance's face hadn't increased my knowledge of human nature. His lips were drawn in tight, and that made his oversized chin even more out of proportion. When Wolfe cued me I had to leave it. I got the seven ties from a drawer, put them in a row on Wolfe's desk, and stood by.

"Those," Wolfe told Vance, "are the seven ties that remained on the rack in your closet. I produce them—"

A growl from Cramer stopped him. It would have stopped anybody. It became words. "So you did. Stebbins, take Mr. Vance out to the car. I want to talk to Wolfe."

"No," Wolfe snapped. "I said there would be no illegal entry and there wasn't. Mr. Goodwin, accompanied by Mr. Panzer, Mr. Durkin, and Mr. Cather, rang the bell at Mr. Vance's apartment and were admitted by Mrs. Fougere. She was in the apartment with Mr. Vance's knowledge and consent, having gone there earlier to talk with him. When an officer came to take him to you she remained, with no objection from him. Is that correct, Mrs. Fougere?"

"Yes." It came out a whisper, and she repeated it. "Yes." That time it was a croak.

"Is that correct, Mr. Vance?"

Vance's drawn-in lips opened and then closed. "I don't think . . ." he mumbled. He raised his voice. "I'm not going to answer that."

"You might answer me," Cramer said. "Is it correct?"

"I prefer not to answer."

"Then I'll proceed," Wolfe said. "I produce these seven ties merely to establish them." He opened a drawer and produced Exhibit A. "Here is an eighth tie. Pinned to it is a statement written and signed by Mr. Panzer, on your stationery. I'll read it." He did so. "Have you any comment?"

No comment. No response.

'Let me see that," Cramer growled. Of course he would; that's why I was standing by. I took it from Wolfe and handed it over. He read the statement, twisted around for a look at Saul, and twisted the other way to hand the exhibit to Stebbins.

"It's just as well I haven't many questions," Wolfe told Vance, "since apparently the few I do have won't be answered. I'll try answering them myself, and if you care to correct me, do so. I invite interruptions."

He cocked his head. "You realize, sir, that the facts are manifest. The problem is not what you did, or when or how, but why. As for when, you typed that envelope and message to Mr. Goodwin, using your own stationery and having found or made an opportunity to use Mr. Kirk's typewriter, at least three weeks ago, since that machine wasn't available after July nineteenth. Mr. Kirk's disposing of it just then was of course coincidental. So your undertaking was not only premeditated, it was carefully planned. Also you retrieved the tie you had given Mr. Kirk before he moved from his apartment. Using the typewriter and retrieving the tie of course presented no difficulty, since you owned the house and had master keys. Any comment?"

No.

"Then I'll continue. Only the whys are left, and I'll leave the most important one, why you killed her, to the last. For some of them I can offer only conjecture —for instance, why you wished to implicate Mr. Kirk. It may have been a fatuous effort to divert attention from yourself, or, more likely, you merely wanted it known that Mrs. Kirk had not been the victim of some chance intruder, or you had an animus against Mr. Kirk. Any of those would serve. For other whys I can do better than conjecture. Why did you take a tie from your closet and hide it in your studio? That was part of the design to implicate Mr. Kirk, and it was rather shrewd. You calculated—"

"I didn't," Vance blurted. "Kirk did that, he must have. You say it was found in a piano score?"

Wolfe nodded. "That's your rebuttal, naturally. You intended the necktie maneuver to appear as a clumsy stratagem by Mr. Kirk to implicate you. So of course a tie had to be missing from the rack in your closet. But if Mr. Kirk had taken it he wouldn't have hidden it in your studio; he would have destroyed it. Why then didn't *you* destroy it? You know; I don't; but I can guess. You thought it possible that the situation might so develop that you could somehow use it, so why not keep it?"

Wolfe's shoulders went up a quarter of an inch and down again. "Another why: why did you send the tie to Mr. Goodwin? Of course you had to send it to someone, an essential step in the scheme to involve Mr. Kirk, but why Mr. Goodwin? That's the point I'm chiefly curious about, and I would sincerely appreciate an answer. Why did you send the tie to Mr. Goodwin?"

"I didn't."

"Very well, I can't insist. It's only that he is my confidential assistant, and I would like to know how you got the strange notion that he would best serve your purpose. He is inquisitive, impetuous, alert, skeptical, pertinacious, and resourceful—the worst choice you could possibly have made. One more why before the last and crucial one: why did you phone Mr. Goodwin to burn the tie? That was unnecessary, because his curiosity was sufficiently aroused without that added fillip; and it was witless, because whoever phoned must have known that he had not already phoned you or gone to see you, and only you could have known that. Do you wish to comment?"

"I didn't phone him."

I must say that Vance was showing more gumption than I had expected. By letting Wolfe talk he was finding out exactly how deep the hole was, and he was saying nothing.

Wolfe turned a hand over. "Now the primary why: why did you kill her? I learned yesterday that you probably had an adequate motive, but as I told Mr. Cramer, that was only hearsay. I had to have a demonstrable fact, an act or an object, and you supplied it. Not yesterday or today; you supplied it Tuesday afternoon when, after killing Mrs. Kirk, you stooped over her battered skull, or knelt or squatted, and cut off a lock of her hair, choosing one that had her blood on it. With a knife, or scissors? Did you stoop, or squat, or kneel?"

Vance's lips moved, but no sound came. Unquestionably he was trying to say "I didn't" but couldn't make it.

Wolfe grunted. "I said a demonstrable fact. To demonstrate is to establish as true, and I'll establish it. Mr. Goodwin found the lock of hair, caked with blood, some two hours ago, in a drawer in your bedroom. He called it a keepsake, but a keepsake is something given and kept for the sake of the giver, a token of friendship. 'Trophy' would be a better term." He opened a desk drawer.

I can move fast and so can Purley Stebbins, but we both misjudged James Neville Vance, at least I did. When he started up at sight of the glove Wolfe took from the drawer I started too, but I wasn't expecting him to dart like lightning, and he did; and he got the glove, snatched it out of Wolfe's hand. Of course he didn't keep it long. I came from his left side and Purley from his right, and since he had the glove in his right hand it was Purley who got his wrist and twisted it, and the glove dropped to the floor.

Cramer picked it up. Purley had Vance by the right arm, and I had him by the left.

Wolfe stood up. "It's in the glove," he told Cramer. "Mr. Goodwin, will furnish any details you require, and Mrs. Fougere." He headed for the door. The clock said 5:22. His schedule had hit a snag, but by gum it wasn't wrecked.

10

A little before five o'clock one afternoon last week the doorbell rang, and through the one-way glass I saw Martin Kirk on the stoop, his overcoat collar turned up and his hat on tight. When I opened the door snow came whirling in. Obviously he was calling on me, not Wolfe, since he knew the schedule, and I was glad to see an ex-client who had paid his bill promptly, so I took his hat and coat and put them on the rack, and ushered him to the office and a chair. When we had exchanged a few remarks about the weather, and his health and mine, and Wolfe's, and he had declined an offer of a drink, he said he saw that Vance's lawyer was trying a new approach on an appeal, and I said yeah, when you've got money you can do a lot of dodging. With that disposed of, he said he often wondered where he would be now if he hadn't come straight to Wolfe from the DA's office that day in August.

"Look," I said, "you've said that before. I have all the time there is and I enjoy your company, but you didn't come all the way here through the worst storm this winter just to chew the fat. Something on your mind?"

He nodded. "I thought you might know—might have an idea."

"I seldom do, but it's possible."

"It's Rita. You know she's in Reno?"

"Yes, I've had a card from her."

"Well, I phoned her yesterday. There's some good ski slopes not far from Reno, and I told her I might go out for a week or so and we could give them a try. She said no. A flat no."

"Maybe she doesn't know how to ski."

"Sure she does. She's good, very good." He uncrossed his legs and crossed them again. "I came to see you because— Well, frankly, I thought that maybe you and she have a—an understanding. I used to think she liked me all right—nothing more than that, but I thought she liked me. I know she was a friend in need, I know what she did that day in Vance's apartment, but ever since then she has shied off from me. And I know she thinks you're quite a guy. Well . . . if you *have* got an understanding with her I want to congratulate you. Of course, her too."

I cleared my throat. "Many thanks," I said, "for the compliment. It's nice to know that she thinks I'm quite a guy, but it's nothing more than that. There's not only no understanding, there's no misunderstanding. It's possible that she actually likes you. It's possible that she would enjoy skiing with you, though in my opinion anyone who enjoys skiing is hard up for something to enjoy, but a woman in the process of getting a divorce is apt to be skittish. She either thinks she has been swindled or she feels like a used car. Do you want my advice?"

"Yes."

"Go to Reno unannounced. Tell her you want her to go skiing with you because if you tumble and break a leg, as you probably will, she is the only one you can rely on to bring help. If after a week or so you want to tell her there are other reasons, and there *are* other reasons, she may possibly be willing to listen. She might even enjoy it. You have nothing to lose but a week or so unless you break your neck."

His jaw was working exactly the way it had that day six months back, but otherwise his appearance was very different. "All right," he said. "I'm glad I came. I'll go tomorrow."

"That's the spirit. I don't suppose you'd consider playing pinochle with her, or dancing or going for a walk, instead of skiing?"

"No. I'm not a good dancer."

"Okay. We'll drink to it." I got up. "Scotch and water, I believe?"

"Yes please. No ice. I think you're quite a guy too, Goodwin."

"So do I." I went to the kitchen.

ABOUT THE AUTHOR

REX STOUT, the creator of Nero Wolfe, was born in Noblesville, Indiana, in 1886, the sixth of nine children of John and Lucetta Todhunter Stout, both Quakers. Shortly after his birth, the family moved to Wakarusa, Kansas. He was educated in a country school, but, by the age of nine, was recognized throughout the state as a prodigy in arithmetic. Mr. Stout briefly attended the University of Kansas, but left to enlist in the Navy, and spent the next two years as a warrant officer on board President Theodore Roosevelt's yacht. When he left the Navy in 1908, Rex Stout began to write freelance articles, worked as a sightseeing guide and as an itinerant bookkeeper. Later he devised and implemented a school banking system which was installed in four hundred cities and towns throughout the country. In 1927 Mr. Stout retired from the world of finance and, with the proceeds of his banking scheme, left for Paris to write serious fiction. He wrote three novels that received favorable reviews before turning to detective fiction. His first Nero Wolfe novel, *Fer-de-Lance*, appeared in 1934. It was followed by many others, among them, *Too Many Cooks, The Silent Speaker, If Death Ever Slept, The Doorbell Rang* and *Please Pass the Guilt*, which established Nero Wolfe as a leading character on a par with Erle Stanley Gardner's famous protagonist, Perry Mason. During World War II, Rex Stout waged a personal campaign against Nazism as chairman of the War Writers' Board, master of ceremonies of the radio program "Speaking of Liberty" and as a member of several national committees. After the war, he turned his attention to mobilizing public opinion against the wartime use of thermonuclear devices, was an active leader in the Authors' Guild and resumed writing his Nero Wolfe novels. All together, his Nero Wolfe novels have been translated into twenty-two languages and have sold more than forty-five million copies. Rex Stout died in 1975 at the age of eighty-eight. A month before his death, he published his forty-sixth Nero Wolfe novel, *A Family Affair*.